Praise for the "Beck" Series

"*The Missing Element* is well-written, the plot is intriguing, and the characters are interesting. Betcher draws you in from page one and holds your interest to the very last. Unlike many recent novels, Betcher takes his time tying up the loose ends and concluding the story. This book is obviously the beginning of an exciting new series of suspense novels for Betcher."

Reviewed by Deb L. Baker for
Reader's Choice Book Reviews

[*The Missing Element*] was a lot of fun. It is the kind of book I love to read and it is the kind of book I try to write. John Betcher has written a real gem. Like a good port, you can enjoy it any time. It is an entertaining addition to the thriller/suspense class of books with just a dash of sci-fi—the style lies somewhere between Carl Hiaasen and Michael Connelly, although the author claims to emulate Robert B. Parker. A difficult task, but he comes close in entertainment value.

Reviewed by Steve Moore for
Bookpleasures.com

"Unlike other thrillers based on an extremely implausible foundation scenario, [*The Missing Element*] uses a very real, even likely situation. The wisecracking dialog between Beck and his wife and the inclusion of the mysterious but very capable sidekick Bull reminded me of the "Spenser" series by Robert Parker. Which is high praise as there are none better in that genre."

Reviewed by Charles Ashbacher,
Amazon.com **Top 50 Reviewer**

. . . if you are also a fan of the late Robert B. Parker and/or fun snappy dialogue, then I move this into the must-read category for you! For myself, you might have already realized that I thoroughly enjoyed the time spent with James Becker, et. al., and look forward to meeting them again in their next mystery!

Reviewed by G.A. Bixler
IPreviewer-bookreadersheaven blog

Books in the Beck Series

The 19th Element, A James Becker Thriller
The Missing Element, A James Becker Mystery

THE 19TH ELEMENT

ELEMENT

A James Becker Thriller

by

John L. Betcher

Published by

John L. Betcher

Red Wing, Minnesota

john@johnbetcher.com

2010

ISBN: 1451521014
EAN-9781451521016

For Lynn, Anne and Kate

PREFACE

The following is verbatim text of an item from the *Presidential Daily Brief* presented to President George W. Bush on August 6, 2001. Redacted material is indicated by brackets.

Bin Ladin Determined To Strike in US

Clandestine, foreign government, and media reports indicate Bin Ladin since 1997 has wanted to conduct terrorist attacks in the US. Bin Ladin implied in US television interviews in 1997 and 1998 that his followers would follow the example of World Trade Center bomber Ramzi Yousef and "bring the fighting to America."

After US missile strikes on his base in Afghanistan in 1998, Bin Ladin told followers he wanted to retaliate in Washington, according to a [--] service. An Egyptian Islamic Jihad (EIJ) operative told an [--] service at the same time that Bin Ladin was planning to exploit the operative's access to the US to mount a terrorist strike.

. . .

Al Qaeda members – including some who are US citizens – have resided in or traveled to the US for years, and the group apparently maintains a support structure that could aid attacks. Two Al Qaeda members found guilty in the conspiracy to bomb our embassies in East Africa were US citizens, and a senior EIJ member lived in California in the mid-1990s.

A clandestine source said in 1998 that a Bin Ladin cell in New York was recruiting Muslim-American youth for attacks.

We have not been able to corroborate some of the more sensational threat reporting, such as that from a [--] service in 1998 saying that Bin Ladin wanted to hijack a US aircraft to gain the release of "Blind Shaykh" 'Umar 'Abd al-Rahman and other US-held extremists.

Nevertheless, FBI information since that time indicates patterns of suspicious activity in this country consistent with preparations for hi-jackings or other types of attacks, including recent surveillance of federal buildings in New York.

*   *   *

Despite this warning from U.S. intelligence sources, the government failed to act.

Less than one month later, on September 11, 2001, Bin Ladin made good on his threat. He brought the fight to America – and thousands died in its first battle.

Even today, the war continues. Are we prepared?

PROLOGUE

Western perceptions notwithstanding, the Afghan War did not put *Al Qaeda* out of business. And despite American bragging to the contrary, *Al Qaeda* has even conducted successful operations *inside* the U.S. after 9/11.

It is true that western forces have succeeded in thwarting a number of attempted attacks. But from *Al Qaeda's* perspective, even worse than failed operations are the West's unbelievably effective cover-ups. Westerners blame nearly all of *Al Qaeda's* successful offensives on internal malcontents. Gang wars. Freedom Fighters. Drug cartels. Anarchists. Radical extremists. These are the "criminals" who receive the credit for attacks that, in reality, are *Al Qaeda's* victories.

Although the premier international terrorist organization is very much alive – and deadly – the name of *Al Qaeda* no longer strikes fear into the hearts of the western world. Of what efficacy is a terrorist group lacking the ability to terrorize? *Al Qaeda* faces a serious public relations problem. World fear of *Al Qaeda* is at an all-time low.

There is only one solution. To regain global prominence, *Al Qaeda* needs an operation so high-profile, and so public, that the world cannot be duped by cover-ups.

It needs something nuclear.

CHAPTER 1

Wednesday, May 6th, at Red Wing, Minnesota.

Tuesday's discovery of a dead body washed up on the Mississippi River shore just north of Red Wing had turned the small town into a press Mecca. Television and print media crews from the Twin Cities and Rochester converged on the murder scene, each vying for the most gruesome, and attention-grabbing, visuals possible.

News helicopters swooped up and down the river valley, past the grassy riverbank where the swollen spring currents at the confluence of the Prairie River with its larger counterpart had deposited the corpse.

The body was that of an older man – in his sixties, the Ottawa County Medical Examiner had estimated. Police hadn't released the probable identity of the victim. And despite photographers' best efforts, the only crime photos that made the nightly news programs were of boaters in small craft, gawking in the river channel, and of four Ottawa County Sheriff's Deputies hoisting a vinyl body-bag from the weedy beach into their covered flatboat.

The remainder of the news footage showcased well-dressed reporters, looking serious, and speaking with concerned voices about the tragic discovery near the small Minnesota town.

But all that was yesterday.

Today was Wednesday and I was at my office. Becker Law Office. James L. Becker, Attorney-at-Law. Nearly everyone who knows me calls me 'Beck.'

I arrived at this lawyering gig via an unusual route. Following my retirement from more than twenty years of *sub rosa* military intelligence operations, my wife, Elizabeth, and I decided to move our family to my childhood home of Red Wing. Beth and I had agreed at the time that the relatively crime-free life in rural Minnesota would be a plus for our girls. Having me working near home more of the time would reduce my family's justified worries for my safety. And I could blend in seamlessly in my old home town.

Lawyering would be a fairly easy professional transition for me. I already held a largely-unused law degree from my pre-Agency days. The segue into small town private practice would not be difficult.

So five years ago, Beth and I, and our two children, Sara and Elise, had picked up our lives and come here to live in Red Wing, a Mississippi River town of about twenty thousand. In this setting, we were able to use our real names. And we hoped to regain for our family a sense of normalcy.

Although being an attorney is not difficult, it can be less than exciting. For the sake of appearances, I maintain the cover – but we really don't need the money.

Our family financial situation is a bit more favorable than most, owing entirely to an invention I had patented during my tenure on 'the Team' – a radically new aerodynamic design for sniper bullets.

A change in the shape of a bullet might not seem like much. But after extensive testing, a government defense contractor had happily purchased my patent for quite a lot of money.

Later, I was pleased to learn that incorporation of my bullet design into new sniper rifles allowed a reliable 'kill shot' at up to a mile and a half – a significant improvement over the traditional .50 caliber long-range projectiles. A win-win for both me and the military.

Of course, the defense contractor got the glory. But that wasn't important. Glory is fleeting and fickle. Neither to be sought nor trusted.

Given our financial independence, my new 'job' is really just my new cover. My true vocation really has no proper name. I guess you could say I am professionally wayward. At least, I like that description. It implies a Huck Finn sort of freedom, combined with a Tiger Woods drive for excellence – minus some of Tiger's extra-curricular pursuits, of course.

My professionally wayward approach allows me complete freedom to select causes and goals; but once chosen, it also requires me to pursue all such matters with utter commitment and maximum preparedness. This combination of dedication and preparation has, thus far, assured my success in numerous challenging undertakings.

I am most certainly *not* a Jack of all trades. I am, however, a master of many.

Professionally wayward. I definitely like that.

At 9:30 a.m. it had already seemed a long morning at the law office. And I wanted to get the inside info on the floater murder. It was time for an informational visit to my friend in local law enforcement.

When I arrived at the Ottawa County Law Enforcement Center, a five minute drive from my office, the atmosphere was still electric in the wake of the previous day's disturbing discovery. So much so, that I had managed to slip through the usual administrative roadblocks and right into Gunner's inner office.

'Gunner' is Ottawa County's Chief Deputy Sheriff, Doug Gunderson. He's in his mid-forties, six foot, 180 pounds and in pretty good shape. Though he displays a hint of a belly, his body is mostly muscle. Gunner's round face, light complexion and short, reddish-brown hair are not atypical of many fourth-generation Scandinavian immigrants to this area of Minnesota.

Gunner is also one of the very few people in town who has any idea of my true life experiences as a covert intelligence operative during my twenty-year absence from Red Wing.

We had known each other in our youth, and had been casual friends in high school, but hadn't kept in contact until my return to Minnesota five years ago. On one occasion, a couple years back, he had pressed me for details concerning my life after leaving Red Wing.

As a professional investigator, he can be irritatingly tenacious.

At the time, it hadn't been my first choice to let Gunner in on my secrets. But he was persistent. My gut told me I could trust him. And a friend in local law enforcement is not a bad thing. So I had elected to come clean about my government past – minus many details, of course. In return, he'd vowed to keep my secrets to himself – a promise he had faithfully fulfilled.

Since then, Gunner and I had 'cooperated' on a few cases. He operated by the book. I, by my own rules. The differing approaches created some conflict. But we shared common goals, and we understood each other well enough to make it work. As a side benefit, being involved with law enforcement activities satisfied my desire for more action than mere lawyering alone could provide.

Gunderson was seated at his desk, deeply absorbed in review of glossy crime scene photographs. He looked up when he heard my voice.

"So what's going on today, Gunner?" I inquired. "Things are hopping around here. Is Oprah planning a visit?"

Gunner looked up from his work.

"Becker. Who let you in here?" He was trying to sound irritated.

"Always nice to be welcome," I said.

Following the exchange of greetings, Gunner answered my question.

"You know damn well what's going on, Beck. Everybody from the Sheriff, to the Mayor, to the frickin' Press is all over our asses to solve this murder case. Deadline is yesterday.

"And of course, the big wigs've gotta fight over the jurisdictional issues. The State guys want in on the investigation. The FBI claims that it oughtta be in charge because the body was found in interstate waters. Actually, our own department has the best claim to the case, since it appears that the murder occurred on our dirt.

"So in short, it's a madhouse right now. No one is in charge. And despite all the activity around here," – Gunner made an arm motion circling his head – "not much investigating is really getting done."

I looked at him, feigning shock.

I'm pretty sure Gunner could sense my lack of sympathy for his bureaucratic hiccups.

Gunner frowned at me for a few moments, then lightened up.

"Oh geez. You might as well have a seat," he said at last. "I need a break anyway."

Gunner motioned me to one of his side chairs.

It was stacked full with manila files.

I raised my eyebrows at him.

He returned the look. But the files didn't move.

So I cleared the chair myself, stacking the manila obstacles alongside a similar pile of files already reclining against the wall. Then I sat down.

Commotion continued in the hall outside his office.

With hands crossed comfortably over his torso, Gunner leaned back in his 1960s-vintage vinyl office chair, looking at me as if waiting for something to happen.

"So . . . ," I began. "Do you know who the unlucky fellow is . . . was?"

I could see that Gunner was trying to project cool and calm – but the butterflies were definitely fluttering in his gut. A murder in Ottawa County was a very big deal. But Gunner wasn't about to let his excitement overtake his professional persona.

"We're pretty sure it was a prof from the U of M Ag Lab at the Ottawa Facility," he said, locking his fingers behind his head.

I noted the obvious perspiration under his arms.

"His wife reported him missing to the Cottage Grove Police early yesterday morning. And he hasn't shown up for work the past two days. Car's missing, too.

"Oh yeah." He paused for dramatic effect. Gunner likes drama. I think he watches too many cop shows on TV. "There's a large amount of dried blood in the Lab parking lot. We're assuming it will match our victim."

I paused for a moment.

"Seems a logical assumption," I said, bypassing the drama. "Have you got a name?"

Gunner looked a little wounded that I hadn't been more impressed with the big blood puddle.

Overcoming his mild disappointment, he leaned forward, referencing the notepad on his desk. "Donald G. Westerman, PhD. Home address is in Cottage Grove. We'll be inviting the wife to the morgue to identify the body as soon as we can make it . . . ah . . . presentable."

The killer had nearly severed Dr. Westerman's head from his body. Some tidying up was prudent before exposing the wife to her husband's corpse.

"Don't s'pose you found a weapon?"

"No such luck. The M.E. is trying to get us a description of the blade. But since it's a slash, that'll probably come back 'inconclusive.' In a stabbing, you can maybe get a cast or something. With a cut, usually its just whether the knife is serrated, and how thick."

Based on my experience with knives, Gunner was probably right about the forensics.

"And at present, no motive either?"

I had all the smart questions.

"Not really," Gunner continued. "Though it is interesting to note that the fellow's lab assistant has also failed to report for work since the murder."

He consulted his notes again.

"One Farris Ahmed. British exchange student in the graduate program at the U of M. Sent a couple deputies by his apartment. No one home. We're working on a search warrant."

In my former military career, I had once encountered a radical Muslim *Jihadist* who went by the name of Farris Ahmed. It was a common enough name in Arab countries – but given my past experiences, one might understand why this name did not sit quietly in my gut.

"What ethnic derivation is Mr. Ahmed?" I asked. "Muslim Brit?"

"Not strictly relevant, Beck. You know there's no racial profiling in this department."

Ah. The company line.

Gunner gave me a steely stare. I waited.

"Officially, we have no word on Mr. Ahmed's ethnicity. We're a small department. We can't do everything at once, for god's sake. Anyway, we try to save the bigotry assignments for the BCA."

The BCA was the Minnesota Bureau of Criminal Apprehension, the branch of the State Police charged with criminal investigations. They would likely take a lead role in the murder investigation, regardless of any Sheriff's Department protests to the contrary.

The mention of the name 'Farris Ahmed,' and the international background of the lab assistant, had further piqued my interest.

"Gunner. You would probably ask the BCA to do this anyway . . . but would you mind checking for any international telephone calls made from the vicinity of the Lab around the time of the murder? I mean, not just the assistant's phone, or the land lines, but anonymous, throw-away cell phones, too?"

"Why?" Gunner replied, leaning forward in his chair. "Do you suspect a connection beyond Minnesota?"

I didn't want to get Gunner off track just because my gut had a twinge – especially with no evidence at all of global foul play. But I wasn't going to ignore my instincts either.

"Well . . . the assistant was from overseas – just thought you'd want to be thorough."

Gunner looked me in the eye before continuing.

Gunner leaned back again in his chair. I surmised I was about to receive some wise advice from the seasoned law man.

"You realize, Beck, that the assistant may be another victim, and not at all culpable in this mess?"

"I suppose that's true," I conceded. "Still, I would appreciate your checking the phone call situation."

"All right, Beck. I'll ask the BCA to do it . . . as a favor to you."

Gunner pretended to think it was a dumb idea. But he has always been a bad actor . . . and a thorough investigator. My concern wasn't so far-fetched that he was going to ignore it.

"'Course I can't guarantee that the BCA'll do anything about it. They don't work for me, you know."

Gunner aimed a forefinger across the desk at me.

"And if I catch any crap for making this request, you will owe me one."

I had gotten what I wanted. No point picking a fight.

"You have a deal. Thanks. And good luck with the investigation."

"Right. Thanks, Beck. I'm sure I'll be seeing you around."

"Oh, I think you can count on it."

And I left.

CHAPTER 2

Somewhere in Germany, one year earlier.

Members of an *Al Qaeda* command cell gathered in a secluded European location. It was late at night. Their *Mawlawi* – their leader – had called this meeting. The four cell members sat in a tight circle on hard wooden chairs in the dimly-lit, dank-smelling room. They spoke in Arabic.

Mawlawi: "It is difficult enough to undertake nuclear action against the Americans without Mullah Omar announcing our intentions to the world. His recent *Al Jazeera* interview threatening nuclear attack on the Great Satan does not make our job easier."

Jamal: "This is true, *Mawlawi*. But at least the Taliban leader has a reputation for making ridiculous claims which, in reality, are seldom achieved. *In'Shallah*, the infidels will pay no heed to his threats."

Mawlawi: "You may be right, Jamal. The Americans possessed far more credible intelligence before the pagan towers fell, and yet did nothing to prevent it. But whether they will or they won't, we must proceed with our plan. We are more than a year in progress already. I only wish the over-zealous fool would keep his mouth shut."

The *Mawlawi* straightened himself in his chair. Swallowing his frustration with the news release, he continued the meeting.

"Jamal." The *Mawlawi* looked, again, in Jamal's direction.

Jamal: "Yes, *Mawlawi*."

Mawlawi: "Without disclosing the exact location, please review for us the chosen target of our action. Will it be sufficiently visible? Will there be ample damage and death to assure international respect for our efforts?"

Jamal: "There exists in the United States a total of sixty-six, nuclear-fueled, electric power plants. Some are much better protected than others. We needed to select a target that would be eminently achievable."

The *Mawlawi* nodded his agreement.

Jamal continued: "Although extreme security measures on the part of the infidels prevented us from targeting New York, Los Angeles or Chicago, our final selection lies proximate to a dense population area in excess of 2,000,000 – more than sufficient for our purposes.

"Furthermore, the attack will strike at the geographical heart of America – where the pagan dogs have always before felt safe . . . and where they will never again sleep deeply. Their misplaced sense of security, of invulnerability, will magnify the psychological impact of our attack at the target site. And American overconfidence will simplify our breach of the facility's lax defenses."

Mawlawi: "Very good, Jamal. We will trust your judgment in this regard."

The *Mawlawi* turned to Ali: "Ali, please review the means of attack."

Ali: "Esteemed *Mawlawi*. The plan is to crash a large airplane, loaded with explosives, into the building in which spent nuclear fuel is stored. Unlike the reinforced reactor towers, this storage building is not well-defended from the air. Yet it contains even larger amounts of radioactive material than the reactors themselves.

"An airport is located only ten kilometers distant from the target. By Allah's will, a plane of sufficient size and strength has been delivered into our hands. Better still, the infidels themselves will unwittingly transport the airplane to the airport at the appointed time.

"These final factors have sealed our decision concerning the target."

Mawlawi: "That is very good, Ali."

Now it was Rashid's turn to report.

"Rashid," the *Mawlawi* continued. "You have assembled the warriors who will carry out this attack. Please enlighten us."

Rashid: "*Mawlawi*. We have among our number a sympathetic American who is actually employed at the target site. We recruited him some time ago and have great confidence in both his motivation and ability as regards this operation. His entire family died in a U.S. nuclear accident. He has sought revenge ever since.

"He is remarkably bright and innovative, though not highly-educated. He also possesses excellent construction skills and has the ability to pilot an airplane. He will be our operational team leader in this endeavor."

The *Mawlawi* frowned. "How can we be certain the American pig will follow through with our plans? It is foolhardy to allow operational control to an infidel."

Rashid: "*Mawlawi*, your point is well taken. However, given the difficulties of inserting our primary forces into America, we must rely on the best personnel available to us in this location and at this time. We have no choice but to make use of the American.

"But of course, we will have an observer in place – someone to ensure the infidel's compliance and to intervene if the need should arise."

Mawlawi: "If we have a trusted fighter to observe, why not let him lead the operation?"

Rashid: "*Mawlawi*, our Muslim brother holds a respected position in the local community. His work hours, visibility and responsibilities are such that he cannot divert sufficient time to lead the operation without attracting unwanted attention. Oversight is within his limitations. But little more can be expected of him as regards this pursuit."

Mawlawi: "I am not yet convinced, Rashid. But please, relate the rest of your arrangements. Then I shall decide."

Rashid: "In addition to the team leader, we have arranged for two American anarchists to provide basic assistance. They will not possess full knowledge of our plans. Instead, we have fed them information aligning with their randomly destructive purposes.

"I have the utmost confidence that these two will not expose our intentions. But their, ah, utility is limited."

Mawlawi: "Limited? In what way?"

Rashid: "*Mawlawi*. To be blunt, they are rather stupid – stupid like sheep. They blindly accept our money and follow our commands. Their role in the operation does not require astute mental abilities – merely strong backs and a willingness to do as we say."

The *Mawlawi's* cold stare pierced the darkness. But he said nothing.

Rashid squirmed on his chair. After a few moments, he spoke again.

Rashid: "*Mawlawi*. You are aware that we require more than one person to mount this attack. These people I have mentioned present our best options."

A tense silence filled the room once more. Finally, the *Mawlawi* spoke.

Mawlawi: "The involvement of the two infidel imbeciles causes me great concern, Rashid. Are you absolutely confident that they will fulfill our purposes without revealing our plans to the American dogs?"

Rashid spoke with all the conviction he could muster.

Rashid: "*Mawlawi*. In all truthfulness, their stupidity may be an asset. They are not smart enough to question commands, or to inquire as to purposes. And from their demeanor, one would not think them anarchists at all. There is no hint of rebellion in them. It is my belief that they are anarchists simply because anarchy is all they know. As I have said, they are like sheep – they follow the flock.

"I *assure* you, *Mawlawi*. These two will suffice."

The *Mawlawi* still did not look convinced. But he possessed a wisdom born of experience. He had been fighting this war as long as he could remember. He knew that compromise and adaptation were parts of real world *Jihad*.

Many times, the *Mawlawi* had prayed for additional soldiers to execute this particular plan – true followers of the Prophet to carry out this mission. But Allah had provided no one else. These infidels would have to do. The *Mawlawi* breathed deeply and slowly exhaled.

Mawlawi: "Very well, Rashid. If you are quite sure we have no other fighters in the area, we will proceed with the personnel you have assembled."

Rashid: "*Mawlawi*. I would be remiss if I failed to mention one other operative in the target's vicinity – an extremely intelligent and skilled young chemist named Farris Ahmed. He sends us useful technical reports on a regular basis. We have been saving his expertise for future undertakings. I do not believe it would be most effective for our long-term cause to unveil his presence as part of this operation."

Mawlawi: "Thank you for your thoroughness, Rashid. If this young chemist is as intelligent and skilled as you say, he may well prove more useful in some future role. You may proceed utilizing your present personnel."

The meeting was over.

The *Mawlawi* stood. He would bestow a benediction upon the assembled faithful.

Raising his right hand, he said: "May the strength of Allah go with you and his blessings be upon you all."

CHAPTER 3

*Thursday, May 7*th*, at Red Wing.*

Today was the day after my meeting with Gunner in his office. My wife, Beth and I were enjoying a sunrise breakfast on our front screen porch at 1011 Jefferson Avenue. Bacon, eggs and toast, with fresh orange slices and coffee. Beth was the cook. I often tried, but seldom succeeded. My heart just wasn't in it.

Jefferson Avenue, itself, is a peaceful street, lined with historic homes and sheltered by mature oaks and maples. In the summer, the trees form a fragrant canopy over both avenue and sidewalks. In fall, they release a swirling sea of red, yellow and brown leaves – the kind kids like to rake into piles and jump in. Automobile traffic on Jefferson is close to non-existent. Pedestrians enjoy walking its shaded length, strolling among the calming smell of freshly-mown lawns. Neighbors push strollers or pull wagons by our home, waving and calling "Hello" as we return smiled greetings from the porch.

"Any big plans today?" I asked Beth as we ate.

"The gals are getting together at Hanisch's Bakery for coffee at 10:00. Then I hope to check the product levels at my art retailers."

Beth has adjusted well to life in Red Wing. So well, in fact, that locals would never guess that, in addition to her top-notch artistic talents, she also possesses high-level government security clearance and unique technological skills. In fact, her computer expertise is so highly regarded in Washington that, between beading, sewing and painting, Beth frequently accedes to desperate CIA requests for her encryption/decryption services. To state it plainly . . . Beth is one of the U.S. Government's best code-crackers.

" How about you?" Beth asked.

"Nothing special." I finished a last bite of toast. "Gotta get going, though. Miles to go before I sleep. No rest for the wicked. Etcetera, etcetera."

Beth and I are soul mates. She knows me better than I know myself, and tolerates my idiosyncrasies – like this morning's hasty departure from breakfast.

"Don't overdo, Babe," she said.

"Never."

I gave Beth a quick kiss. Then steered my dark grey Honda Pilot down the vacant, early-morning streets of Red Wing to Becker Law Office, arriving at the door a few minutes after six o'clock.

One of my preferred professional strategies was doing my legal work outside of normal working hours. I knew from prior experience that, if I arrived at the office before clients and secretaries knew I was there, I could actually accomplish quite a lot without interruption.

By the time my legal secretary, Karen, showed up at 9:00 a.m., I had worked my way through substantial stacks of client files accumulated from the previous day and had already decided that my work day at the law office was finished. I wanted to know more about the death of Professor Westerman.

I was also concerned about young Mr. Ahmed. The uneasiness hadn't left my gut. And no one in law enforcement had, as yet, displayed any concern over possible terrorism.

My intercom beeped. It was Karen. "Will you be taking any appointments this afternoon, Beck?"

"Sorry, Karen. Can't do it today. Full calendar."

I glanced down at the same blank calendar page that Karen was no doubt observing. "Last minute. Meetings all day outside the office. Forgot to get it on the calendar. Sorry again."

"When shall I say you will return calls – tonight after midnight? Or tomorrow before breakfast?"

Did I detect a touch of sarcasm?

"Let's just go for: 'I'll tell him you called.' Does that work for you, Karen?"

"Your wish is my command. Could I get a few signatures from you though, before your, ah, meetings?"

"Sure thing. I'll swing by your desk on my way out."

The intercom clicked off.

Without Karen, I don't know how I would ever get so much legal work done.

So as not to appear too sluggardly, I hung around my office with the door closed listening to jazz and reading online newspapers for another couple hours. When the time felt right, I grabbed my jacket from the back of the door and headed for Karen's desk, a spring in my step.

A pile of correspondence and a number of bank checks awaited my signature. I worked my way efficiently through the stacks, signing without reading.

I inquired to whom the checks I had just signed were payable. Being satisfied with the responses, I thanked Karen for her good work.

Then I doffed my imaginary hat in her direction, and ducked out.

Meetings . . . all day.

CHAPTER 4

Since I had promised to be in meetings 'all day,' and it was only 11:15, I had some serious meeting to do. My first meeting was with a sandwich at The Smokey Row Café. They baked the best breads in Red Wing. It didn't really matter what you put between two slices. It was all good.

Today I was motivated by the turkey club on toasted sunflower bread. I sat in a booth by the window and ate my sandwich, washing it down with a cup of Sumatran Dark Roast, black. As I ate, I checked out the local daily newspaper, which hadn't been available online, to see if it contained any additional info on the obvious murder. It came as no surprise that the paper knew even less than I did.

Fifteen minutes and one delicious sandwich later I was back in the Pilot, headed for the University Ag Lab – the place with the bloody parking lot.

It was about a forty minute drive to Rosland, the entirely rural township which was home to the University of Minnesota Agricultural Research Facility. When I arrived at the Facility, a tan and white Ottawa County Sheriff's cruiser was parked at the driveway entrance, facing outward and ready to greet visitors. Two uniformed deputies occupied the front seat. I recognized their faces from around the cop shop in Red Wing. But we weren't close.

Turning the Pilot into the Facility drive, I pulled slowly alongside the cruiser – our driver's side windows adjacent to one another. His window was already down. I lowered mine.

"Can I help you, Mr. Becker?" he asked, stifling a yawn.

He was thirtyish with brown hair, cut close in military fashion. His left arm, from elbow to hand, rested on the cruiser door. His partner leaned forward, looking my way . . . checking out the action. Probably the most they'd seen all day.

"I am doing some private legal consultation for the University about the other day's, ah, unfortunate business," I lied.

I smiled. Highly engaging.

The driver gave me a quick look up and down. I don't think he figured me for a threat.

"We've got a chunk of the parking area, the main entrance and one of the labs taped off."

A full yawn this time.

"Stay away from those spots and you should be okay."

"Thank you very much, Deputy. I'll make sure to avoid the taped area and stick strictly to my business with the U," I lied again.

I flashed another smile, then reached my right hand across my body to wave at the cops. Both had already returned to whatever they had been doing before. Without looking my way, the driver did manage to lift a finger from the car door as acknowledgment of my departure.

It was a short driveway. Almost immediately, I could see the boundaries marked with yellow 'Crime Scene' tape. Besides the deputies, the exterior of the Lab Facility property was nearly deserted. In fact, the only other person I could see outside was a man wearing a tan groundskeeper's uniform and a dirty-white panama hat. He was on his hands and knees, spreading wood mulch around some shrubs near the building.

I was careful to park the Pilot between the largest blood stain and the cruiser – but not too close to the yellow tape. Maneuvering outside my vehicle, I leaned through the back door, appearing to rummage for some papers. Once below the cops' line of sight, I turned around, contortionist fashion, and snapped a few quick pics of the parking lot blood and the crime tape. There wasn't much to see. But one never knows when a photo might come in handy.

Returning to a normal body position, I withdrew from the back seat. Damn. The groundskeeper was looking my way. He was pushing his wheelbarrow across the parking lot, presumably in pursuit of more mulch for the bushes. I wondered how much of my photography performance he had seen. His face wore a strange expression.

When our eyes met, I smiled and gave him a friendly wave. He looked away, then picked up his pace crossing the lot.

With the groundskeeper gone, I returned to my planned activities. Reaching back into the Pilot, I withdrew my trial case – essentially the result of mating a briefcase with a steamer trunk. I smiled and waved respectfully at the cruiser as I traversed the space to the Lab's only unblocked entrance.

Just a friendly guy doing his job.

Once inside the Lab building, I located a wall sign identifying the Facility's Administrative Director as one Charles Downing, PhD. I found the main reception area and entered.

The cute co-ed receptionist looked up from her computer. "May I help you, sir?"

"Please let Dr. Downing know that Attorney Becker is here to see him. He is expecting me."

Lying can be habit-forming.

"Very well, sir." She punched a button on her telephone console and announced, "Dr. Downing, Attorney Becker to see you. He says you're expecting him."

There were a few moments of silence during which I examined the aerial photos hanging on the reception area walls. Without exception, they depicted farm fields, all of which looked strikingly similar to one another – at least as far as my untrained eye could discern.

"Yes, sir. I'll tell him," the receptionist said into her phone.

Then, turning to me, "Dr. Downing will be out to see you shortly."

"Thank you very much."

More thoughtful examination of crop photos.

A minute or two later there was a voice behind me.

"Mr. Becker is it?" The voice belonged to a man.

"Yes," I said, turning away from the pictorial tillage to face the professor.

Dr. Downing looked just like an administrative PhD should look. Tall, slim, with brilliantly white hair and a distinguished posture. He wore navy-blue dress pants, with an open collar on his light-blue, broadcloth dress shirt. No sport coat.

We approached each other.

"James Becker. Pleased to make your acquaintance," I said warmly, switching my trial case to my left hand, while extending my right in greeting.

Dr. Downing accepted my large hand in his even larger, calloused one. He had a firm handshake. Despite his academic credentials, the man clearly had not spent his life in an office.

"I must apologize, Mr. Becker, but no one notified me that you would be coming today," Dr. Downing said.

I gave him the perplexed brow, shifted my weight to my left foot and put my right hand on my hip. "I don't understand," I said. "The University President called me just this morning and asked that I meet you here at 12:30."

I looked at my watch. Right on the dot. I shook my head.

When in doubt, it's frequently smartest to say nothing. I continued to shake my head and shift my weight back and forth from one foot to the other.

I gave him seriously perplexed.

"Well," Downing said, after considering the situation, "these sorts of things happen all the time in large institutions when the chiefs act outside normal channels. I apologize. May I see your credentials?"

I showed him the laminated card from the Minnesota Supreme Court identifying me as an 'Attorney-at-Law' and backed it up with the photo on my driver's license. He seemed satisfied.

"Fortunately, I have some time. Shall we meet in my office?"

"Perfect." I smiled.

The doctor ushered me through a door, down a white-walled institutional hallway and into his private office.

"Please have a seat," he offered, as he rounded the side of his desk.

I did. And he did as well.

"Now . . . how may I help you, Mr. Becker?" He rolled his metal office chair closer to the drab-green-topped metal desk.

"Beck, please," I said.

"Very well, Beck. Please call me Chuck."

"Okay. Chuck it is."

I had been holding the trial case on my lap. I leaned over and placed it on the floor on my side of the desk. As I opened the case, I flipped the switch on a small digital audio recorder. There's no substitute for verbatim recollection. A second later, I popped back up into Chuck's view with a yellow pad. Removing a pen from my shirt pocket, I established a ready position.

"Chuck. First of all, I think it's fair to say that we are all horrified by the apparent murder of Dr. Westerman."

Chuck nodded sadly.

"The President is, of course, devastated by Dr. Westerman's death. But he also has a responsibility to protect the University from potential liability exposures, what with the death occurring on University property and all. Hence, my involvement."

I spread my arms, palms up.

Chuck nodded.

"I'm hoping I can count on your complete cooperation in this internal investigation. There could be a good deal at stake. If this matter isn't put to rest with the University coming out squeaky clean, who knows the ramifications?"

Chuck shrugged. He didn't know the ramifications.

"Donors might withhold contributions. There could be funding cuts for Ag programs."

No change of expression on Chuck's face.

"Employee positions could be in jeopardy – especially managerial and administrative jobs. And you can imagine who could end up the scapegoat for this whole fiasco." I looked Chuck in the eye with purpose.

That got Chuck's attention.

He rolled even closer to the desk and sat up straight. "I'll certainly do anything I can to assist in your investigation, Mr., ah, Beck."

"Thank you." I paused thoughtfully – my pen and pad poised for action. "Could you please describe your relationship with Dr. Westerman? Were the two of you close?"

"Actually," Chuck began, "although we've worked under the same roof here at the Lab for these past many years, he and I seldom spoke. Technically speaking, Dr. Westerman reported to me as his supervisor. But he had tenure. And he was extremely productive, self-directed and reclusive. I saw no reason to bother him."

I raised an eyebrow.

Chuck began fidgeting. "I mean, his written progress reports were all in order. And his work was very impressive, I might add. Very impressive. He really needed no supervision, *per se.*"

Taking advantage of Chuck's cooperative attitude, I continued with my questions.

"What had Dr. Westerman been working on recently?"

"His last report, filed about a month ago, indicated that he was continuing to make progress toward developing improved agricultural fertilizer compounds."

My experience with fertilizer was limited to Miracle Gro, manure and truck bombs. "Can you give me more details? I really have neither a chemistry nor agricultural background." That wasn't completely true. I actually knew quite a lot of very specialized chemistry. But I wasn't planning to share.

"Of course. Where should I start."

It was rhetorical. I waited.

"Many farm crops require significant amounts of the chemical, potassium, in the soil in order for them to grow. The problem is that these crops permanently remove relatively large quantities of the potassium from the land each growing season. The soil's natural reserves of potassium deplete quite rapidly."

"So the crops wear out the soil. And then what?"

"Well. For years, farmers have added potassium compounds to their fields to supplement the depleted soil levels. Typical supplements are: potassium chloride, potassium hydroxide, potassium sulphate and potassium magnesium sulphate. There are a few others. But those are the most common supplements, or fertilizers, if you will."

Chuck continued his speech. I had gotten him into lecture mode.

"The chemical reactions between the other soil components, the sun, the rain and the plants themselves, liberate . . . ah . . . separate the potassium from its compounds to make the potassium available for the plants to use as food.

"Are you following so far?"

"I believe so." Actually, the talk of fertilizer components had taxed my concentration. I needed to re-focus.

"What does this have to do with Dr. Westerman's work?"

"I'm just getting to that." Chuck's voice was patient now, and less flustered.

"Until very recently, sources of potassium compounds were plentiful, making them available to agriculture at very low prices. If a farmer needed more potassium, he could afford to just order up a load of potash and spread it on his field.

"But with broad international development of more sophisticated farming techniques, notably in the Republic of China, the global demand for potassium compounds has sky-rocketed. There are actually shortages in many parts of the world today."

This was turning into a longer manure dissertation than I had hoped for.

"Again . . . Dr. Westerman's role in all this?" I pressed.

"Dr. Westerman was working on new ways to encourage farm soil to retain more potassium, and to ensure that crops could make the most efficient use of lower soil potassium levels, should that become necessary. His latest project involved reducing potassium fertilizer to pure potassium metal, and then constructing entirely new potassium compounds with the desired characteristics, from scratch. It's a novel approach and has not been tried anywhere else in the world – at least that I am aware of."

I scratched my head with the end of my pen. I hadn't actually written anything down on the yellow pad. Nothing seemed relevant enough to be noted – and I did have the digital backup.

"Again, I'm no chemist, but it seems like someone else would have considered this approach before. Don't scientists break apart compounds and make new ones all the time? I mean, they take the salt out of seawater. And I remember doing an experiment in high school where we separated hydrogen and oxygen gases out of distilled water. What made Dr. Westerman's work so 'impressive,' as you described it earlier?"

"Well, Beck," back to lecture mode, "many chemical elements are easily separated from their molecules or compounds – electrolysis of water to produce hydrogen and oxygen being one example. Other elements are so volatile or unstable in their elemental form, that segregating the pure element is extremely difficult. Potassium is one such element.

"Potassium metal is a solid at room temperature, so one might think it would be easy to handle. But in reality, elemental potassium reacts so violently with water, including the water vapor present in all air, that it's not practical to either make, or retain, pure potassium in a small lab. But Dr. Westerman found a way to do it – at least in theory.

"He designed a unique lab apparatus for the process. And then he built it himself! Most chemists would never consider such a thing. But developing innovative laboratory tools and devices was one of his specialties. As of a month ago, he had completed assembly of a reaction chamber that, in my professional opinion, was capable of producing pure elemental potassium metal.

"Once the device was proven, his experiments with new potassium isotopes and compounds could move forward very rapidly."

I doubted the part about new isotopes. I could see potential advantages to new compounds, though. Finally, this was getting interesting.

"Can you think of any military or terrorist applications of the doctor's invention?" I'd spent most of my life thinking like a terrorist. I wasn't about to stop now.

Chuck thought for a moment. "Actually, no. Elemental potassium can only be manufactured, stored, transported and I suppose deployed, in an air-free and water-free environment.

"And if you're thinking that any potential new potassium compounds might be highly explosive or unusually dangerous, again the answer is 'no.' There are many more forceful explosives easily made in much safer fashion than anything anyone might want to make from potassium.

"Any chem student could cook up nitro-glycerin in her basement. Dynamite is only one or two steps farther down the same road as nitro. Internet websites even boast recipes for making plastic explosives. *The Anarchist's Cook Book* is one example. I can think of absolutely no reason anyone would use potassium in place of any one of these other, more stable, explosives."

"What about other uses? Could potassium potentially form an unusually potent acid? Or an exceptionally lethal poison? Could a tiny amount contaminate a large water supply, for example?"

Chuck paused for a very short time, then continued.

"Again, 'no.' Potassium hydroxide, also called caustic potash, is corrosive, but not extraordinarily so. And based on the nature of potassium bonds in existing compounds, development of a more highly caustic one is unlikely. In addition, there are already many extremely caustic acids and bases that any chem student could acquire or concentrate with little risk or expense. Why invent a new one?

"As far as poisons go . . . while some new potassium compounds certainly could be toxic to humans, cyanide, iodine and arsenic are all more deadly. And the formula for sarin nerve gas is not complex – just four ingredients. I can't imagine that any potassium compound might be more lethal.

"I'm sorry, but I just don't think Dr. Westerman's fertilizer research is useful for military or terrorist purposes."

Seemed a reach for me as well.

Of course, I knew that Timothy McVeigh had used a mammoth truck-bomb made from fertilizer and diesel fuel to blow up most of the Federal Building in Oklahoma City. But that was a nitrogen-based explosive. Nothing to do with potassium. Still, one should never underestimate the ingenuity of one's enemies.

"I'm sure the President will be relieved that the University doesn't appear to have any liability exposure owing to uses of the professor's work product," I said.

I was running out of ideas for things to ask Chuck.

"Is there anyone else at the Facility who may have known Dr. Westerman more intimately – and I'm not implying anything improper here?"

"His lab assistant, Farris. But he hasn't shown up for work since the professor's death. I can get you his address?"

"Thank you. I'll take the address and anything else you have on Farris: resumé, job application, social security number, cell number, pictures, whatever. I'll also need copies of Dr. Westerman's reports to you for the past three years."

Chuck didn't sense my urgency. Academia has its own timetables.

"I'd like to tell the President that I have them in hand *today*?" I added.

That moved Chuck out of the starting gate. "Of course. I'll have Rita ready them for you right away." He reached for his desk phone to relay the instructions.

"Thank you very much for your assistance. Shall I wait for the copies in the reception area?" I said, when he hung up the phone.

Chuck looked a bit perturbed at my lack of patience, but not enough to risk irritating the University President.

"The documents will be ready very soon. The reception area is fine."

"Nice to meet you, Chuck," I said.

"And you as well . . . Beck!"

There may have been a tinge of unnecessary emphasis on my name. No matter. I didn't need Chuck to be my buddy.

Departing Chuck's office, I returned to the reception area where Rita, the cute co-ed, was already efficiently producing the documents I had requested. I admired the photographic fields a while longer.

In a few minutes, the documents were ready. I thanked Rita for her assistance and headed out the office door.

CHAPTER 5

Three days earlier, Monday, May 4th, nearly midnight at the University of Minnesota Ottawa County Agricultural Research Facility Lab.

Farris Ahmed's journey to the University Agricultural Lab in Ottawa County, Minnesota had been a long one. At the age of eleven years, his father enrolled Farris at a *Madrassa* in a remote Saudi village. There he was taught the strict principles of militaristic Islam. In addition to academics, the teachers spoke untiringly of the Great Satan – a foreign entity with immense earthly power to do evil – which Farris later recognized as the United States.

It was every Muslim's solemn duty to fight for Allah in the *Jihad* against the Great Satan. And the teachers at the *Madrassa* made sure each pupil left their care with that message drilled deep into his brain.

After departing the *Madrassa* at age eighteen, Farris moved to the United Kingdom, where he attended and graduated from Cambridge University, with an emphasis in chemistry. During his final year at Cambridge, Farris had applied and been accepted to the post-graduate chemistry program at the University of Minnesota School of Agriculture.

It was there that he had met the professor – the man he was convinced could help him take the next step toward ultimate service to Allah among the infidels.

The same man whose throat he had slit only minutes ago.

It was truly unfortunate that the professor had to die. But he had caught Farris rummaging through the professor's locked desk. Though he felt no pity for the infidel, Farris recognized that he had learned a great deal of creative chemistry from the professor – so his death had, indeed, been a loss of sorts.

Only two months ago, Farris had filed a report with his command cell, describing the new apparatus the professor had designed to isolate potassium metal, and its successful testing. He didn't know if the *Mawlawi* had found this information significant. But Farris, himself, was very impressed.

Now, following the unanticipated need to kill the professor, Farris had to re-group. There were plans for such contingencies. But he wasn't pleased to employ one already, and certainly not for this exigency. Nevertheless, using the prescribed emergency communication method – in this case, a disposable cell phone – Farris had contacted the command cell for direction.

After Farris offered some disposal alternatives, the *Mawlawi* had instructed Farris to deposit the body and the professor's car in the Prairie River. Afterward, Farris was to return to the Lab on foot to pick up his own car – the distance from river to Lab was only a few miles. Then he would drive to the designated safe house via the most inconspicuous route possible. While he was on the way, he would receive further information and instructions on his laptop, via its wireless connection to the web.

Farris had done as he was told. The professor and his car went into the river. And Farris departed the Lab for the safe house, taking the potassium apparatus with him.

CHAPTER 6

Thursday, May 7th, late afternoon. Location unknown.

The *Al Qaeda* operative needed to report the attorney's Lab visit to his commander. Mr. Becker's presence at the crime scene was troubling. It may be that some action would need to be taken to deal with this unanticipated development.

Encrypted communications were exchanged.

Ultimately, the operative was told that he had done well and should not concern himself further with this situation. He should stay on task. The commander would handle Mr. Becker's intrusion.

CHAPTER 7

Tuesday, May 5th, early morning near the safe house.

After traversing what seemed like a thousand miles of rutted dirt roads through the darkness, Farris finally arrived at the end of the safe house driveway. It was just after dawn on Tuesday . . . a mere six hours after the professor's murder.

He was still driving his own car. He knew there had been some risk in that. But his route had been largely on hardened dirt roadways bordered by farmland. The risk was acceptable.

Farris also knew that, once the professor's murder was discovered, he would be the prime suspect. Besides leaving his fingerprints everywhere, he had no doubt left bloody foot-prints and all kinds of DNA evidence at the scene. Not to mention the obvious fact that he was absent from work and nowhere to be found today.

Farris didn't really care that everyone would know he was the killer. Actually, he was rather proud of himself. The *Mawlawi* had praised his valor and applauded his decisive action. Farris had already acquired the knowledge and equipment he needed from the professor, the *Mawlawi* had said. Farris's presence in mainstream America was no longer required. From this day forward, his service to Allah would take a new form – one that would take full advantage of his lab skills, and would have an immediate and decisive impact on the Great Satan.

Farris was excited about this new opportunity.

Parked near the end of the driveway, he checked his web connection. The information had downloaded as promised. There was a lot to read. He skimmed for the high points.

Farris should expect to find three 'colleagues' at the safe house. They would not be Muslim. They served Allah's will as unwitting soldiers in the *Jihad*.

Farris had been given complete background information on each of them. All of it was stored, encrypted of course, on his laptop hard drive. He would learn and memorize every detail about his three colleagues later. For now, he had read enough to know how to interact with them without upsetting the council's plans.

Two of his co-workers had come to Minnesota from a remote compound in Idaho. The Idaho group was a collection of *posse comitatus* types, mixed with all manner of vigilantes and government haters. The two here at the farm were of the government-hating variety. They held no particular religious prejudices and no strong racial convictions.

They had been told that Farris was an American Indian who had a gripe with the government over tribal land. *Al Qaeda* saw no benefit in disclosing his Arab connection when it was not necessary to do so.

The third member of the group would be a local of Ottawa County. He would know the plan completely, and also of *Al Qaeda's* role. And he would know that Farris was Arab, though he would go along with the American Indian cover story for the benefit of the government-haters.

Farris proceeded slowly up the narrow dirt road. A deep ravine paralleled the rutted road tracks to the right. Farris glanced backward as he drove. The curvature of the hills and the thick growth of sumac, prickly ash, bur oak and box elder trees, totally obscured his view of, and presumably from, the public roadway.

Ahead, dense and unkempt vegetation encroached on the driveway, hiding it almost completely from the morning sun's rays. Even from inside the car, Farris could smell the fresh moistness of the leafy trees and the dew-dampened undergrowth. He thought this remote valley an excellent hiding place.

Proceeding farther up the drive, Farris could see some buildings ahead.

The safe house, itself, was not much to behold. An 1800s-era, two-story farm house with peeling white clapboard siding and dark-green trim, it seemed to tilt a bit to one side. The roof ridge displayed a clearly discernable sway-back.

Most of the out-buildings were similarly dilapidated – some in a near state of collapse. The exceptions were what Farris assumed to be the former milk house, and two open-sided structures beyond the milk house that were partially blocked from his view.

The milk house appeared to have benefited from some recent reconstruction. The concrete block sides looked substantially repaired. There was a new metal door and the galvanized metal roof shone bright silver. The two open-sided structures appeared to be entirely new.

As Farris continued forward into the graveled driveway turn-around, there were no signs of his colleagues. He saw no people and no vehicles. His superiors had prepared him for this eventuality.

Per his electronic instructions, he pulled into the turn-around, stopped the car and put it in park. With all four windows rolled down and the engine off, he honked the horn three times, paused a few seconds, then honked twice more. Now he waited, seated in the car with his hands in plain sight at the top of the steering wheel.

Before long, there was movement to his right. A red-bearded man emerged from behind a barn-red granary building. He wore shaggy hair, a flannel shirt, denim jeans and over-the-ankle brown boots with leather laces. Drawing on his extensive cultural training, Farris thought the man looked like something out of a lumberjack movie. He was muscular and pretty big – maybe six one or six two, probably 220 pounds – much larger than Farris.

Following closely behind the man was a blond woman. Farris figured her for maybe forty years old, five foot six, and a fairly flabby one hundred eighty pounds. Her face would probably have been attractive without the extra weight.

The two stood motionless about thirty feet from Farris's car.

"Are you Mr. Eagle Claw?" the man called tentatively.

"Yes, sir," Farris replied, with equal trepidation.

His name for the rest of his stay in Ottawa County was to be Farris Eagle Claw, member of the Northern Cheyenne Indian tribe. Farris had asked whether his first name should also be altered; but the council had assured him there was no need, so 'Farris' it remained.

"Okay if I get out of the car?" Farris asked through the open windows.

The couple moved closer. Though the woman was still a bit behind the man, they both looked more relaxed.

"Sure. Let's get acquainted," the man said.

He sounded harmless enough.

Farris got out of the aging white Ford, stepped around the front and offered his hand toward the man.

They shook. The man had a strong grip. He smiled at Farris, displaying uneven, tobacco-stained teeth.

"Urland Umber, and this is my wife, Brenda." He gestured over his shoulder with his left thumb as he introduced her.

"Farris Eagle Claw," said Farris, thinking the name sounded absurd.

Now Brenda stepped alongside her husband.

"How!" she said, raising her left hand as if signaling a right turn on a bicycle.

Farris was not quite sure what to do. His indoctrination to western culture had not included viewing 1940s westerns.

He extended his hand toward Brenda. "And how are you, as well?"

Brenda shook with her right hand as she slowly lowered her left, pretending she had never made the ridiculous gesture.

"Pleased to meet you," she said.

Brenda was bursting to say more.

"I just want you to know how much we respect you Indians and all that you have done for this country. You were the first revolutionaries. And you're still standing up to Uncle Sam. Fightin' for casinos and independence and all."

She displayed a genuinely warm and admiring smile.

Great! How should Farris respond to that statement?

"Why, thank you, madam," he managed. "We Indians try to do our best. After all, we cannot let the folks in Washington run things."

This was a strange conversation.

"That's for damn sure," Urland joined in. "Politicians and judges been runnin' this country into the ground for over 200 years. Time we took it back for ourselves."

Urland obviously had no appreciation of what "take it back for ourselves" would mean to an American Indian, if he were actually speaking to one.

Farris maintained his pleasant facial expression. Underneath it though, he was deeply concerned. Could these be his colleagues? Not only infidels – but idiots? No wonder it hadn't been necessary to change his name. These dolts wouldn't know Arab from Algonquin.

May Allah save him!

As Urland moved alongside the car, he noticed the boxes of lab equipment in the back seat. "I'll give you a hand with these," he said, reaching through the back window.

"Stop! Please!" Farris said, a note of urgency in his voice.

Urland looked chastised. He removed his hands from the car. "What'd I do?" he asked.

"Sorry," Farris said. "Very sensitive. Very dangerous. Please do not touch the boxes. You know I am a chemist, right?"

Urland nodded, still a little confused.

"Very delicate chemicals in there. I am really sorry. You can help me move the boxes when we decide where they need to go. Until then, we are all safest if the boxes stay where they are."

"Okay," Urland said, his head hanging. "Just tryin' to help."

"How 'bout something to eat?" offered Brenda, changing the subject. "We don't have any wild turkey or corn-on-the cob or . . . or cranberry sauce. But I could make steaks and eggs?"

She was trying to be culturally sensitive.

Farris became suddenly aware that he was hungry. "That would be most kind," he replied.

Urland was not to be outdone in making his new Indian friend feel at home. "And I can see about maybe gettin' some venison for tomorrow. I put a salt lick out for the deer up behind the barn. They seem to come by pretty regular. How would that be?"

"Very thoughtful of you. But please, do not put yourself out for me," Farris said. He had no idea what deer meat might taste like. And he had no desire to find out.

Better finish reading up on my colleagues as soon as possible, he thought to himself.

"Let's get on inside now," said Brenda, shooing the two men along the cracked sidewalk toward the kitchen door.

CHAPTER 8

Tuesday, May 5th, somewhere in Europe.

With the new developments freeing Farris to work on the nuclear project, the *Mawlawi* had decided to call an emergency meeting of his technical advisors. A change in logistics might be in order.

The original plan had called for dynamite to be used as the primary explosive. It could be easily manufactured by non-chemists. And the raw materials were readily available. The main disadvantage to using dynamite was that it would take a lot of the stuff to accomplish their goal. And even with mass quantities, given the lack of confinement for the explosion, there was no guarantee of success.

When Farris had first reported the invention of the professor's potassium electrolysis device several months earlier, the *Mawlawi* had wondered if a chemical explosion might not accomplish the attack with a higher degree of confidence than dynamite.

Consultation with the chemists at his disposal had indicated that a chemical reaction was, indeed, a viable and potentially more effective approach to achieving the goal. But the scientists had recommended sodium instead of potassium. Sodium was substantially more stable than potassium, was easier to isolate and could be manufactured in a fairly basic lab by any competent lab technician. The American could be given the necessary instructions.

At that time, the *Mawlawi* had taken the decision to use sodium as the explosive. The council directed the American operative to modify the lab facilities to accommodate the additional requirements for sodium production. His chemists had assured the *Mawlawi* that the team in place would be capable of making the sodium bomb without the need of a chemist.

Now, two months later, the *Mawlawi* was convinced Farris's sudden availability was a sign from Allah that the operation should take advantage of the young man's unique talents. The *Al Qaeda* chemists continued to be wary concerning the complexity of processing potassium. But they had to agree that, if processing and delivery could be accomplished, elemental potassium offered significant explosive advantages over sodium.

After considerable prayer and reflection, the *Mawlawi* had made his decision: Potassium it would be. Allah had spoken.

CHAPTER 9

On March 28, 1979, an 'incident' occurred at the Three Mile Island Nuclear Generating Station near Harrisburg, Pennsylvania. Metropolitan Edison owned the facility. But its design and operation were closely monitored, and to a large extent controlled, by the federal government through the Nuclear Regulatory Commission, or NRC.

John Sigler knew the entire debacle was the government's fault. The administration's energy policy had not only driven entire coal mining communities out of work, but had also deposited the American public on the doorsteps of Hiroshima.

It was only a matter of time before something horrible happened. And in fact, it had taken a mere three months after TMI's commissioning for the disaster to occur.

After the total melt-down of TMI Reactor Unit 2, the government and the utility had both assured neighboring residents that there was "no significant release of radiation." Everything had been safely contained. Multiple government-sponsored "investigations" had concluded that, although the incident was extremely unfortunate, and TMI's neighbors had suffered substantial psychological distress, the melt-down posed no physical health risks to surrounding communities. Eventually, the government even allowed TMI Unit 1 to resume nuclear operations, while Unit 2 remained a pile of rubble filling a hole in the ground where the "incident" had occurred.

But John Sigler knew the radiation leak had not been "insignificant." He and his family lived just east of TMI, in the small community of Elizabethtown. When John turned twelve in June, 1979, just three months after the disaster, he had already seen some of the radiation's hellish effects.

His mother was pregnant with his brother, Jacob, at the time. She had lost most of her hair and was frequently so weak she couldn't get out of bed. The doctors assured the family that pregnancy hormones were the likely cause of her hair loss and weakness. She should remain bed-bound until delivery, just to be safe.

When Jacob arrived on July 4th, 1979, his family was in shock when the doctors sympathetically told them that Jacob had been born with an unusually small brain. Mental retardation was likely, they said. They were sorry, they said.

Less than three years after Jacob's birth, both he and his mother were dead. Each had died of lung cancer, though no one in the Sigler family ever smoked. The doctors could offer no explanation for the coincidence. But fourteen-year-old John and his dad knew the reason. It didn't take a genius to know that two-year-olds don't die of lung cancer.

TMI was the cause.

A few years later, John's father developed leukemia. Not common for a man his age, the doctors said. But it happens, they said.

The cancer progressed inexorably through his body. Evilly patient. Excruciatingly earnest. John had dropped out of school so he could remain by his father's bedside as the cancer silently ravaged his organs. John's father finally died, after months of agony, in October, 1985.

John was eighteen.

John wished he had died, too. Dying would have been easier than drowning in his family's pain, gasping for a breath of relief.

Even after the shock of the nuclear assault on the Sigler family had subsided, there were the nagging questions. Pursuing him. Unrelenting. Why had he, alone, survived? For what purpose?

John never forgave the United States government for torturing and murdering his family. Ultimately, he concluded there was only one possible reason he had been spared – to take vengeance for his family's suffering.

But John was no fool. He knew he couldn't defeat, or even seriously damage, the nuclear juggernaut by himself – especially not as a boy of eighteen. He needed collaborators, others who hated the nuclear establishment as much as he.

For years he sought out anti-nuclear organizations to aid him in his mission, to feed his pathological need for revenge. He posted his contact information in chat rooms on the rapidly expanding internet. He joined in anti-nuke rallies and attended meetings.

But without exception, these nuclear opponents were far too passive. He wanted to send a serious message. He wanted clear retribution for the death of his family at TMI.

John was patient. John was pragmatic. While he searched for help, he also maneuvered. Years passed, then decades. He attended trade school, served an apprenticeship and eventually developed a high degree of skill as a metal worker and welder. He earned a good living.

But he never forgave. And he never forgot.

Finally, an opportunity arose for him to infiltrate the enemy. Willing to leave his hometown for this chance, he accepted a job as a Plant Engineering and Systems Repair Specialist at the Prairie River Nuclear Power Plant near Red Wing, Minnesota.

Initially, John was very excited about his new job. He had assumed that his employment with the utility would surely present chances for revenge. But he soon discovered that even his status as a nuclear insider did not afford him the opportunity he sought. The facility's design included too many back-up systems, obstacles, counter-measures. For John by himself, assaulting the plant was still impossible. He needed to reach out farther, beyond his comfort zone. He still had to find a co-conspirator to lend him aid.

Then he suffered a devastating setback. Although at the time of the TMI incident John had appeared to suffer no serious radiation effects, he now learned that radiation damage can be subtle and sometimes slow to make itself apparent. At the age of forty-one, with his lust for revenge as great as ever and still unrequited, John was diagnosed with a malignant melanoma.

He first underwent radiation treatments and then chemotherapy. After twelve long months of treatment, his cancer was cured. The doctors declared it to be in remission.

But despite his apparent victory over the cancer, John knew his time to take retribution might be running out. He desperately needed to take action soon. The nuclear bastards had to pay!

Then one day, seemingly out of the blue, he had received a telephone call. By the man's accent, John would have guessed the caller to be English, or possibly Australian. Although no one mentioned the organization by name, when the group the caller actually represented became clear, John was taken aback. He had always considered *Al Qaeda* the enemy. But in this case, his interests and theirs aligned perfectly.

What was the saying he had heard during the Gulf War? "The enemy of my enemy is my friend?" After some consideration, John decided he didn't care if they were *Al Qaeda*, Nazis or Martians, so long as they would help him achieve his goal.

Al Qaeda had done its research on John before making contact. They knew his family background at TMI. They knew he wanted action, not passive protest. They assured him they had a plan – a plan that would devastate the nuclear industry. When he indicated an interest, they acted swiftly.

Within days after the initial call, John received a package at his home near Red Wing, Minnesota containing $250,000.00 U.S. in cash, together with instructions that he should acquire a specific, secluded, rundown farmstead in Ottawa County. The farm would be used as a safe house and bomb production facility.

John felt energized by his new collaboration. There was renewed hope for retribution.

He bought the farm property for less than $150,000.00 using a commercial money order he had purchased in St. Paul, and titled the land in his name. The rest of the money he put aside for future use. The organization instructed him to take care of the farm, such as it was, and said they would contact him when their plan was ready for implementation.

That was all about a year ago now. It had seemed an eternity to John. To make matters worse, his cancer had returned. He feared that he wouldn't survive to see the plan through to completion.

To be so close and not to finish? The thought was unbearable!

But recently, John had received another message from *Al Qaeda*. Plans for the attack were moving forward. The date had been set. The final act was only months away. Maybe he would yet survive to avenge his family's suffering.

The communication directed John to build a laboratory on the farm property. The initial lab construction plans called for a simple concrete block building, containing only lab tables and basic equipment.

It would be an easy project for a man with his construction and mechanical background. And when it came to beginning the actual construction, it got even easier. He could use the concrete-block milk house already present on the farm as a foundation. He didn't need to start from scratch.

He immediately began work in earnest.

From time to time John's ongoing cancer battle slowed his progress. But his determination for revenge countered the ever-present ache in his gut, and he pressed on.

When he wasn't at his regular job, he was at the farm, building the lab. He was making good progress, too. So he was a bit disappointed when, about two months after beginning construction, he received another communication from *Al Qaeda.*

The demands for the lab had become significantly more complicated. He could still use most of the construction he had already completed, thank god. But he would need to obtain additional construction materials, build two additional structures to complement the lab, and obtain substantially increased quantities of certain specific lab equipment and supplies.

The changes definitely made the project more challenging. But after the initial letdown, he decided he was up to the assignment. He would have to be.

There were no explanations for the design changes. None were necessary. As long as he was actually progressing toward a conclusion, any approach suited him fine. In his book, the ends amply justified the means.

CHAPTER 10

Wednesday, May 6th at the Ottawa County farm.

Farris knew that John Sigler was supposed to be the head of this group and in charge of operational logistics. Farris prayed John would have the intellect and sense that Urland and Brenda seemed to lack. And hopefully, John would be able to get Farris the materials he needed to perform effectively in the lab. Now that he was free to fight the Great Satan, he had embraced the role and was eager to begin.

When John stepped into the farmhouse kitchen early Wednesday morning, looking more or less like a normal human-being, Farris was relieved. Brief introductions were made.

John had been advised of Farris's arrival and knew of his talents as a chemist. The council had also informed John of the change in chemical processing, and that Farris would bring with him both the necessary laboratory apparatus, and the technical expertise, to make the potassium bomb a success.

John had plans for the day all laid out. Farris would begin to set up the lab in the concrete block building. He would inventory the current lab equipment and provide John with a list of any additional items that were needed. If Farris wanted it, John would get it – one way or another.

John also had an assignment for Urland and Brenda. They were going to steal a fertilizer truck filled with potash and drive it back to the farm. John had given careful thought to the whole truck-stealing procedure. He knew he needed to explain their duties as simply as possible, so as not to confuse Urland and Brenda. And they were easily confused.

Hopper cars of potash arrived at the Red Wing train terminals daily, mostly from the vast potash mines of Saskatchewan. Urland and Brenda were to select a fertilizer truck after it had filled up with potash for delivery to some small-town elevator operation. Then they would follow the truck to a remote location (of which there were many) and relieve the driver of his vehicle.

John explained all of these details, and more, to the Umbers. They seemed to comprehend. This was not unlike some of their operations back home . . . though after stealing a truck, they usually would burn it.

"Looks like we get some action today, Sweetie," Urland said, hacking tobacco juice into an empty beer can. "I'm takin' my gun."

"What do I wear for stealing a truck in Minnesota?" Brenda was serious. "Are jeans okay?"

"Come on Brenda," Urland said. "You'll look great whatever you wear. Where'd you put my ammo belt?"

Judas Priest! John thought. Of all the anarchists in the damn country, he had ended up with Snuffy Smith and Daisy Mae Yokum. He hoped they could at least steal the damn truck.

As Brenda and Urland prepped for their mission, John and Farris walked to the concrete building. Farris would survey the lab.

The facilities here were better than Farris had feared. The building interior had been thoroughly power-washed and smelled of industrial cleaner. The ventilation system seemed adequate. Lab tables, beakers, flasks and miscellaneous lab supplies were present in abundance. The fluorescent ceiling lights provided ample illumination. And multiple electrical outlets were powered by a diesel generator Farris heard rattling behind the barn.

One wall held multiple gas hook-ups. The gas fittings were set into two stainless steel panels. The panels lay flush with the wall on the inside and would connect to gas sources outside the concrete structure. Farris thought segregating the gas supply lines from the lab proper was a wise design decision. Much less danger of an inadvertent explosion.

Some of the gas fittings were labeled. Oxygen. Propane. Acetylene. A few spare connections were available in case other gases were required.

"I will need a dozen cylinders of argon gas hooked into the wall," Farris said. It was more an order than a request.

Little shit thinks he's in charge.

"Twelve tanks. I may have to be creative getting that much argon without attracting attention," John said. "But I'll get it. When do you need it by?"

"The argon is for the last step in the process. It will be at least a few weeks, maybe longer, before we get to that point."

John took Farris outside and pointed him toward the adjacent facilities, then left Farris to explore on his own. The Umbers probably needed further instruction.

John didn't like Farris. And Farris merely tolerated John. Each considered the other a necessary evil.

Farris began to explore. Leaving the lab and walking to the side farthest from the house, Farris could see the full extent of the new construction. He noted that the oxygen and acetylene gas lines were connected to a smallish metal shed nearly abutting the lab on one side.

Farris unlatched the metal door. Inside the shed were multiple canisters of each gas. The argon would fit here, too.

Alongside the shed was a steel-framed, tin-roofed lean-to which sheltered four, large cast-iron cooking grates with sizeable gas burners beneath each. Two five-hundred-gallon pressurized gas tanks located a short distance up the hill behind the lab provided propane to these grill burners, and also to the propane wall fixture in the lab.

Hand-adjustable flow regulators – much like the knobs on a back-yard gas grill – controlled the propane flow to the grills. On each of the four burners sat an empty, four-gallon, stainless steel, covered cooking pot.

Farris continued his assessment of the premises. Another, much larger lean-to lay perpendicular to the first and opened toward him. This empty structure had a concrete slab bottom and was nearly forty feet in length. Substantial steel poles supported the roof in three locations along the front.

Farris looked at all the structures again. None of them was built with any wood at all. Unusual. Wood would certainly have been a typical choice for the lean-to structures, and maybe the lab as well. Wood is much easier to work with than metal.

The person who built these structures preferred cutting and welding metal over sawing wood and pounding nails.

Interesting. At least he wouldn't need to worry about the buildings catching fire.

Having surveyed the surrounding facilities, Farris returned to the lab and set about compiling a list of additional chemicals and equipment he would need. Reagents. Buffers. Acids. Bases. Solvents. And some further specific lab tools and instruments.

By now, John had returned from the house. Farris was sitting at a lab table, pen in hand.

"The facilities will suffice," Farris said to John. "With the items on this list, and an extreme quantity of potash, I can begin."

He tore several sheets off the yellow pad and handed John the multi-page list.

John looked at the handful of papers. "Sure this is all?" he asked sarcastically.

Farris just stared at him.

John considered slapping the insolent kid – then thought better of it. "I can get most of this stuff for you within the next few days. Will you be able to stay busy setting up 'til then."

"I will need to do a good bit of preparation and testing before I can actually begin production. I must *know* that all the equipment and connections will work flawlessly before I start doing anything dangerous."

"Good. I'll be checking in every day to see if you need anything more. In the meantime, good luck with the inbred comedy act!" John slipped out the metal door, closing it behind him.

Infidel!

Snot!

Alone in the lab, Farris felt a surge of energy and purpose that he had not felt since the incident with the professor. He could feel Allah's will upon him.

Now . . . where to start?

CHAPTER 11

Friday morning, May 8th at Red Wing.

I had gotten quite the education from Chuck at the Lab. I now knew considerably more about farming and fertilizer than I would have cared to. But the potassium apparatus and its abilities interested me. Exactly how much potassium production was it capable of? And where was it now?

Maybe Gunner would have some answers.

By this time, law enforcement would have completed some of the background investigating – questioning the family members of the deceased, interviewing Ag Lab Facility employees, searching for the decedent's car – all of the time-consuming, and usually boring, services that police perform so well.

The Episcopal Church carillon in downtown Red Wing rang out the hour as I entered the front door of the Law Enforcement Center. Eight o'clock. Time for donuts. And I had a large box of Red Wing's finest pastries in hand.

Approaching the uniformed secretary at the front desk, I asked to see Doug Gunderson. "Please inform the Chief Deputy that I come bearing gifts."

I smiled.

The secretary gave me a sideways look; but she put my request through to Gunner. "He'll be down in a bit. If you'd like a seat . . . ." She gestured at the uncomfortable-looking plastic chairs lining the wall across the lobby.

I had seen alleged criminals sitting in those chairs on many occasions. I had always assumed the rigid plastic was part of the interrogation process. No water-boarding. Plastic chairs only.

"Do you need to cuff me before I sit there? Because I can't part with this box until I am assured it will get to the Chief Deputy."

She threw me a fake smile and turned back to her computer.

I remained standing.

After a couple minutes, Gunner appeared in the doorway to the inner offices. He first confirmed that I, indeed, held bakery products, which I lifted in his direction. Then, leaning against the open door, he waved me inside.

I led the way down the hall to Gunner's office, entered and ceremoniously placed the donut box in the center of his cluttered desk. Paperwork could wait for a few minutes when donuts were within reach.

Gunner poured himself a styrofoam cup from the Mr. Coffee in the corner. He gestured with his thumb that I was welcome to help myself to one also – which I did.

"So to what do I owe the pleasure of this visit," Gunner asked, as he expertly opened the donut box, folding the white cardboard top carefully under the bottom, exposing the entire selection. He chose a cream cheese danish. I took a cake donut.

"I was wondering if you have anything new on the floater murder? The *Red Wing Daily* says you have a 'person of interest' in the case."

Gunner had his mouth full of cheese danish.

I waited patiently for mastication to conclude.

Gunner choked down the danish and cleared his throat with a swallow of coffee. "Never a free lunch . . . or donut, apparently," he said. Then, "Why should I tell you about an ongoing investigation?"

"Gimme a break with the 'ongoing investigation' shtick. I brought donuts. I asked politely. Whatta ya' want from me? Try the eclairs, by the way. Still cool from the fridge. The custard filling is unbelievably smooth."

Gunner had polished off the danish in record time. He refilled his coffee. Topped mine off, too.

"Okay," he said.

"Okay what? Eclair or info?"

"Both," he said, carefully acquiring the eclair while resuming his position behind the desk. "Here's what we've got."

He wiped his fingers on a paper napkin.

"The perp is almost certainly the lab assistant. DNA evidence, footprints his size in the blood, fingerprints on the outside wall where the blood trail starts. We got his prints from INS. The Brits conveniently include a thumb in their passport records.

"But here's the clincher. When we found the professor's car nose-down in the Prairie River, we also found the lab assistant's prints on the *inside* of the trunk – one was even pressed in the good doctor's blood."

Gunner was clearly pleased with himself over this last statement. When I didn't look impressed, he continued.

"Plus, the assistant has disappeared and nobody has a clue where he went. He had no friends we could identify. And there were no other profs he was close with.

"We don't have the murder weapon. But that's minor.

"I'd like a more concrete theory of motive. The old man might have stolen credit for the kid's work? Maybe there was a woman we haven't yet discovered? Maybe the kid was doing the professor's wife – but that's a picture I'd prefer to keep out of my mind.

"I don't know. You got any theories?" He took a bite of eclair.

"Have your science guys reviewed the professor's work activities just before he died?" I asked.

"Yeah. Fertilizer research," Gunner said, his mouth still full of eclair.

Gunner's "Fertilizer" had sprayed me with pastry bits. I wiped my face with a paper napkin.

He sipped some coffee and swallowed. "Sorry about that," he said. Then . . . "Are you suggesting there's a murder motive in making artificial cow dung?"

"I don't know what I'm suggesting."

I paused a moment in thought.

"What about the piece of lab equipment the professor created? What is that like? Does it have any nefarious uses?"

Gunner looked at me baffled. "What the hell are you talking about? There wasn't any unusual or created equipment in the professor's lab. The BCA science geeks said it's all standard stuff. What makes you think there was something else?"

"Did your guys look at the professor's reports to the Administrator? Chuck Downing? Or interview him? When I talked to Chuck, he told me that the professor was some kind of genius with inventing lab devices. And Chuck has drawings of a recent invention in his files."

"You spoke with Dr. Downing?" Gunner looked at me disapprovingly.

"Yeah. We happened to be in the same place at the same time. Anyway . . . what about the invention?"

"The science guys said something about a *theoretical* invention referenced in the old guy's reports. But it didn't seem like something that had ever actually *made* anything. No one implied to me that it should've been in the lab when we inventoried it.

"Are you thinking this missing invention thingy is more than . . . what's the word?"

"Peripheral?" I offered.

"Yeah. Peripheral." Gunner took another bite of the eclair.

"Well, the thing is gone," I persisted. "If your guys didn't find it in the lab, the assistant must have taken it. Why?"

A pause for Gunner to sip his coffee.

"Lots of possible reasons," he said nonchalantly, leaning back in his chair. "First of all, maybe the professor decided the gizmo didn't work right after all and shit-canned it himself – possibly weeks ago."

I nodded, conceding the point.

"Second, even if the contraption was still in the lab when the professor was killed, it's hard to guess all the potential reasons why the assistant might have taken it: To sell it? To melt it down for precious metals? To play mad scientist in his garage? To stockpile his own custom manure supply?

"And if it *is* actually missing, maybe somebody else took it. We'll look at it some more, Beck. But I doubt it's relevant."

Gunner had a point – several, actually.

"You're probably right. No big deal. It's just something, you know, anomalous. Why was it there before and now it's gone?"

"I see what you're saying," Gunner said. "And I *will* check into it."

I knew this invention would haunt me until I had discovered why the thing was missing, and what someone might do with it. Maybe Gunner would figure it out.

We each had another bite of pastry and sip of coffee. The coffee wasn't bad today. Sometimes Gunner's brew will make your lips pucker.

"Can you tell me anything else about the kid . . . the assistant?" I asked after a few moments.

"Well, like I told you a few days ago, his name is Farris Ahmed. He is a dual Saudi and British citizen here on an unlimited student visa. That's the usual practice with citizens from the U.K. Graduated Cambridge near the top of his class. Started as a grad student at the U of M about three years ago. Twenty-five years old. Arabic descent."

Arabic. Not a surprise. But that feeling in my stomach was becoming more uncomfortable.

"Do you know anything about his education before Cambridge?" I continued.

"Let me see."

I waited patiently as Gunner again wiped his sticky fingers on a napkin, then began digging through a pile of papers. He pulled one sheet from the stack.

"Cambridge records indicate he attended The Riyadh Science Academy. From what I can find out, it's a prestigious school. Supposedly top flight. I haven't gotten any official records from the Academy itself. His father . . . we are communicating with him regularly . . . lives in the U.K. by the way – very concerned . . . confirmed his son's attendance at the Academy. The father claims that the high-class prep school is what got him into Cambridge in the first place.

"The father also assures us the boy is no radical. Just a normal kid trying to get the best education possible. According to Dad, the kid's fondest dream is 'to improve agricultural production in the barren Saudi soil.'

"Sort of sad, isn't it?"

"Yeah. Sad."

My stomach was churning, and it wasn't the donuts.

"So Dad says he's just a normal kid," Gunner went on. "Life's ambition? To improve on manure. And yet, here we are. No apparent motive. And little doubt about the boy's guilt. The Homicidal Horticulturist?"

"And how about international calls around the time of the murder?" I asked. "Did the BCA have any luck with that angle?"

"I don't know that I would call it an angle; but yes, there was one international call made from a cell phone off the tower in the area of the Lab around the time of the murder. Not many towers out in the boonies, so it was the only one they needed to check. Even so, the BCA told me I was a pain in the ass because, apparently, they needed to contact each cell phone company separately to get the info. So you *do* owe me one.

"What's the significance of the call?"

"Where did it go to?" I asked, ignoring Gunner's question.

"Somewhere in Germany . . . best they could do. Now . . . why do you care?"

"Just a hunch." I stood. "Thanks Gunner. Got to go. Keep the health food."

Before Gunner could chew and swallow his last bite of eclair, I was gone.

CHAPTER 12

Friday, May 8th, late afternoon at Red Wing.

Back at Becker Law Office, I was finishing up some legal work that my wayward adventures had delayed. It was about four p.m. when my intercom beeped.

My receptionist's voice announced, "Mr. Becker, it's Mrs. Becker on Line 1 for you."

"Thank you, Debbie," I said, as I answered the call.

"Hi, Doll. What's new?"

"Thank God you were there to answer!"

There was panic in her voice.

"What's the matter?"

"Sara just sent me a text. She thinks someone's following her around campus. I tried to reach her on the video-conferencing set-up, but no answer."

Our daughter, Sara, was attending college out of state.

"Beth. Relax. Breathe.

"It's probably nothing. I'll be home in a few minutes. Try to calm down. We'll figure everything out when I get there.

"Love you. Bye."

I would have stayed on the line with Beth on my way home from the office; but frankly, I was just as likely to cause more distress as I was to alleviate any. Thankfully, there was no such thing as congested traffic in Red Wing and I would be home shortly.

During the brief drive, my mind vacillated. Was this a real threat? Or just a young adult's active imagination. There certainly were those who might seek revenge against me for some of my prior intelligence activities. That is precisely why pains had been taken to hide my true identity while I was on Agency business. It is also why our daughters had received training from the Agency on how to identify potential threats, and what to do if they perceived danger.

Both girls were smart, strong, active, athletic and trained in self-defense. I had seen to the last part. But there was no way to be sure about the current situation with the little information I had at present.

As I approached Jefferson Avenue, I tried to relax. Clear my mind. Be calm. Help Beth be calm. Panic never helps anything.

The Pilot rapidly decelerated to a stop in front of our home. I jumped out, racing up the sidewalk and steps and continuing through the front door. Beth was sitting in the living room on the red leather couch with her head in her hands. She looked up at me. I could tell that she had been crying, but she had made herself stop. She knew the same things about clearheadedness and calm that I knew. She was controlling her emotions.

"Thank God, you're home!"

She got up from the couch. We held each other tightly.

"Okay. Let's sit and catch our breath," I said, as calmly as I could muster. My heart was beating in my throat.

We sat together on the edge of the couch, facing each other.

"This is probably nothing," I said. "But obviously, we have to treat it seriously. I need you to tell me everything you know, everything Sara said in her text, and what, if anything, has changed since we spoke on the phone."

Beth took a deep breath, holding back more tears that fought for release. Marshaling her resources, she gave me her report.

"First of all . . . what has changed since we last spoke . . . .

"I returned a text message to Sara telling her to be extra careful and that you and I would discuss things and get back to her as soon as possible. I didn't want to cause any panic."

"Good. She knows we're in the loop. That knowledge alone should make her feel better."

"I'm afraid I have nothing else new. But here's Sara's text," she said, handing me her SmartPhone. I accepted the phone from Beth, holding it in my right hand, with my left arm around her shoulders.

As I manipulated the phone with my thumb, the digital screen displayed the following message:

M&D,

> Please don't freak out or worry or anything. But I was told to contact you if I felt uncomfortable about any situation. So that's what I'm doing. I'm texting because I'm in the library and can't use the video link. At least I can still use my laptop. If I had to use my thumbs, you would need to decode this message twice. Ha.

Good. She still had a sense of humor.

I'm texting you because I think a man may have been following me around campus for the last couple days. Maybe I'm being paranoid or something. But I have seen him in the caf, at the library and in the fitness center. Whenever I look his way, he pretends to be reading a book, or listening to music, or whatever.

Normally, I wouldn't think anything of it. But the guy doesn't look like a college kid, you know? He has too many rough edges, if that makes any sense. And I can't find his picture in the college snoop book either.

He has a sort of oriental look. But not like my Chinese or Japanese friends. More prominent cheek bones maybe. He could almost be Native American; but I still think probably oriental, because of his eyes. He's maybe five foot ten and pretty muscular, about 190 pounds. Black hair, jeans, usually white shirts, running shoes. Sorry I can't describe him better.

I thought she had given a very detailed description. That would help a lot.

Oh yeah . . . he has a large tattoo on his right forearm. We were both working out and he was wearing a T-shirt. I saw it clearly, even from twenty feet away. Not that some guys here don't have tattoos, because they do. But this looked different. Not typical college guy stuff. Or even fake gangster ink. It contained three letters that looked to me like: capital "O," number "6" and small "r." But they didn't look exactly right – like some sort of archaic script or something.

Below the lettering was an image of a sword with a snake wrapped around it. And it looked as though he had

had the tat for awhile. It had bled and faded some. Sorry I can't do better.

It's probably nothing. But just to be safe, until I hear back from you, I'll try to stay with at least one friend all the time when I'm not in a very public place. And I'll be totally careful. So don't worry.

Lots of love,

Sara

I looked up from the screen.

When Beth saw I had finished reading, she asked, "Does this message mean more to you than it does to me?" There was a hint of quaver in her voice. "I can't make any connections with the tattoo or the oriental look."

I paused a few seconds, assessing Beth's emotional capacity at the moment. She could handle what I was about to tell her.

"I'm afraid it *does* mean something to me," I said.

"What Sara interpreted as 'O-6-r' on the tattoo, is likely 'O-B-G' in Russian, or Cyrillic, lettering. And Mongolians have the sort of facial features Sara describes."

"So you recognize those initials?" Beth asked. "Or a Mongolian connection?"

I looked directly into Beth's eyes, holding her hands in mine.

"The letters stand for Ovog Borjigin Gansükh. The English translation would be something like 'Gansükh of the Borjigin Clan.'

"Gansükh used to be a prominent Mongolian gun dealer. At one time, Gansükh headed perhaps the largest private arms brokerage in the world. He had hundreds, maybe thousands, of minions. All of them wore that tattoo. I played a substantial role in putting him out of business. In the process, I probably also made his life a bit . . . uncomfortable."

"Uncomfortable? How exactly?" Her expression betrayed her concern.

"My Team commandeered a freighter in the Indian Ocean near the horn of Africa. The cargo consisted of 30,000 crates of small arms, mostly Russian-made Kalashnikov assault rifles and grenade launchers, together with a lot of ammunition. The shipment was en route from the Ukraine, via the Black Sea and Suez Canal, to a ruthless rebel group in Kenya. The Kenyan rebels and Ukrainians were well-established trading partners at the time.

"With regard to this particular shipment, the Kenyans had paid half in advance, with the rest due on arrival. When the ship disappeared at sea, each trading partner suspected Gansükh of making off with the goods. Since my Team had blown up the ship with no witnesses, Gansükh was screwed. He couldn't recover the arms, and he couldn't afford to repay the Kenyans or the Ukrainians. Given the reputations of his two trading partners, I would have assumed that Gansükh would be long dead by now."

"So you're saying that this Mongolian arms trader may be trying to kidnap Sara?" Tears welled in Beth's eyes, but once again, she fought them back.

"I m afraid that's very possible. Yes."

I knew that I, too, wore a look of concern.

"I need to pay Sara a visit to check things out. I'll book the earliest flight I can. In the meantime, see if you can raise her on video conferencing. Otherwise, texting will have to do.

"Our main message to her is not to worry, but to remain calm, cautious and vigilant. Obviously, if she sees the man again, she should avoid contact. She should also surround herself with as many fellow students as possible until the man is gone. She should *never* be alone. In addition, please ask her to see if she can sleep in a friend's room tonight.

"Oh yeah . . . tell her I'll meet her at the caf at 8:00 tomorrow morning. I bet she'll be thrilled with that."

She likes to sleep in.

CHAPTER 13

Wednesday, May 6th, at the Ottawa County farm.

Farris had kept busy arranging the existing lab supplies and testing out equipment, gas lines and power circuits. Everything was checking out so far. Apparently, someone other than Urland and Brenda had built this set-up. Probably John. The infidel had some uses after all.

About 4:00 in the afternoon, Farris heard a car coming up the drive. He looked out the door. It was John's Chevy. The car made a 'Y' turn on the gravel and backed toward the lab. John parked just outside the lab doorway, turned off the car and popped the trunk.

As John unloaded additional lab supplies and brought them inside, Farris placed each item in its appropriate location in the lab. They repeated the routine with items stowed in the back seat. John was still missing a few of the more esoteric components and the argon. But for the most part, he had fulfilled Farris's order from this morning.

"I was wondering about this folding army cot and pillow," John said as he passed them along to Farris. "They don't look very scientific to the untrained observer."

"Well, ah, I will probably be keeping long, odd hours out here. Once the chemical reactions start, it is not as though I can just put them on hold and go take a nap in the house."

"Couldn't stand any more face time with Frick and Frack?" John said. It was half question, half statement.

"Something like that, maybe," Farris said, continuing to unpack the boxes. He had no desire for small talk.

At that moment, they heard the sound of a powerful diesel motor down on the public road. Both men stepped outside the lab and looked in the direction of the sound. The grinding of down-shifting gears and the intermittent revving of the diesel got louder, then changed direction – moving straight toward them.

Presently, a yellow semi-truck appeared, slowly making its way up the dirt drive. Blue smoke blasted from its vertical exhaust pipes. As the truck lumbered closer, they could see that attached behind the truck was an equally yellow trailer. The trailer looked like a coal tender – heavily reinforced metal sides with unloading shoots angling to the left along the bottom. Soon, they could make out Urland's tobacco-stained grin behind the wheel.

Pulling the semi alongside the Chevy, Urland gave the truck's horn one long blast.

John and Farris both cringed at the sound.

The driver's window was down. Urland's elbow rested confidently in the opening.

"How'd it go?" John yelled, over the diesel's rumble.

Urland shut off the truck.

"Slicker than owl-shit, if you'll pardon my French. When that trucker saw Brenda with the hood up on the Buick, looking all helpless, he pulled right over to assist. A damsel in distress. She's real good at that. All I had to do was ring his bell and we had 'er."

"I hope you didn't kill him," John said, a look of concern on his face.

"Nope. No need. I just gave him a rifle butt to the back of the head. Then I drug him off into the weeds. He's gonna have a bad headache when he wakes up. But he'll survive."

"Sounds good," John said. "Let's take a look at your cargo."

Urland was already out of the truck, strutting around like a peacock. Brenda was just coming up the drive in their blue Buick sedan.

John walked around to the back of the trailer.

He suspected there was a problem as soon as he smelled the ammonia. Farris smelled it, too. They looked at each other. Maybe the smell was left over from a prior load?

John grabbed the heavy metal crank affixed to the truck box and climbed the ladder until he could see over the top of the trailer. The ammonia smell was stronger here. He used the crank to roll the canvas trailer-cover partly open.

"What the fuck!"

Urland stopped strutting and looked blankly at John. "What's the matter?"

The Umbers had heisted a load of fertilizer all right. But it wasn't potash. It was nitrogen. God knows what it was mixed with.

"Uh, Urland?" John said, as calmly as he could manage. "This isn't the right stuff."

"Whatta ya mean?" Urland asked. "It's gotta be."

"The bulk potash we get around here comes from Canada and it's either orange or pink," John told him. "This stuff is white. And potash is the consistency of sand. This load is more like water-softener crystals."

Urland was totally deflated – like a boy who had just wrecked his bicycle.

"But this is the same stuff we used out west to make diesel fuel bombs. It worked real good for us." Urland was whining and it made John want to spit.

Instead, he took a deep breath before speaking.

"Urland, we're looking for something a little different here. Farris is going to cook the fertilizer up in the lab and we'll get a real fancy explosion," John explained. "This stuff you got today just won't work for what we have in mind. We're going to need to try for another truck tomorrow."

Urland seemed to be getting over his disappointment. He was probably used to screwing up.

"Okay. You want pink, we'll get you pink."

"And Urland . . ." John said. "Please. Next time . . . just get the potash. Don't improvise."

"Absolutely. Yessir!" Urland saluted.

John turned away from Urland and rolled his eyes. If the Bobsy Twins don't get it right this time, John thought, I'm going to have to do *this* myself, too. We can't just steal a whole convoy of fertilizer trucks.

Shit!

CHAPTER 14

Friday and Saturday, May 8th and 9th, between Minnesota and Sara's college.

The earliest flight I could catch out of Minneapolis/St. Paul International was at 10:15 that evening. I had booked a seat in first class. From ticketing to baggage claim (I had to check my gun and ammo), the flight took about four hours.

After collecting my luggage, I took the VIP lane to pick up the rental car. I had selected a red Ferrari F430 Spider convertible. Although I knew the Ferrari wasn't a great choice if I planned to inconspicuously tail another vehicle, I expected to acquire my target on campus. And the college community was far too small for Gansükh to have an operations center there. So I wouldn't need to surreptitiously follow the mark to home base.

I tossed my overnight bag on the passenger seat, removed the gun and shoulder holster, slapped in a full clip and strapped the Beretta under my light jacket. Once you get used to carrying a gun, you sort of feel naked without it. I felt better now that I had it on.

I set the navigation system for my destination and peeled out of the rental lot. The drive to Sara's college took another two and a half hours. When I arrived, with the time change, it was 2:45 a.m.

It was too early to do anything else. So I parked in the Visitors' lot, put the top up, reclined my seat as much as possible, and went to sleep.

Being able to sleep under adverse circumstances is a potent weapon. It can allow you to persist while your opposition falls victim to fatigue. I intended to employ all weapons at my disposal to neutralize Sara's stalker.

The night went quickly. I awoke at 7:00. I was starting to feel my age. That sucked. I massaged the kinks out of my sore neck.

My face felt grizzly and my clothes probably looked like I'd just slept in them. I couldn't see Gansükh moving on Sara in broad daylight. So I decided to freshen up before breakfast.

Locking the car behind me, I lugged my duffle down to the athletic complex. Once I found the men's locker room, I made myself at home. I took a long, hot shower, shaved a dark growth of whiskers and brushed my teeth. I raised and lowered my eyebrows in the mirror. Checked out my clear brown eyes, straight nose and strong jaw. Made sure my thick hair was properly organized. A winning smile for confidence.

I was ready to go meet Sara.

The Student Center was in the middle of the smallish campus. It was an uphill hike of about five minutes from the athletic facility. I entered the Center through the main doors and walked up a wide flight of stairs to the cafeteria level. By the time I had arrived outside the caf, it was 7:50 a.m.

I like being a few minutes early. Having extra time at your disposal can help you deal with unanticipated circumstances. I took a seat in a soft chair outside the caf and watched and waited.

A short time later, I checked my watch. It was 8:00 a.m. and nothing unusual had happened. As I looked up, I saw Sara and two friends coming through the aluminum and glass front doors. Right on time. Great kid.

Sara is an elegantly athletic five foot nine, with straight blond hair, like her mother's, but a bit lighter.

When she saw me, I subtly waved her ahead into the cafeteria with her group of friends. She caught my motion and continued as if I weren't there. I waited behind to see if anyone was following. There were lots of college students, but no gun-smuggling Mongolians.

Fifteen minutes later, having identified no one of interest, I strolled into the caf, scanning the tables for anyone matching Sara's description of the stalker. I saw no likely candidates.

Sara was seated at a table for four with three other co-eds. As I approached her, I smiled.

"Sara. There you are. I was afraid I'd missed you."

I was standing beside the table now. Sara stood up.

"Hi, Daddy." She gave me a hug and introduced me to her friends. I was cordial . . . charming, even . . . but in a fatherly way.

"Your mother sent a CARE package and I'd like to get it to your room before your classes start, if possible. May I steal you from your friends?"

"Sure. See you guys later!"

Sara collected her backpack and cafeteria tray and led me out. On the way, she placed her tray and dishes on a conveyor.

As we cleared the caf door, she tried to turn to me to speak. But I gently guided her near arm forward, keeping her moving until we were outside the building.

Once clear of the Student Center we stopped. I turned to her and asked, "Is there a good place for us to talk privately?"

"How about the Library?" Sara said.

"Too quiet. We might be overheard. And your room might be bugged."

Sara's eyes grew larger and the corners of her mouth dropped. I wished I could take that one back.

"Probably not. Just being extra careful," I said, trying to look relaxed.

She thought a moment.

"How about a gym? There are usually basketball games, or dance classes, or both, going on in one gym or the other. The echoes make it almost impossible for anyone to eavesdrop."

"Sounds good. Let's just stroll down there. But I want you to keep your eyes peeled for this guy you think might be following you."

We made our way across campus along a winding pathway shaded by august oaks and elms, down the hill to the athletic complex. Once there, it was pretty easy to find a noisy gymnasium in which we could privately visit.

The gym was much larger than the portion that was being used for the dance class. We staked out two folding chairs in a corner. No one cared, or appeared to even notice. Under the cover of big band swing tunes, we talked.

"Daddy. I know you wouldn't be here if you didn't think there might be some danger. I also know that if I *am* in danger, there's no one better in the world to watch out for me. I've been a little nervous since talking to Mom last night. I feel safer now that you're here."

Sara appeared genuinely reassured by my presence.

"That's good," I said, "because I promise that I will see to your absolute safety. You know that, don't you?"

"Of course I do, Daddy." Sara smiled. "You're the best."

"Okay. First off, I want to get a look at this man you think is following you."

Sara frowned.

"I don't know how to do that," she said, a hint of frustration in her voice. "I just see him around every once in a while."

"If he's watching you, he knows your routine, your class schedule, when you eat, where and when you study . . . that sort of thing," I explained. "Then he stakes out places where he can discreetly observe your movements. I'll follow you at a distance and watch for his hiding spots."

I could tell that the whole idea of someone stalking her, following her every move, felt uncomfortable and invasive to Sara. Who could blame her?

"But I don't see him very often," she protested. "It doesn't seem like very good odds to find him quickly that way."

Sara didn't understand how surveillance works. I was glad that she hadn't needed to learn.

"The times you see him are his mistakes," I said. "When he's doing his job correctly, you won't notice him at all. Trust me. If there's someone following you, I will find him this way . . . probably."

She raised an eyebrow at the 'probably,' but she knew I was most likely right. I did have experience in these sorts of things.

"Okay," she agreed, a hint of relief in her voice. "I just do my usual thing and you watch out for me."

"Yes. And now, you should make sure to walk alone, at least sometimes. Seeing you apparently vulnerable, might make him overconfident. He doesn't want to harm you. He's only interested in using you to get to me. If he tries anything, I will . . . ah . . . intervene. Got it?"

"Yessir." She saluted.

We'd have to work on her salute some day.

Even though it was a Saturday, academic classes were in session. Sara's first class that morning was Modern European History at 11:00 a.m. It was 9:00 a.m. right now. She planned to take a short nap in her room before class. As I mentioned, she likes to sleep in. Not a morning person.

We walked from the athletic complex straight back to her dorm, remaining separated from one another as we approached the building. She let herself inside with a key card. I walked up to the entryway about thirty seconds later. A smiley co-ed on her way out of the dorm kindly held the otherwise-locked outside door open for me.

Great security!

I jogged up the stairs to the third floor, two steps at a time. Sara was waiting for me in the corridor. I remained on watch at the far end of the hall while Sara opened her room door. She left it ajar, stepped in, then leaned back out and gave me a thumbs up.

Seeing that she was all set, I went back outside the dorm and found a suitable location from which to keep an eye on both dorm entrances/exits. I chose to recline on a grassy slope, pretending to read a student publication I had glommed onto in the dorm entryway.

Surveillance still felt natural.

For quite a while I saw nothing interesting. A steady stream of college students entered and departed the dorm. Most toted backpacks containing obviously heavy textbooks and laptop computers.

I continued watching. Nothing seemed out of the ordinary.

Then at about 10:45, Sara exited the dorm. She looked around briefly, probably trying to see where I was. Sorry, Dear. You won't be seeing me. Proper surveillance is one-way only.

I waited a few moments more, watching for any suspicious characters in pursuit. No joy. So I stood up with my paper and struck out after Sara. I could barely see her in front of me. But I knew where she was headed.

He would, too.

Sara had passed the Student Center and was nearing the history building when I spotted him. It was almost too easy. Mongolian features, white long-sleeved shirt, jeans, tennis shoes. He was lurking in an alcove of the Administration Building across the commons from Sara's classroom.

I stepped sideways behind the boughs of a convenient spruce and continued observing the stalker.

As soon as Sara disappeared into the history building, he left the alcove and headed my way. That was helpful. I was between him and his apparent destination.

When he passed my position, I followed. He wasn't expecting a tail and that made him easy to pursue. He continued away from the academic buildings and past the dorms. He was headed for his car.

It turned out to be a long walk. He had parked in an outlying lot, apparently to avoid attracting either unwanted attention, or campus parking tickets. The remote lot would be a great spot for us to get to know each other.

He approached, then unlocked, the driver's door of a green Hyundai. Gansükh had been reduced from international arms dealer to sub-compact status. I almost felt sorry for him.

As soon as he opened the door and began to sit, I broke from my latest position in a row of bushes. I had about fifty feet of pavement to cover and arrived at the Hyundai just as the door was closing.

Before he knew what was happening, I had jerked the door open and leaned into the car. I acquired a firm grip on his throat with my left hand.

"Let's get out and have a little talk," I said coolly, just as he thrust the heel of his right hand up toward my nose.

I turned my head in time . . . barely . . . but he still caught me pretty hard in the left eye. And the hand to the face had distracted me enough for him to wriggle out of my throat grip.

He was tougher than he looked. Fortunately, so was I.

As I assessed my next move, he dove for the glove box on the passenger side of the dash. I knew he had a gun in there and I didn't want to have to shoot him. He was just a flunky. I needed Gansükh himself. As he fumbled to open the compartment, I grabbed his belt, yanked him from the car and flung him onto the asphalt.

He scrambled to a crouch, then tried sweeping my legs with one of his. He made contact; but I had braced myself for the impact and didn't go down.

I waited for him to get to his feet. He tried a left-footed head kick, which I ducked, landing a firm right fist to his left kidney as he rotated.

He was down again. But not for long.

This time he popped to his feet, jabbing at me with a right. I deflected the punch. He followed with a left hook, which I ducked again, this time using my momentum to drive my left shoulder into his solar plexus.

Churning forward with my legs, I pinned him hard against the car parked two spots over. He groaned. With my head still down, I gave him two quick jabs to the stomach, putting all my weight into them.

Then I backed away – my body poised in a defensive stance, boxing-style. He wasn't coming any more. I watched as his back slid slowly down the side of the car until he sat on the dirty black pavement, a limp and dusty mess. He struggled to catch his breath.

Not allowing him time to recover, I reached down and pulled him up by the front of his shirt, turned him against the car and bent his right arm high between his shoulder blades. He groaned again.

I looked around. Apparently, no one had noticed our scuffle. And this remote location seemed as good as any for our chat. With his right arm still pinned against his back, I escorted him into a sheltered area of evergreens, just off the lot and out of sight from everywhere but up.

"Like I said," I repeated in his ear, "we need to talk."

CHAPTER 15

Friday, May 8th, late evening at the Prairie River Nuclear Plant.

Acetylene torches generate such extreme heat that many metals, including many grades of steel, turn to liquid when the torch is applied. The result is commonly referred to as 'cutting,' though 'melting' is a more accurate description.

John's project at the nuclear plant this evening was a cutting job, requested not by his employer, but by his conspiratorial superiors. He pulled the two-wheeled torch cart out of the storage shed and across the concrete pad to the pump house. Opening the door to the metal building, he turned on the interior light and wheeled the cart in behind him. The door swung shut with a clank.

This building held a three-dimensional maze of pipes, junctions, pumps, connections and valves of various types and sizes. Each had a specific purpose. John knew them all.

He moved directly to the valve he would be adjusting tonight. This particular valve controlled the flow in a twelve-inch-diameter water line. John knew exactly why this line was important. It should definitely be properly maintained.

Although there was no water flowing in the line at present, John needed to close this valve before working on it. He knew that if he closed the valve without taking preventive measures, he would set off an alarm in the Plant Operator's control room. Since he didn't want to trigger any bells or buzzers, he bypassed the remote monitoring system with a short length of wire. With this adjustment in place, the valve would always register as 'open' in the control room, whether it was, in fact, open or not. Now he could proceed with his work without interruption.

Frequently, maintenance of a valve requires removal of its bonnet, the metal housing that holds the valve's parts together. John used a large socket wrench to remove the one-inch nuts that joined the bonnet's two sections, then lifted the top of the bonnet from its seat. He would repaint the nuts and bolts when he was done, leaving no evidence of his activities.

Using a fair amount of effort, and steeling himself against the cancer pain that stabbed through his gut, John rotated the two-foot diameter wheel at the end of the valve stem clockwise until it wouldn't turn any more. Now this valve was fully closed.

Next he opened the hand valves on the gas tanks on his cart – first the oxygen, then the acetylene, which had a left-handed thread to assure that welders wouldn't open this cylinder of highly explosive gas by mistake. He pulled the gas flow trigger on the cutting torch, simultaneously squeezing the striker to create a spark. One spark was all it took and the torch was lit.

A throaty hiss emanated from the lit torch-head – like air jetting from a compressor. John made fine adjustments to the gas flow to assure optimum combustion mixture. For a moment he looked back and forth between the torch and the water valve.

This project would be evilly satisfying.

Flipping down his shaded welder's mask, he set to work.

CHAPTER 16

Saturday, May 9th, at Sara's college.

Having acquired the location of Gansükh's present hideout from his assistant, I dragged the Mongolian flunky back to his Hyundai.

Damn! No trunk. So much for a nice tidy package.

By this time, the Mongolian was totally passive, having perceived the benefits of submission. I encouraged him to take the Hyundai's driver's seat. Using several sturdy plastic zip-ties, I secured his arms around the steering column. Then I fastened his feet to the brake pedal in similar fashion.

With his arms and legs immobilized, I rolled up his right sleeve to confirm what I already knew. There it was: "O-B-G" in Cyrillic lettering, together with the clan's sword-and-snake tat. Sara had described it perfectly. Smart kid!

I was quite practiced at using plastic ties for binding captives. But just to be extra sure, I jogged back to the Ferrari and acquired a smallish cloth bag from my luggage. Then I returned to the Hyundai.

Using substantial lengths of grey duct tape, I further secured the Mongolian's hands and legs. With the remainder of the tape, I circled his head and mouth, twice. By the time I had finished, he looked like a handyman had wrapped him for mailing via parcel post. Finally, I removed the Mongolian's gun from the glove box and stuffed it in my belt.

Now I had to make sure the authorities would handle this package properly. I closed and locked the car doors, then made two identical paper signs. Using a bold marker, which I had brought with me, and a couple sections of the campus press, which were still folded in my pocket, I wrote clearly:

DANGER! INTERNATIONAL FUGITIVE!

STAY AWAY!

CALL INTERPOL AT

[I gave the number.]

I affixed one sign to each side window.

I was pretty sure Interpol would have a file on this guy. But without some prompting, I couldn't trust the local FBI to find it before they let him go.

I waved bye-bye to the Mongolian.

No response.

Returning to the Spider, I dropped the top. Comfortably seated in the Ferrari's driver's seat, I needed to make a few telephone calls. Beth would still be worried. I called her first, just to give her a status report and ease her mind. After telling Beth the whole story, I asked her to contact Sara to let her know I had solved the problem. She was safe. I would give Sara more details later.

I had other work to finish here. But I also wanted to get back to Red Wing to continue working the potassium puzzle. The right government authorities could help me out with the Mongolians.

Using a disposable phone, my next call was to the FBI's main office on Pennsylvania Avenue in D.C. It was the private line of Daniel Trew. Dan had one of the longest official titles of anyone I knew. Executive Assistant Director for National Security Branch/Associate Executive Assistant Director for National Security Branch, Counter-Terrorism Division. I knew Dan from a case in which we had both been involved a few years back, when he was just a 'Special Agent.' He wasn't really an agent at all anymore. But I trusted him, and that meant everything.

He answered his telephone, "Executive Assistant Director Trew."

"Dan," I said. "I can't say who this is. But you probably remember my voice from the ops team in the Bolivar drug bust about ten years ago."

There was a moment of silence.

"Say: 'On the ground, Shithead, or you're dead meat,' with authority."

I obliged.

"I'll be damned! How're you doing? Never mind. I bet you didn't call just to catch up, especially since you can't even give me your name. What's up?"

I told Dan about the Mongolian guy strapped to the Hyundai in the college parking lot. I told him about the tattoo and the arms dealer connection. I told him the Hyundai guy was dangerous and might still be armed. And I asked if Dan would personally see that this fellow was properly arrested and checked out for international wants, warrants or alerts.

"There should be plenty," I said.

"I'll make sure the gentleman receives appropriate attention. I know the counter-terrorism SAC in the local office out there. I'll talk to him right away. He'll do a good job.

"What about Gansükh himself? You got anything on him?"

"Nothing concrete," I lied. I hated lying to Dan. But he didn't want to hear my plans for Gansükh. "I'll let you know if I get anything more. Thanks, Dan."

"No problem. Be good."

"Yeah, Dan . . . like always."

"Right."

With the Hyundai Mongolian covered, I still needed to take care of Gansükh before he heard about the fate of his operative and fled the country. I couldn't take any chances that Gansükh might escape, or even be arrested and then weasel out on some legal technicality. If that happened, my family would be in danger once again.

To ensure that Gansükh didn't evaporate, I called my best contact at the CIA and told him Gansükh's exact location, as extracted from the Hyundai guy. Another favor. He would have some of his people keep an eye on Gansükh for now and leak his whereabouts to the Kenyan rebels and the Ukrainian Secret Service as soon as possible.

After receiving assurances that the CIA would baby-sit him until his business partners arrived, I was pretty confident I wouldn't be hearing from Gansükh again. My CIA contact would let me know later, just to confirm.

I was troubled that I had no idea how Gansükh had found Sara. I wouldn't rest easy until I had figured that one out.

With the Mongolian job completed in record time, and no flights home until evening, I called Sara's cell from my disposable. Maybe we could go out for dinner before I had to leave.

I was lucky enough to catch her at a time when she could answer.

"Hey, Sara. It's Dad."

"Hi, Daddy," Sara said. "Mom called and told me that you have 'abolished' the bad guy and all is well with the world."

"That's pretty much true. But I'd like to visit with you before I leave. Any chance we could do an early dinner?"

"Sure. Let's go downtown to The Dregs. They have the best burgers in town. Can you meet me at my dorm at 5:00?"

"Sure thing. Love you."

"I love you, too, Daddy. And thanks for everything."

"No sweat. See you soon."

*   *   *

I picked Sara up promptly at five. She was standing in front of her dorm as I arrived in the Ferrari.

"Nice ride," she commented as she hopped into the passenger seat. "Having a mid-life crisis, are we?"

"Ouch," I said, and headed for the restaurant.

The burgers were all that Sara had promised. But I wasn't really there for the food.

"Sara, Honey. What your Mom told you is true. I located your stalker and have made sure that he will cause you no further consternation."

"Thanks again, Daddy."

"But Sara," I continued, "just because I got rid of this goon, that doesn't mean we're completely in the clear."

Sara listened calmly, showing no undue anxiety.

"I don't know how this guy found out about me, or you, or where you go to school. So that concerns me a little and I must ask that you raise your alert level a tiny bit – just in case the leak hasn't been completely plugged.

"Do you understand what I am saying?"

Sara remained composed.

"I'm pretty sure I get it. You've done away with the current threat. But you want me to be a little extra careful until you can find out why it happened in the first place."

"Exactly," I said. "Can you do that for me?"

"Of course, Daddy. I'm not worried anymore. But I will, as you always say, 'remain vigilant' in case of unanticipated developments."

"Great."

We finished off our burgers and fries. It was time for me to head back to the airport to catch my return flight.

When I dropped Sara off in front of her dorm, we both got out of the car. I walked over to her side and we gave each other big hugs.

"Love you lots," I said softly into her ear.

"Right back atcha," she said into mine.

I departed for home.

CHAPTER 17

Saturday, May 9th, at the rural Ottawa County farm.

A couple days after their first truck-jacking, Urland and Brenda had better luck. They delivered a truck filled with potash to the farm. (Under John's instructions, they had parked the first truck, the yellow one, out of sight, up a winding field road, between the trees. It was well-hidden, even from the air.) Urland pulled the new truck forward until the potash hopper doors were alongside the large, empty lean-to.

The three co-conspirators, Urland, Brenda and Farris, stumbled over each other trying to construct a potash feeding system to transfer the load from the truck-trailer into three sections of the concrete-floored structure – the three sections farthest from the lab.

The result was utter failure.

Fortunately, when John arrived on the scene, he made short work of the project, designing and installing a more efficient feeding system than any of the other three had thought possible.

After solving the potash unloading dilemma, the splinter cell had no further need for John at the farm, so he left to attend to errands elsewhere.

With John's potash feeder in place, Farris and the Umbers made fast work of transferring the pink sand from truck to lean-to. The potash now lay in three separate piles inside three of the lean-to's four bays.

After Urland had closed the tender's bottom doors, Farris instructed him to hide this truck next to the yellow one. Urland complied.

Once the second truck was safely hidden away, Farris needed to get Urland and Brenda out of his hair. He informed the infidels that from here on, the advanced chemistry he would be undertaking was very delicate. He really could not use their help in or about the lab. Furthermore, their mere presence inside the lab risked contamination of both the chemical processes and themselves.

Urland and Brenda seemed convinced of Farris's sincere concern. As for Farris, separation from the Umbers would make his work, and his life, immeasurably easier.

When the Umbers departed for the house, Farris knew his first order of business was to test the potash to see exactly what he had. Not all potash is the same.

Retrieving the necessary lab supplies from their cabinets, Farris prepared six different solutions in six separate test tubes. He spooned a bit of the pinkish potash powder into each. After corking the tubes, he shook them gently, then allowed all of them to rest in their holders on the lab table for sixty seconds.

Based on the compounds that had precipitated from solution in each test tube, Farris knew that the predominant ingredient in this potash was potassium chloride. Other compounds he needed to eliminate before processing the potassium were: an iron compound, a fair amount of sodium nitrate and some lime.

He knew how to remove all of these impurities. Employing the four-burner grill in the smaller lean-to as his mass production facility, he set about doing so on a wholesale basis. Using shovels and pots instead of lab spoons and flasks, he attacked the huge mounds of pink sand. He intended to purify as much of the truckload of potash as possible.

This would take a while. But he had learned patience long ago, at the *Madrassa*. Hadn't he already lived among his enemies for more than three years without being allowed to fight?

With resolve and determination born of religious zeal, he set about this first major task.

CHAPTER 18

Around noon, Tuesday, May 12th, at Red Wing.

Ever since hearing of the murderer's Arab connection and the international call, I hadn't been able to get terrorism off my mind. I'd spent most of my life thwarting terrorists. I anticipated a terrorist around every corner and in every situation. Maybe I had developed terrorist paranoia. Then again, sometimes a little paranoia can be a good thing.

I needed to gain some perspective. Sitting outside the office in the Pilot, I pushed a button on my cell. I was calling my friend, Terry Red Feather, aka 'Bull.'

The phone rang twice. Then Bull's voice came out of my earpiece.

"Yeah?"

"You have won a free lunch for one at Fiesta Mexicana – casual dining in an authentic Mexican atmosphere. This offer is good for the next half hour. You may redeem by meeting me there within that time."

"Important?"

"Yeah. I think so."

"Okay," Bull said.

Click. No need for niceties.

I don't remember when I first heard Terry called Bull. But the name fit his six-foot-four, 235 pound muscular frame, and his tendency toward stubbornness as well. So I had adopted the nickname and had called him by it ever since – probably more than four years now. He didn't seem to mind.

Bull is a full-blooded Mdewakanton Dakota American Indian. Born on the local Prairie River Reservation, he left his home and family at the age of sixteen to join the army.

At the time, he was required to be at least eighteen to enlist. But documentation of his birth on the reservation was non-existent. And he was big enough and strong enough. So the army was pleased to have his assistance.

After he left the Rez to "be all that he could be," Bull's family and friends heard nothing from him for more than twenty years. Based on Terry's behavior as a teen, they assumed he had been killed in a knife fight at some bar.

Then one day about eight years ago, he had shown up on the doorstep of his parents' home on the Rez. By the time of his return, he had become the imposing figure I had come to know.

Bull never told anyone where he had been for twenty years. And after a few altercations, folks quit asking. Based on his military knowledge and the way he carried himself, I'd formed my own conclusions. I might ask him for details some day. Probably not soon.

Bull didn't live on the reservation. He owned a recently-built, log-style house on a Wisconsin bluff overlooking the Mississippi river valley, together with forty acres of mostly wooded land to spare. A modern-day Native.

I drove to the restaurant. It took two minutes – traffic was horrific.

I got us a booth near the back and ordered two Coronas, *con limón.*

As luck would have it, Bull was in downtown Red Wing when he got my call. I had barely settled into the booth when he appeared around the corner of the restaurant entryway. His massive frame hiked down the aisle between tables toward where I sat – his long black hair somehow blowing in the breeze. I pulled the table closer to my side of the booth to make room. Bull sat down across from me just as the beers arrived.

Speaking in Spanish, I told the waitress that we would need a few minutes before ordering. She nodded and left.

Neither of us said anything at first. I squeezed the lime wedge into my Corona and took a pull, taking care to let the lime float out of the way so the clear yellow beer could flow freely. Silence was comfortable with Bull. There was no need to speak unless you had something to say.

"Well. Other than tacos, why am I here?" Bull asked presently, following the question with a swallow of Corona.

I leaned over the table and spoke quietly. "I think I'm seeing terrorist ghosts," I said.

"Huh?"

"Here's the deal. I've spent so much of my life chasing terrorists, that I think I'm seeing terrorists behind every mystery, even when they may not be there. Does that ever happen to you? Even after all these years?"

"'Course. Been drilled into us. Terrorists 'til proven otherwise."

He took another pull on his Corona, then rotated the bottle on the table a few revolutions.

"You didn't drag me down here to shoot the crap about the old days. And you sure as hell aren't looking for any bullshit psychology from *me*. What's buggin' you?"

I thought for a moment.

"Do you remember the floater they found on the river a few days ago?"

"Dumb question."

"Yeah. Well, it turns out the killer is from Saudi Arabia. He was a graduate assistant agronomist at the U of M Ag Lab where the guy was killed. And the cops have looked, but they can't locate him."

"Nothing new there." Bull finished his Corona and waved two fingers at the waitress. *Dos mas.*

"Cops almost never find the doer, 'cept if it's the spouse or the lover. Hell, you know that. Kid's probably in Mexico by now."

"Another interesting tidbit," I continued. "There was an international cell call made to Germany, on a throw-away phone, from the vicinity of the Lab, at the same time as the professor's murder."

"Hmmm."

"And one other thing I think might be important. The cops have found no motive. But . . . a novel piece of chemistry equipment the professor had invented disappeared from the Lab the night he died. According to the Lab Administrator, this invention is supposedly unique and highly sophisticated. He told me what this apparatus is for, that is, what it does. But he also assured me that it didn't have any military or terrorist applications."

I paused.

"So why am I still feeling a terrorist in my gut?"

Bull considered what I had just told him.

"The international call is weird. How many of those d'ya 'spose get made in the middle of the night from the Ottawa County boondocks – especially from a dime store phone? And the missing lab gadget is interesting. What's it s'posed to do?"

"It makes elemental potassium metal."

Bull raised an eyebrow as he finished off the Corona.

"Huh. That *is* something new. Elemental potassium. Tricky stuff. But I gotta go along with the Lab guy. Doesn't sound like a weapon of mass destruction."

"Would make one hell of an explosion in the river, though," Bull went on, thinking out-loud. "Reacts with water like a sonofabitch. But you'd have to get the stuff to the target without it blowin' up in your face. Not easy to transport. Reacts with water in the air, too. Way too unstable to be used as an explosive in any traditional sense."

I couldn't remember ever having heard Bull speak so many words consecutively. He usually said little. His interest confirmed that my suspicions weren't entirely baseless.

"And yet . . . my gut," I said, as two new Coronas arrived to replace the empties.

We ordered our food. I had *Dos Enchiladas Verdes*. Bull had the *Mole Burrito*. The waitress left to fill our orders.

More silence.

I respected Bull's opinion in the area of explosives. I knew no one with more knowledge of things that blow up. Bull had worked with everything from crude ammonia/diesel bombs, to

C4 plastique, to specialty pyrotechnic ordnance. He knew his bombs.

"Cell call to Germany," Bull said, mostly to himself, shaking his head as he held the second Corona in both hands.

The waitress brought our food. After she left, I restarted the dialogue.

"Okay. Let's look at this from another angle. If you were a terrorist stationed in Minnesota, and you could pick any target at all, what would you choose?"

Bull washed some burrito down with a swallow of Corona. "Easy. One of the nuke plants – Prairie River or Canton."

"I was thinking the same thing. And one of those nukes is just a stone's throw from Red Wing – and from the University Lab."

Bull thought some more.

I waited.

Bull finished off his lunch before speaking.

"Those plants have pretty heavy security. No idea what weapons are inside that fence."

Bull thought some more. I waited again.

"'Course, you might be able to crash a private plane into one of the reactor towers. But they're built like a brick shit-house. Plane would squash like a bug on a windshield. And no way *Al Qaeda* is gonna get another commercial plane close enough. New rules of engagement since 9/11."

I nodded my agreement with Bull. But I persisted. "Every target has a soft spot somewhere. If I were going to attack a nuke, I'd find it. It might be a challenge without inside information. But there could be an insider."

"Could be," Bull conceded. "And that cell call is unusual. But you've got a lot of question marks."

"Bull, I need to find out more about the Prairie River Plant. It's right here in Ottawa County. And it's also the larger of the two nukes. Any ideas?"

"Got some contacts on the Rez. Can maybe find out some that way. But you never gonna know nothin' for sure."

"Okay. That'll be my problem to deal with," I said.

Bull raised his Corona in a toast in my direction. "Good luck with that." He drained the bottle.

CHAPTER 19

Still Tuesday, May 12th, in Red Wing.

After having lunch with Bull, I told Gunner about my theory that terrorists were planning an attack on the Prairie River Nuclear Plant. To put it tactfully, he was skeptical.

I had to admit that hard evidence was scarce. But he did do me the favor of connecting me with Dana Winston, a chemist at the plant. Dr. Winston agreed to meet me for a beer at the Hog and Jowl after her shift ended at 3:30 that afternoon.

The Hog is a mid-western imitation of a British pub. Lots of dark wood and dim lights. At the appointed time for our meeting, I was seated at the bar, a pint schooner of Bass Ale in front of me.

As I waited, I leaned one elbow on the bar and checked out the terrain. Burgers sizzled on a metal grill in the back corner. Booths and chairs were tightly upholstered in imitation red leather with rows of brass rivets around the edges. The atmosphere was discreet and comfortable. Even at four in the afternoon, couples groped one another over small round tables in the corners.

I inhaled. The smoky aromas from the sandwiches toasting on the grill completed the ambience.

At five after four the outside door opened, slashing a shaft of light across the smoky room. After the door swung shut, I saw a well-dressed, middle-aged woman standing in the doorway, squinting.

I had told Dana I would be at the bar. I turned halfway on my bar stool and gave a subtle wave, the heel of my hand resting on my thigh. Responding to the gesture, the woman headed my way.

I stood.

"James Becker," I said, offering my hand to Dr. Winston. "Please call me Beck."

"Dana Winston," she responded. "And Dana is fine with me."

After the introductions, the barkeep drew us a couple fresh ales and we sat at a table for four, as distant from other patrons as practical. Neither of us wanted to broadcast the discussion we were about to have.

After we had settled in, Dana spoke first.

"So Deputy Gunderson says you need information about the nuke plant. Obviously, there are limits to what I can tell you. But I hope you will keep even the facts I am able to disclose to you in confidence. We – that is, the utility company folks – like to keep as much information about the nukes as close to the vest as possible."

I decided to play the attorney confidentiality card.

"Dana," I said. "I am a lawyer. I can assure you that I fully understand the meaning of confidentiality. No one will hear from me any hint of the topics we discuss today."

Dana had been sitting primly on her chair – back straight, with her hands in her lap. Now she allowed herself to relax into the backrest.

"Okay. So how can I help?" She picked up her schooner smoothly and sipped the ale.

"Let's start with the basics. Tell me about the plant in general. Give me Nuclear Power Plant 101."

"Okay." She replaced her glass on its cocktail napkin. "Let me think a minute."

I tipped my schooner, enjoying a swallow of the cold Bass, then dabbed the foam off my upper lip with an extra cocktail napkin. While I waited for Dana to organize her thoughts, I watched the bubbles rising in lines inside my glass. Like my terrorist paranoia, they seemed to emanate from nowhere.

"Okay. Let's start with electric power in general.

"The vast majority of electric power in the U.S. is made with steam. Nearly all electric plants use fuel of one type or another to boil water and make steam.

"The boiling water expands dramatically as it becomes a gas. The expansion creates tremendous pressure and forces the steam through a turbine – basically a series of fan blades mounted on a steel shaft – which rotates as the steam forces past them. After exiting the turbine, the water cools to its liquid state and is recycled through the boiling process."

"Got it," I said. "Water turning to steam spins the turbine. Then the steam is cooled again, like going through a car radiator, and continues through this boil and condense cycle indefinitely."

"Very good. Now . . . connected to one end of the turbine is a generator. The generator is a device that converts the mechanical energy present in the rotating turbine – the spinning fan shaft – into electrical energy. The generator transmits the electricity through various circuits to sub-stations which meld it with the electricity already in the power transmission lines – the grid."

I nodded my understanding.

"The main difference between types of electric generating stations," Dana continued, "is the kind of fuel used to turn the water into steam. Gas plants use methane. Coal plants use mixtures of coal ore. Nuclear plants use uranium, though as soon as the reaction begins, plutonium is also present, and that also 'burns.' Obviously, each type of plant needs to burn its fuel in a different way."

Dana hadn't actually told me anything that I hadn't known for twenty years. But she was being thorough and I appreciated that.

I have always endorsed the theory that a sound understanding of the fundamentals leads to better execution of more advanced skills. That theory applies equally whether you're involved in the military, academics, sports, business . . . just about anything.

Preparedness is next to godliness. Cleanliness isn't actually next to anything.

I let her continue.

"For coal and gas, you light what amounts to a huge barbecue grill and surround it with water pipes. The fire heats the water in the pipes to make the steam. In the case of nuclear fuel, the uranium actually burns itself. So you don't need to light it.

"By the time the nuclear fuel arrives at electric power plants, the uranium pellets have already been formed into rods and coated with a zirconium alloy. The zirconium is strong and reacts very little with the uranium, so it makes the fuel easier to move around. The fuel rods are typically about thirteen feet long and a centimeter or so in diameter. Long and thin.

"Fuel rods are bundled together in rectangular metal frames to give them structure and stability. A bundle might typically contain around 150 to 200 fuel rods. Collectively these framed bundles are called 'fuel assemblies.' A nuclear reactor in an electric plant might have up to 200 of these fuel assemblies in its reactor vessel at any given time."

"Just a moment, please." Now I was learning new stuff and I wanted to get it right. "What is a reactor vessel?"

"The reactor vessel is the oven of the reactor. The fuel assemblies are precisely racked in this oven space to produce maximum heat, with minimum risk that the nuclear reaction will get out of control.

"More terminology here," Dana continued. "Once placed in the reactor vessel, the collection of fuel assemblies is called the 'reactor core.' Normally the reactor core will be suspended in the center of a radioactively insulated space. The core will also have control rods strategically placed to interrupt the nuclear reaction if it needs to be reduced or shut down – like for repair or to adjust power output."

"I'm sorry. I need to stop you again. How do the control rods affect the nuclear reaction? I understand that they shut the reaction down; but how do they do that?"

Dana thought for a moment. I had another swallow of Bass.

"To answer that question, I need to first explain how nuclear fuel burns. You see, the uranium in the fuel assemblies is inherently unstable and is constantly releasing neutron particles into its surroundings. In the reactor core, the freed neutrons slam into uranium atoms in other fuel assemblies. Every time a neutron/uranium collision occurs, another uranium atom splits, releasing more neutrons, and so on. Every collision releases heat.

"As long as there are unstable atoms like uranium and plutonium in the area, the reaction is self-sustaining. To control the intensity of the reaction, 'control rods' are inserted between the fuel assemblies."

"What are these control rods made of and how do they work?" I asked.

"Control rods are typically encased in stainless steel and contain obscure elements, like gadolinium or hafnium, that will withstand bombardment by the neutrons without fissioning – that is, splitting apart. As the control rods intercept and absorb free-flying neutrons in the core, the reactor cools. The farther the rods are inserted, the more neutrons they absorb, and the cooler the reactor becomes."

"Okay. I think I understand the basic idea. We may have to come back to this for more details later. Okay?"

"Sure." She sipped her ale. After wiping excess condensation from the table with an already soggy cocktail napkin, she replaced her drink in the semi-dry spot.

"How are the reactor vessels protected from sabotage?" I asked. "What keeps someone from bombing them or flying a plane into them or something?"

"Well," Dana continued, "the reactor core is totally enclosed within a theoretically bomb-proof containment structure. Many feet of steel-reinforced concrete. More steel. Then more concrete, etc. And no one is allowed in or out of containment except to conduct repairs or to re-fuel the reactor."

"You said 'theoretically bomb proof.' Only 'theoretically'?"

"Well, the engineers and the physicists are pretty sure . . . very sure actually . . . that the containment structures can survive conventional explosives, or even an airliner crash. But of course, no one has actually tried flying a commercial airplane into a containment structure. So their imperviousness remains theoretical.

"I didn't mean to imply that the structures are unsafe or anything. From all the data I've seen, the reactor containment towers seem pretty impregnable."

"Okay. Got it. What happens to the uranium fuel when it is burned up, for lack of a better term?"

"About every year-and-a-half, when the nuclear fuel is 'spent,' the reactor must be re-fueled. Usually about a third of the oldest fuel assemblies are removed from the reactor core and replaced by fresh fuel.

"Although the fuel that has been removed is considered 'spent,' it remains highly radioactive and the nuclear reaction still needs to be controlled. For this reason, the spent fuel assemblies are placed in a pool and surrounded by circulating water infused with boric acid – the 'spent fuel pool.'

"The circulating borinated water is a closed loop. The heat the cooling water absorbs from the fuel dissipates through a heat exchanger, like the car radiator you mentioned before. A continuous supply of river water provides the coolant.

"The spent assemblies remain in the pool until the utility gets government authorization to move them elsewhere. That was supposed to be Yucca Mountain. But there is no permanent storage site for spent fuel at present."

"Can regular water without boron be used to fill the pool?"

"If ordinary distilled water were the only coolant in the pool, you could keep the fuel cool, as long as the water kept circulating through the heat exchanger; but there would be little margin for error. The boron is the real 'control rod' in the pool.

"Boron absorbs the flying neutrons. Plain water wouldn't slow the nuclear reaction, just carry the heat away. If the water stopped flowing for even a few hours, the pool could boil dry."

That was interesting.

"So what happens when the spent fuel pool gets filled with fuel assemblies?" I was catching on to the terminology.

"If the spent fuel pool is full, the reactor must be shut down and decommissioned. We were close to that a few years ago. The spent fuel pool at Prairie River was nearly full. At that time, the NRC, the Nuclear Regulatory Commission, allowed us to re-rack the fuel assemblies in the pool – basically, packing the fuel closer together.

"Re-racking helped for a while. But you can store the fuel assemblies just so close to one another without risking over-heating. If they're too near each other, there isn't enough boric acid between them to absorb the flying neutrons.

"A few years after re-racking, the pool was almost full again. At that time, the utility again received permission from the NRC, and the State of Minnesota, to store some of the coolest, least radioactive, fuel assemblies in 'dry casks' outside the plant. The dry casks each contain a couple dozen fuel assemblies in a stainless steel container. Every container is encased in tons of concrete.

"The concrete casings of the casks provide nuclear insulation, preventing radioactivity from leaking into the outside world. And the fuel assemblies in the casks are sufficiently inactive that they no longer require water to keep them cool. Simply radiating heat through the concrete shell into the air provides adequate cooling.

"The spent fuel just sits there in these casks on a concrete pad near the plant – waiting for the government to determine a final storage destination."

"Is there any way the casks could blow up?" I didn't think so – but I wanted to be sure.

"It is impossible for a dry cask to explode. The nuclear reaction inside the cask has slowed to such a degree that it is, to the extent possible, constantly exploding. The neutrons are interacting with fissionable atoms as rapidly as the depleted fuel will allow. Nothing can make these spent fuel assemblies react more violently."

I had already done some dry cask research. I knew the casks were huge and massive – typically about twenty feet tall, ten or eleven feet in diameter and weighed in excess of 150 tons each. They couldn't be stolen, and it would be very difficult to even break one open. So I didn't need more info on that subject.

"What secures the spent fuel pool from sabotage?"

Dana looked at me for a long time without responding. Then she said, "I'd prefer not to say more about the pool beyond what I've already told you."

What she declined to say spoke volumes. I may have found the soft spot I was looking for.

"Just one more question . . . and you don't have to answer if you are uncomfortable."

"Go ahead."

"The spent fuel is cooled by circulating water laced with boron. What would happen if the treated water stopped circulating?"

"That's no secret. The water would eventually boil away and bad things would be the result. But there are backup systems in place to prevent the water flow from being interrupted. And there are backup tanks of both distilled water and boric acid."

"What kind of bad things?" I asked.

"No one can say exactly. That precise scenario has never occurred. Some scientists theorize that the fuel assemblies could get so hot that they would ignite their zirconium alloy coatings, creating a zirconium fire. That would be a tough fire to put out. Zirconium burns at about 1000 degrees Celsius."

"Other than fire control, why is burning zirconium a concern? Is it radioactive?"

"It's not so much the fire that's the problem – though that would certainly be a localized danger. It's the lethal elements the fire would release that create the larger concern. Along with the uranium and plutonium, the fuel rods contain at least two other extremely toxic elements in substantial quantities. The first is iodine. The second is cesium 137 – a highly radioactive gas.

"While the fire burns, some scientists theorize that large amounts of iodine and cesium 137 would be expelled into the atmosphere, creating a deadly plume which would expand and travel with the prevailing winds. "

"Exactly how bad would that be?" I asked, fearing that I knew the answer.

"Let me put it this way. In 1986, the Chernobyl Nuclear Plant meltdown resulted in the release of a *maximum* of 2.4 million curies of cesium 137 into the air. That cesium was still present in the atmosphere at measurable levels over Scandinavia – after circling the globe.

"A typical spent fuel pool in the U.S. today might contain anywhere from 20 million to 40 million curies of cesium 137. The NRC has estimated, in a paper released to the public, that a zirconium fire could release up to 100% of that cesium.

"You do the math.

"I'm afraid that's all I care to say about the pools, Mr. Becker. Are there other questions I can answer?"

"Yes. Just one. How comfortable are you living within six miles of a nuclear power plant?"

"Completely comfortable. Safest, most cost effective and environmentally friendly method of electrical production ever invented."

"Thank you so much for your time, Dana," I said. "I'll make sure to keep this discussion between us."

We both stood.

"I'd appreciate that," Dana said. "Have a nice evening."

Nice evening, indeed.

CHAPTER 20

Still Tuesday, May 12th, in Red Wing.

Dana Winston had certainly given me some interesting questions to think about. But just because the consequences of a nuclear plant attack would be horrific, that didn't mean a plot to assault the plant was in progress. Those same potential consequences had been present for decades – since the inception of the nuclear age. No terrorist had yet successfully attacked a nuke.

Gunner was probably right anyway. No reason to suspect terrorism. As gruesome as it was, the murder at the Lab seemed merely a murder. It wasn't unusual for the motive to be unknown. And several experts had already counseled me that the professor's work, and his potassium machine, did not constitute a terrorist threat. Even if an attack on the spent fuel pool *might* be possible, that did not mean plans for such an attack were underway.

Then again, in the midst of the investigation, the Mongolians had coincidentally reappeared in my life. I have never been a believer in coincidences. And there was still the missing lab device to be considered.

I needed a break. A dinner with my lovely wife.

I was still at the Hog and it was just before five in the afternoon when I called Beth on her cell. She answered the call with exaggerated heavy breathing, stalker-style.

"Umm," I said. "I think that's supposed to be my line."

"With caller ID, it works both ways. Catch up with the times, Babe."

"I am calling to request the pleasure of your presence at a dinner for two this evening at The Norton's. Fine wine. Gourmet food. Sparkling repartee. And did I mention, fiendishly sinful chocolate dessert?"

"Sounds irresistible. How about 7:30? I'm doing research at the Clothes Horse right now. They're about to close-up shop for the day. Then I need to go home, shower and apply a few breath-taking touches to my appearance before dinner."

"7:30 it is."

This time for eating dinner would have once sounded foolishly early. But in a community where most diners hit the restaurants in time for the 'early-bird special,' seven-thirty is just about perfect. Any later and you risk being trapped inside the restaurant when they roll up the sidewalks.

I had a little time to kill. It wouldn't take me quite as long as Beth to morph into my dinner persona. A final Bass seemed a reasonable idea. I caught the bartender's attention with a raised finger. He brought the ale and a fresh cocktail napkin to my table.

Staring down at the frothy schooner, I resolved to put all thoughts of guerilla warfare, terrorist plots and world domination aside for now. I sealed the resolution with a cool swallow of the Bass, dabbing the foam off my upper lip. A new man.

I nursed the ale in a state of self-hypnosis for the next half-hour. Then I walked home – six blocks. Small town living has its perks.

When I arrived at the house, Beth was busily trying on various top and bottom combinations, seeking the right *je ne sais quoi.*

I tried to be supportive.

"That looks terrific," I said.

"I don't know. The jacket isn't quite right with the skirt."

"Now I really like that choice," I offered, upon seeing the next ensemble.

"I think I might like the last combination better."

There really was no helping Beth pick out clothes. So while she persisted in her search for the perfect outfit, I showered, shaved and donned my grey slacks, white oxford shirt and navy blazer. A grey and navy tie with red accents. A splash of cologne. My signature oxblood penny-loafers completed the look.

I know the loafers are not exactly high fashion; but I've had my fill of lacing and tying over the last couple decades. I like slip-ons. These loafers look nice – fantastic, even.

It was 6:30 and I was set. Beth had selected her attire, at least preliminarily. While she showered, I went downstairs, picked up the local paper and lounged on the red leather couch, feet up on the old wooden bass drum case that served as our coffee table.

It wouldn't take long to read the paper. Usually twelve pages or less. So I took my time. I read every article and even some of the Classifieds.

One day a month, anyone could post a short classified add for free. Today was the day.

"Lawn mower for sale. Used to run great. $20 obo." I used to run the hurdles.

"Slightly used queen mattress set. $10." Yuck!

"Three cross-country skis with poles. Make an offer." Hmmm?

I scanned the page of obituaries, traffic accidents, speeding tickets and miscellaneous items of local interest. Readers fondly refer to this page as "the Briefs" and it is by far the most widely followed, and closely scrutinized, page in the paper. Everyone wants to know if someone they know has died, or is in trouble with the law, or has had their car window broken. If one doesn't know such things, what would one talk about?

On page two of the paper, next to the editorial for the day ('Should garbage collection fees increase?') a short article about a fertilizer truck heist caught my eye. The truck-jacking happened last week. Apparently, the driver had stopped to help a motorist in need. The next thing he knew, his truck was gone.

I pictured a semi-load of manure and wondered how the economy had gotten so bad.

Then I remembered that 'fertilizer' might also include the makings of truck bombs. Near the end of the article, the reporter identified the cargo as nitrogen. That's the bomb-making stuff . . . but no discernable connection to either potassium or the nuke. A truck bomb would never get close enough to do damage before being repelled, or detonated, by plant security. Of that much, I was certain. The truck-jacking probably was not relevant to my concerns.

After finishing the paper, I went out to our (and by that I mean, Beth's) garden and cut some early-blooming tulips to present to my date. I found a vase and arranged the tulips quite nicely, I thought.

Beth came down the stairs. I met her as she entered the kitchen.

"I brought you flowers, my love," I stated as I held the tulip-filled vase out toward Beth, presentation style.

She looked stunning as always. She had chosen an outfit I can't accurately describe because of my lack of vocabulary in the area of women's attire. But it looked perfect in every way. It tastefully accentuated all the right parts. And her scent was enticing.

"How lovely!" She accepted the vase of tulips, pretending to inhale their sweet aroma, of which there wasn't any. Tulips are not aromatic. "You are my gallant prince."

"Never let it be said that I didn't do the least I could do, my sweet," I replied. Then motioning toward the front door, "Shall we?"

"Indeed."

I took the vase from Beth, and set it down, featuring it prominently on the kitchen table.

It was a short walk to the restaurant. Almost everything of import in Red Wing is a short walk from our house. As we strolled, we visited about her day. An hour at the law office chatting with Karen. A stop at the grocery store to lay in some staples. A short CIA cyber-decryption project. And an afternoon of serious art, jewelry and clothing research at multiple locations.

We arrived at the restaurant precisely at seven-thirty and the hostess seated us promptly. The Nortons is my favorite location for fine dining in Red Wing. The decor echoes the roaring twenties, when times were good and dining was elegant. The menu is fairly brief; but it offers something for every discerning palate. The restaurant owners, not surprisingly, the Nortons, had created each recipe themselves and personally assured that every meal was prepared to perfection.

I selected a bottle of Merlot from the wine list and relayed my choice to the waitress. The wine, together with a basket of sliced baguette and a small dish of iced butter patties, arrived at our table shortly. The waitress uncorked the wine, handed me the cork and poured a small amount in my glass. I sniffed the cork as she poured. After swirling the wine in sophisticated fashion, I tested its aroma, then tasted a sip.

"This will be just fine. Thank you."

The waitress poured Beth's wine, then mine. She left the bottle on the table, and with a bow, departed.

"To soul mates," I offered, raising my glass.

"And lovers," Beth added. Our glasses met, ringing a clear tone in the quiet room. We raised them again toward one another and each enjoyed a sip of the Merlot.

"Delicious," Beth said, placing the wine stem back on the white cloth. She unfolded her linen napkin and laid it gracefully across her lap. "We've talked enough about my day. What adventures do you have to share?"

I wasn't sure if my conundrum was right for dinner conversation. But Beth and I share everything. So I thought I'd give it a shot.

"I've got kind of a mess. Are you up for helping me sort through it?"

"Let's give it a try, shall we." A slight British accent. She liked to do that to lighten the mood. I found it endearing.

"Here's what I've got." I relayed the details about the murder, the international cell call, the probable killer, potassium, my visits with Bull and Winston.

"And in tonight's paper, I read about a fertilizer truck hijacking. A whole semi-load. And it was the kind of fertilizer that anti-government types use to make bombs."

Beth sat watching my eyes intently as I spoke. Her facial expression confirmed that I held her complete attention as I plodded through the details of my quandary. I could be reciting Dr. Seuss and Beth would still give me her undivided attention, if she thought it was important to me. I loved her for that, too.

"You certainly have a lot of dots to connect," she said when I had finished. "Let's see . . . you have a murder suspect who your gut tells you may be a terrorist. The nuclear plant, and particularly the spent fuel pool, you think may be his target. Potassium may be part of the means of attack. Mongolians may, somehow, be related. And someone stole a truckload of fertilizer that could be used to make a bomb, but that type of bomb doesn't appear to threaten the nuke plant.

"Is that about it?"

"Yeah. Oh, and Gunner probably thinks I'm certifiable. Any thoughts?"

Beth looked across the table. She sensed my frustration and would try to relieve it.

"Yes," she said momentarily. "First of all, in the many years we have been together, I have found your gut to be one of the most reliable indicators in the universe. Don't ignore it just because nothing makes sense *yet*.

"Secondly, no one is going to take you seriously with the evidence you've accumulated so far. It's all too circumstantial. Crying 'wolf' at this point will only undermine your credibility when you do have more evidence. So I wouldn't share any further theories with law enforcement right now.

"Finally . . . a suggestion. Nobody could possibly be a better terrorist than you. You have fought and defeated terrorist operations for most of your life. Think like a terrorist. Given what you know now, how would you attack the target?"

Beth was right, as she almost always is. I needed to approach this question from the other end. If I could devise my own plan to assault the nuke plant, using the materials and information I already knew about, I could work backwards.

Excellent idea!

Our hands joined across the table. Our eyes held one another's.

"You are as insightful as you are beautiful," I said.

"That might be tough," Beth replied.

"True."

We ordered dinner and dessert, enjoying the rest of the evening without further thought or mention of my dilemma.

CHAPTER 21

Wednesday, May 13th, at Becker Law Office.

It was a Wednesday morning and the law office was in high gear. My eccentric office-sharing mate, Frank, was telephoning frenetically. And my second office-sharing mate, Bill, had a legal brief due. Between connecting callers to Frank and deflecting them from Bill, our receptionist, Debbie, barely had time to copy and collate the brief.

We three lawyers had devised this office-sharing arrangement to save on our collective overhead expenses and consolidate staff personnel. I rented the office space and hired the employees. The other guys rented space and secretarial time from me. It worked particularly well for my practice, because I needed a secretary at the office at all times to deal with clients. I assumed the other attorneys reaped similar benefits.

Beth frequently helps out at the office, too. She was at her desk preparing accounting reports this morning. The journal entries were finished and she was in the process of running trial balances.

I understand accounting fine. But its excitement coefficient is something even less than lawyering. I didn't pay much attention to the credits and debits, though I did kill an accountant once, in the line of duty. He was a very bad man. Probably a bad accountant, too.

Anyway, I was thankful that Beth took on the accounting responsibilities. She had an undergraduate accounting degree and actually enjoyed the symmetry of coaxing the numbers to balance. I allowed her to process the business data uninterrupted.

Alone in my private office, I perched tentatively on my infinitely-adjustable, comfy lawyer chair and stared at the piles of legal files. My mind kept drifting back to the terrorist activities I suspected to be in progress.

Although it was early, and I hadn't actually accomplished anything, I knew I'd already reached my maximum legal work potential for the day. Exiting my office, I leaned over the oak-trimmed half-wall toward Beth. "I gotta get out of here."

I gave her twitchy.

She looked up and flashed the smile that made my heart turn to mush. "Have fun, Babe. I'll be through here soon. Then I'm leaving as well. Think I'll hit the Fine Arts Center. See if inspiration strikes."

"Great idea," I agreed. "See you later. I'm heading out."

I made a beeline for the receptionist's desk. "Gone for the rest of the day, Debbie. Please route my calls through Karen."

"Yes, sir. Have a nice afternoon."

I said a quick goodbye to all, then exited the legal miasma in search of investigational enlightenment.

CHAPTER 22

Friday, May 15th, in Red Wing.

Two evenings later, while perusing the paper in our living room, I discovered something very unusual and disturbing. Another fertilizer truck had been hi-jacked later last week – sometimes it takes the news a while to hit the local paper. Two fertilizer trucks stolen within a few days? This *could not* be a coincidence.

What kind of fertilizer was this truck carrying? I read on. Potash. The main ingredient in potash is . . . potassium!

Another star in my constellation. The stolen potash somewhat confirmed that potassium was to play a part in whatever plan was unfolding. But what part? And how the hell was I going to find out?

"Beth. Is it okay if I skip dinner tonight and do some work at the office. I need to get a handle on this nuke thing and I can focus better there by myself."

"Do what you need to do, Babe. You know I'll be here. Any idea how long?"

"Probably going to be late. Don't wait up."

I kissed her on the lips and headed out the door.

Unlike almost everything else in Red Wing, Becker Law Office is not within comfortable walking distance. I took the Pilot.

Once at the office, my ceiling fluorescents were the only sign of life. No Frank. No Karen. No pool. No Pets. I turned to my computer. I needed to do more research.

First, I confirmed what Bull and Chuck had told me. Elemental potassium is highly reactive with water, even water in the air. Although it is the eighth most common element on earth, because of its tendency to react readily with other elements, pure elemental potassium does not exist naturally *anywhere* in the world.

Manmade potassium has a few industrial uses. The potassium isolation processes employed to make large quantities of the element available for industry involved highly complex, technologically advanced, and very large, equipment – not to mention enormous processing facilities.

I reclined in my comfy lawyer chair for a moment. It didn't seem likely that any terrorist group could operate a potassium production facility of such magnitude in Ottawa County and still escape notice by law enforcement.

Yet there was the professor's invention. Might that provide enough pure potassium for some specialized purpose? I knew nothing of its production capacities.

Leaning forward into my keyboard, I next researched nuclear power plants. Much technological information that had been easily accessible on the web before 9/11 was no longer available. Many web links led to blank pages where the juicy design and engineering details had once resided. But I *was* able to find out a few things.

Liberal scientific groups had already warned the NRC concerning the vulnerability of spent fuel pools. Many pools, including those at Prairie River, were in fact, located *outside* the heavily reinforced containment buildings. And because Prairie River had not one, but two separate reactors, its fuel pool was larger than most, and contained more of the dangerous fuel.

I also learned something surprising about spent fuel storage pools. Many of them are located entirely above-ground. The elevated design was intended to allow plant operators to monitor any leaks that might develop in the pool. In my mind, it also made the pools susceptible to sabotage.

Although the pool walls and floor are usually built of five-foot-thick concrete, such material does not pose the same sort of barrier as the heavy steel reinforcement of the containment buildings. A precisely-placed chunk of C4 might well crack the pool, allowing the water to drain out. Even a crude fertilizer bomb could have the same effect. But you would have to get that bomb to the pool. And direct access to the pool area must surely be guarded – at least from land.

One web article contended that the spent fuel pools were completely safe – including from air attack. According to this author, a well-directed airplane crash into a typical, metal spent fuel building would not create enough force to damage the pool. Nor would the resulting fire generate enough heat to boil off the pool's protective water. Since the pools are a minimum of forty feet deep, with only a forty by forty foot surface area, the author argued, there simply wasn't enough surface area for a fire to boil the water off fast enough to cause a problem.

The article went on to say that most of the fuel in commercial planes is stored in the wings. And being made of light-weight aluminum, the wings would most probably peel off the fuselage as the plane penetrated the spent fuel building, leaving the bulk of the burning fuel outside.

My own knowledge of aircraft agreed with the analysis of their structure. I didn't know whether the boiling issue might be a problem.

I broadened my web search to other topics.

I located several conceptual diagrams of nuclear reactors that illustrated what Dr. Winston had told me about their design and function. I read a lot more about potassium. I viewed a short video clip showing a tiny pinch of potassium being tossed into a barrel of water. The pyrotechnic explosion was visually impressive, even given the minuscule quantity of potassium involved.

I leaned back in my chair and checked my watch. It was well past midnight. Trying to absorb all this chemistry and nuclear technology made my head hurt.

Refocusing on the task at hand, I tried to combine my previous knowledge with the new information I had just learned from the web. It seemed plausible . . . barely . . . that a terrorist might breach plant security from the air, crash a small plane into the spent fuel building and start a fire. *Maybe* if you had enough potassium aboard, *if* the potassium hit the pool, there *might* be an explosion big enough to crack the pool and make it leak.

That didn't seem like much of a plan. At least, I wouldn't attack a nuclear plant that way. Chances of success seemed slim. How would you get a big enough plane even close to the plant? There must be all kinds of red flags that would go up if a commercial flight were in the air below 10,000 feet. And I *knew* the plant had at least *some* anti-aircraft capability. A small plane wouldn't have a snowball's chance.

Even if you somehow managed to steal and crash a commercial plane, would the lightweight aluminum airframe penetrate the steel building with sufficient fuel aboard to boil away the water? Would potassium make a significant difference? And how in the world would you get elemental potassium through airport security? That was simply not possible on a commercial flight.

Security for cargo flights had become just as strict – not to mention the fact that the potassium would probably blow up when some forklift operator dumped it onto the plane. 'Fragile' has no meaning to cargo carriers.

I still couldn't make it add up. All I could theoretically accomplish was a nuclear nuisance. I could maybe shut down the plant for a few days while they scraped my charred remains from the building roof.

I checked my watch again. Three-thirty a.m. I would nap in my comfy lawyer chair for two hours. Then I'd go home, make coffee and take my best shot at preparing a nice breakfast for Beth.

Loving husband. Breakfast in bed.

CHAPTER 23

Monday, June 1st, in Red Wing.

Two weeks had gone by since my all-nighter and I still had not been able to formulate a reliable plan to cause a significant nuclear incident at Prairie River. Nor had Gunner made any progress locating Mr. Ahmed.

I was at the office today.

I depressed the "Intercom" button on my desk phone. "Karen, intercom please," I said, in the general direction of the built-in microphone.

"Yes, Beck," Karen's voice replied from the speaker.

"Could you come into my office for a moment."

"Certainly. I'll be right in."

Moments later, Karen knocked once on my door, opened it and entered the room. "Open or closed?"

"Ah, leave it open please." She let the door swing open all the way.

Efficient, loyal and capable legal secretary that she was, she had come equipped with a yellow pad and pen in hand to record any instructions I might give her.

"Karen. How's your workload today?"

"About normal. No real rushes. What may I do to assist?"

"You see these piles of paper and file folders all over my office?" I extended my upright palm and swivelled my comfy chair 360 degrees. "It would really be a wonderful thing if these papers found their way into the right files, and the files into the correct cabinets." I gestured again, this time at the rows of wooden laminate file cabinets whose specific purpose it was, in theory, to provide lots of filing room – so my office wouldn't get messy.

Karen was still standing unruffled, near the door, paying close attention to my every word. I don't know how she puts up with me.

"Do you think you could take a stab at making that a reality?" I asked.

I gave her needy.

"Of course, Beck. Is there a deadline?" Karen said it as if it were her mess to clean up and not mine. Part of the job. This was just one more work item for Karen to prioritize among drafting and filing legal documents, talking with my clients, writing my letters and performing lots of other tasks I didn't even know she did, because she did them so well.

"Do you think you could work this in by the end of the week? I know it's a big job."

Smile. More needy.

"I believe I can, Beck." A pause. "But may I ask a favor?"

"Sure. Fire away."

"Frank has got me organizing a dinner party for him. He wants formal invitations, a seating chart, place cards . . . so the right people don't sit next to the wrong ones . . . English party crackers, individually-wrapped party favors. And he wants me to buy him a 'festive belt.' I don't even know what a 'festive belt' would look like. Any chance you can get some of that off my plate?"

"No sooner said than done. Fear not!" I rush in where even fools fear to tread – never mind the angels.

"Bless you," said Karen, now ready to leave. "Door open or closed?"

"Let's leave it open. I think I'm heading out soon. Long day already, you know."

"Open it is." Karen returned to her desk.

Frank was in his office right now. I might as well do the deed and have it over with. I rose from my comfy lawyer chair, departed my office and knocked firmly on Frank's door, three times.

Frank motioned for me to enter. When I was half-way through the door he greeted me. "Come in, Jimmy boy. What's up?"

I closed the door quietly behind me. Turning to look straight into Frank's eyes, I held my index finger to my lips. 'Confidential.'

Frank duplicated my gesture.

"I just wanted to give you a heads up," I whispered, moving away from the door and balancing on the edge of one of Frank's client chairs.

"How's that?" Frank whispered back.

I leaned forward over the desk, furtively glancing at the door as if someone might be spying on us. "Well. Karen has a bad sinus infection today. She wouldn't tell anyone. She just soldiers on. You know Karen." I was still whispering.

"A real team player." Frank was still whispering, too.

"That's for sure. Problem is," I continued, "the last couple files I gave her to organize for me this morning? Well, they came back to me a mess. Everything out of order. Sub-files intermixed. Typos on the manila folder tabs. I think the sinus infection is affecting her concentration."

"Yikes!" Frank's worst nightmare.

"Anyway, I just wanted to warn you maybe not to have Karen do anything that requires a lot of organizing today. Maybe just stick to dictation and stuff. And make sure to proofread everything!"

"Thanks for the heads up, Jimmy Boy." Frank looked a bit distracted. "I was going to have Karen . . . well I had asked her to . . . get me a new belt for a festive occasion. Do you think she could do that?"

"Frank, if I were you, I'd choose your own attire. Relying on Karen's judgment today might not work out so well."

Frank breathed deeply while appearing to stare at something on the ceiling. "Right you are, Jimmy Boy. Thanks again."

"No problem."

Frank was practically on my heels as I left his office. He waited for me to return to mine before approaching Karen. I peeked out my door – snoop that I am.

Frank was leaning over, speaking very quietly to Karen. Her head was cocked a bit to one side, eyes on Frank's mouth. She blinked once, then said something that looked like 'Okay.'

Frank did an about-face and returned to his office. Karen put her thumb on her temple, fingers on her forehead and elbow on her desk. Then she saw me peeking from my doorway. She smiled and shook her head.

Mission accomplished.

Before leaving, I wanted to check on the status of Gansükh. I called my CIA contact. It hadn't taken long for the Ukrainians to take advantage of their opportunity. Gansükh would no longer be a problem. That was good to know. One potential threat from my past extinguished.

Unfortunately, the CIA had no idea how Gansükh had found Sara in the first place. So that remained an open question.

Time to leave the office.

"Another day, another dollar," I announced as I strode for the door. "Please take messages. Carry on. As you were."

And . . . I . . . was . . . out!

CHAPTER 24

Tuesday, June 2nd, at the Ottawa County farm.

Farris had lived on the farm for a little less than a month. Time flew when he was working in the lab, and dragged endlessly when he had to interact with the others.

By this time, he had completed preliminary purification of the potash. The large lean-to now covered two sizeable piles of dry chemicals.

The pile nearest to the lab was almost pure potassium chloride. It was white, made up of small clear crystals, and sat on the clean part of the concrete slab – the part that had not been contaminated by the raw potash.

The other was the waste pile. It consisted of mixed iron powders, salt crystals and a few miscellaneous trace chemicals that Farris had extracted from the raw potash. The waste mound sat in the center of the lean-to, actually on top of an area where the potash had previously lain. But since it was all waste material anyway, the extra impurities wouldn't matter. The waste pile resembled a huge, multi-color marbled Dairy Queen creation.

Farris summoned Urland and Brenda and informed them that it was their responsibility to clear away the waste pile. He needed the room for storing containers of finished product. This wasn't technically true. Actually, the pure potassium would be kept safely out of the weather, inside the enclosed lab. But the waste pile project would keep the Umbers out of his hair.

Farris distributed to each of the Umbers a 3M fabric face-mask. These masks would protect them from the chemical dust as they shoveled and wheel-barrowed the waste to its destination. The waste material needed to be dumped in a specific area, away from the buildings, and not in a ditch where it might be washed away by gushing rain water. He couldn't allow colorful pollutants running down the gully to the neighboring creek to draw unwanted attention to their little enterprise.

Farris selected the perfect waste disposal area, about a hundred yards from the lab, and just slightly uphill. That should keep them busy.

Brenda and Urland looked back and forth between the waste pile and its intended destination.

"Well Brenda. If it's gotta be done, it's gotta be done."

More standing and looking.

"The shovel is right here and the wheel-barrow is in the garage," Farris offered, then headed into the relative serenity of the lab.

Tomorrow, Farris hoped to start on the truly dangerous part of this project – electrolysis of gaseous potassium chloride. He had already set up the professor's invention and it looked pretty good. If it worked as well for him as it had for the professor, he should be able to produce a sizeable amount of pure potassium – given time, fuel and a lot of electricity.

CHAPTER 25

Late evening, Wednesday, June 3rd, near Red Wing.

It was 10:30 in the evening and John had just finished watching the evening news in his recliner when the phone rang.

For John, receiving any telephone call at all was unusual. To receive one this late in the evening was unprecedented. He checked the caller ID. "Unknown Name. Unknown Number."

"Yeah?" he said, answering the call.

"John Sigler?" a man's voice asked. The man had a mid-western U.S. dialect.

"Who wants to know?"

"Don't get smart. You know who I represent. And I need some answers."

John was still baffled. The caller must be from *Al Qaeda*. But the accent . . . . Who did they have in this area?

"Okay. This is John," he said. "What do you need?"

"Well first off, what the hell is going on with the truck-jackings? We knew you needed fertilizer. But two trucks?"

"The first one was a mistake by one of the dopes you assigned to help me with this thing. I can't help it if they don't know shit from Shinola!"

"Well for god's sake, have you got what you need now? Or am I going to be hearing about more stolen fertilizer?"

"We're set at this point," John said tentatively. He still couldn't figure out the caller's connection to the operation.

"I sure as hell hope so. Now . . . I've got something else you need to know.

"There's been a lawyer named Becker nosing around the professor's murder. Seems he's a bit more than just a lawyer, though. Some sort of military background. We were able to divert him for a while. But he's back in town and may be lookin' to cause us trouble. So keep your head down and your eyes open. Got it?"

"Who is this exactly?" John asked.

"This is the person who's been assigned to watch your ass and make sure everything happens like it's s'posed to. You'll probably be hearing from me again before we're through."

John was confused. He had understood that he was in charge of the operation. And he didn't like being second-guessed on every move.

"So do you have things under control?" the man asked harshly. "Or do I need to intervene?"

"Oh, I've got everything under control all right," John replied. "Just make sure that your ass-watching doesn't get in our way!"

"You do your job and you won't have problems from me. Just don't steal any more goddamn trucks!"

"You done?" John was hot.

"Yeah, I'm done. Just keep this thing moving. We've got a schedule, ya know."

"Got it," John said, and hung up the phone.

What the hell was *Al Qaeda* up to? Could he trust them to complete the attack on the nuke? They had been pretty decent to deal with so far. But now this call? He needed to give it all some thought.

John shut off the TV and went to bed. It was a fitful night's sleep at the Sigler residence.

CHAPTER 26

Saturday, June 6th, at Red Wing.

It had now been more than a month since the murder. Maybe my gut had been wrong. I'd been wrong before.

Well, not really – at least not when it came to terrorism.

When one is stumped, I have found that it sometimes helps to look at things from a new angle.

I called for Bull.

A woman answered. "Who shall I say is calling?"

"George Armstrong Custer."

"One moment, Mr. Custer."

Bull's voice came on the line. "Ready for another whuppin' General?"

"Not today, Chief. I still have an arrowhead in my gluteus from the last time. How about a plane ride?"

"Your plane or mine?"

Bull. Always the comedian.

"Um, since I don't have a plane, how about yours?"

"Sounds like fun," Bull said, "or is this business?"

"A little of both."

We decided on a time to meet at the airport and hung up.

I wondered how Bull occupied his time when he wasn't in my company. He always seemed to be available for my calls, and was willing to participate in my escapades regardless of their apparent foolishness. I'd have to ask him some day.

I pulled the Pilot into the Red Wing Airport parking lot at the specified time. I didn't see Bull's Cherokee. So I decided to reconnoiter. I used to do a lot of that back in the day.

On the way into the airport, I had seen no security checkpoint, no cameras, no fences, not even Barney Fife snoozing in a chair leaned against a wall.

I knew from previous visits that there were no large planes resident at this airport. The locals were recreational users only.

I entered the main terminal. No one was there. The airport had only one employee and he had duties that often took him outside the terminal. So basically, the airport was 'self-serve.'

The main terminal at the Red Wing Airport is a brick building about fifty feet square. It has a main level and a lower level, also known as a basement. On the main level are: a pair of rest rooms; a general public area with comfy chairs and a television set, used mostly by pilots to hang out or sleep while their business passengers are in meetings; a formica counter with airport communication equipment behind it 'for airport personnel only'; a medium-sized conference room, in case you had just flown in for a business meeting and you needed a convenient place to meet with the locals – which, believe it or not, happened quite often; a flight center with maps, charts, up-to-date computerized weather information and flight-plan forms; and a couple small office areas not accessible to the public.

I gave the basement a quick check. It was basically an overnight pilots' dorm, complete with showers and single beds. Here, too, there was a lounge area with a television set.

As I walked the interior perimeter of the first floor public area, I observed that it held a very nice view of the sole runway at the airport. One could watch all the take-offs and landings one wanted, as long as there were planes flying. There weren't any at present. I did notice one security camera near the runway-side window, pointed out at the runway. I couldn't see a monitor.

Still, no 'airport personnel' were in evidence.

Bull stuck his head halfway into the terminal doorway and called to me. "Let's go."

Besides the brick terminal, the other structures at the airport consisted of either private hangars, or airplane maintenance facilities. Nearly all were constructed from corrugated sheet metal hung on wooden framing. The entire group of buildings formed a sort of village around the three sides of the terminal away from the runway.

Taxiways ran up and down between the rows of hangars and up to the fueling pumps – one with AvFuel, for the jets, and one with 100 octane low lead, for everything else. In the end, all the small taxiways led to the main taxiway, and then to the runway.

We walked past Bull's bright-red Cherokee on the way to his hangar.

"What's with the Cherokee anyway?" I prodded. "I thought you were Sioux."

"And you're Japanese?" he said, referring to my Honda.

He had a point.

"Besides, I'm not Sioux. Sioux is what others call us. I'm Dakota."

"But a Cherokee?"

"Hey. It's got the sun roof. I get close to nature . . . shoot stuff through the top." He paused, then added, "It's my culture."

It was hard to argue with Bull.

Bull's hangar was just a few buildings away from the terminal, and five hangars distant from the runway. Bull unlocked the hangar access door and flipped the switch to raise the overhead. We stepped inside.

"Hey, you got a new plane!" It was white and sleek.

"Yeah. You like?"

"Love it. Give me the specs?"

"It's a Diamond DA40. 180 horses. Four seats. Composite frame with a 39 foot wingspan. She'll do 140 knots pretty easy, and cruises nicely at 120."

"You're clearly moving up in the world," I complimented.

Bull smiled slightly – at least, I think it was a smile.

I watched as Bull went through his pre-flight checklist, circling the plane, jerking on the propeller to make sure it was soundly attached, testing fuel purity for possible water in the gas, kicking the tires, etc.

Then he attached a metal tow handle to the front wheel. Leaning back to use his mass as leverage, he began pulling the plane from the hangar. The front wheel was attached to the plane by a freely rotating caster, so steering was not a problem. The plane rolled easily onto the taxiway.

When the plane's tail was clear of the hangar, Bull detached the metal wheel handle, tossing it back through the open hangar doorway. He and I climbed into the small plane through the clamshell cockpit canopy. It was comfortable; but there was no wasted space in either front seat.

We put on our headsets for the dual purposes of communication and sound control.

Then Bull yelled out the window, "Clear!" and started the engine. The propeller spun smoothly. At least there was less vibration than I expected.

Before moving, Bull continued with his pre-flight routine: oil pressure, altimeter, radio, GPS, fuel. I'm not sure what else. Bull was very thorough when it came to airplane safety – paranoid even. I felt good about that.

Having completed the items on his list, Bull increased the throttle speed and we began to roll forward. Outside the plane, the weather was perfect. Sunny skies and a light wind out of the west – straight down the runway.

Red Wing is a Class E airport. There is no tower or air traffic control. There may or may not be someone to answer on the airport radio if you tried the Unicom frequency. But whether airport personnel were present or not, you needed to announce your take-offs and landings, just in case some other plane had conflicting plans for the only runway.

Bull spoke nonchalantly into his headset microphone.

"Red Wing traffic. This is November 3-6-3 Delta Sierra taxiing for departure on Runway 27."

We headed slowly down the taxiway toward the east end of the runway. Although there is only one runway at the airport, it has two numbers, 9 and 27, depending on whether you will be moving on the runway toward the east (90 degrees) or toward the west (270 degrees). We were taxiing to the east end of the runway – Runway 27 – to take off into the light westerly wind.

When we reached the point where the taxiway last intersects the runway, we made a turn into the wind and stopped. There were some final engine checks. With his feet on both brake pedals, Bull revved the engine up to operating rpms. Everything looked good.

"Red Wing traffic. This is 3 Delta Sierra entering Runway 27 for departure."

Hearing no objections from the radio, we proceeded onto the runway and made another right angle turn, taxiing down the runway toward the east. Near the end of the concrete, we rotated 180 degrees. We were now pointed straight down the runway to the west.

"Red Wing traffic. This is 3 Delta Sierra departing Runway 27."

Bull released the brakes and eased the throttle forward. Steering at low speed was accomplished with Bull's light touches to the brake pedals. Once we got going, the rudder and ailerons took over directional control through the pilot's control stick. We accelerated quite quickly. Within about eight hundred feet, we were in the air and climbing fast.

"This baby sure is smooth," I commented into my headset microphone.

"Um hmm. Burns less than ten gallons an hour, too."

Was there a touch of pride in Bull's voice?

"As long as we're headed west anyway," I suggested, "why don't we head up toward the nuke plant. I want the eye-in-the-sky view."

"Roger that."

I glanced over at the instrument panel in front of Bull. We had already climbed to an altimeter reading of about 2800 feet. We were actually only about 1900 feet above the ground, since the land below us was approximately 900 feet above sea level.

I could feel the plane level off and glanced over at the attitude indicator. It was nearly centered. We were in level flight.

"You want 'er?" Bull asked.

"Absolutely!"

I placed my hand on the control stick between my legs. As soon as Bull felt the plane pull up a bit, he released his stick. I leveled off again and aimed for the highly-visible nuke plant, just up the river valley.

"What are the rules for flying around the plant?"

"500 feet above all structures. No loitering."

Bull was not one to make lengthy conversation. Straight to the point.

I checked the altimeter again. Still around 2800 feet. We were plenty high. Not wanting to give any trigger-happy security guard a reason to shoot at me, I decided not to fly directly over the plant – instead, proceeding straight past to its southwest.

From our airborne vantage point, I could see the whole plant layout distinctly through the clear cockpit canopy. I could have even taken a picture if I had wanted to. But I had already seen enough aerial shots on the web, so that wasn't necessary.

The spent fuel building was the large green metal structure between the two reactor containment towers. If I were a terrorist who wanted to approach the pool building, I would fly low and from the north.

I could be as low as I wanted over the river and not be violating anything. But about 600 feet above the ground seemed the right altitude for an attack. From there it would be possible to dive at 45 degrees straight into the center of that building.

I was not technically a pilot; but even I could do it easily. 600 feet down at a 45 degree angle doing 160 knots would take less than three seconds.

That's three seconds from legal to lethal!

I would give that scenario some more thought later. Right now, I had a chance to fly.

After we were well clear of the nuke, I climbed to just under 3000 feet, the maximum altitude at which I could still fly wherever I wanted, and any direction I chose.

"Will this thing let me do a 45 degree dive at full throttle?" I asked Bull.

He smiled. "That'd be less than two negative Gs. No problem."

"Okay. Tighten your seat belt. We're going down."

I nosed the plane downward while I opened the throttle. As the downward pitch on the attitude indicator approached thirty degrees, I could feel the seat belt pressing on the top of my lap, and my buttocks began lifting off the seat. When the indicator reached 45 degrees, I was pinned firmly against the lap belt and shoulder restraint, and not touching the seat bottom at all.

It felt suicidal – which I guess it was.

I didn't leave the plane at 45 degrees very long before I began to pull back on the stick, gradually lessening our rate of descent until we were, once again, flying flat and level. Our present altitude read 1800 feet on the altimeter. We had only been diving for about 8 seconds. Our maximum airspeed had topped 180 knots.

It would definitely be possible to impact the fuel building in a plane like this one from 600 feet aloft. But what sort of damage could it do to the plant? I would do the math later.

Bull flew us around the countryside, staying below 3000 feet on the altimeter, and doing some impressive acrobatics. "Hang on," Bull said. He leaned us over into a 60 degree left bank. My body pressed severely down into the seat. I tried to lift my right arm. It felt like lead. Bull held the turn for a full 360 degrees, then leveled off.

"Two Gs," he said, with no discernable inflection.

"Impressive."

CHAPTER 27

Monday, June 8ᵗʰ, at the Ottawa County farm.

An objective name for the professor's invention might be a 'potassium electrolysis separator.' The theory was relatively simple. The execution, exceedingly risky.

Farris would use the professor's device to extract pure potassium from the pile of potassium chloride outside. This is how it would work:

1) Farris would boil the potassium chloride, trans-forming it from a solid to a gas;

2) Electricity would separate the potassium element in the gas from its chlorine companion atom;

3) The pure potassium gas would cool until it be-came solid potassium metal.

It sounded easy enough. But the details made the pro-cess much more complicated. This is a more precise description of the professor's device, and how it really would work:

The bottom section of the device was the 'burner.' Made from heat-resistant stainless steel, graphite, and glazed porce-lain, it could withstand the full brunt of the oxy-acetylene flames. The mixture of acetylene and oxygen gases fueling the burner would have to be in perfect proportions to generate enough heat to boil the potassium chloride.

The electrolysis chamber was the 'cooking pot.' The temperature in this chamber needed to reach 760 degrees Celsius (1400 degrees Fahrenheit) to boil the potassium chloride. The body of the electrolysis chamber was made of heat-resistant materials similar to the burner's. The working parts were a bit more exotic.

Suspended in the 'pot' were the terminals of an incredibly powerful electro-magnet. The anode, or positively charged pole, was made of graphite. The cathode, or negatively charged pole, was titanium-encased mercury. When the flames brought the potassium chloride to a boil, and the compound turned into a gas, the electro-magnet would rip the positively charged potassium atoms from the negatively charged chlorine ones.

Making a strong enough electro-magnet to tear apart the molecules required four of the largest diesel electric generators on the market. They were situated behind the barn. Together, they could produce more than 1.1 megawatts of electricity – enough to power a small village.

Next to the pot, but separated from the heat by a half-wall, was the 'cooler.' Inside the cooler, the temperature of the gaseous potassium dropped, changing the potassium first into a liquid and then a solid. As it condensed, the liquid potassium dripped down a ceramic plate into white ceramic collection trays, where it cooled further, solidifying into ingots of pure potassium metal – like muffins in a muffin pan.

The poisonous chlorine gas by-product vented through a port on the opposite side of the pot, where an exhaust fan channeled it through a PVC-lined duct and to the open air outside the lab.

To a chemist, the whole arrangement was something to behold! A farm milk house, converted to a hi-tech chem lab, complete with a fantastically fierce super-heater, an unimaginably strong electro-magnet, and an elegant and effective elemental separator.

A little more than a month ago, Farris wouldn't have thought it possible. Praise be to Allah!

Finished admiring the look of the lab, Farris decided to try out the equipment to see if it all would work as designed. The heating system was first.

He confirmed that both the acetylene and oxygen lines were pressurized and securely connected to the combination valve on the 'burner.' He inserted his striker into a hole in its side, opened the valve slightly, and gave the striker a click. A spark flew from the striker, but no flame ignited. He clicked it again. One more spark and the burner flared to life.

The radiant heat was instant and dramatic. Distortion appeared in the air above the chamber almost immediately. Even at this low setting, the heat was uncomfortable. Farris gradually increased the intensity of the flame. The burning oxy-acetylene plasma was a bright bluish-green in the center, surrounded by a bushy, secondary flame, purplish yellow in color. The heat rapidly became unbearable.

Farris dialed the gas down, then off. He was going to need a more robust cooling and ventilation system in the lab, or he, himself, would cook. He opened the lab door to let some fresh, cooler air into the room. He would direct John to arrange the enhanced cooling and ventilation he needed.

Although he knew that testing the electrical system was also crucial, he didn't want to activate the actual electrical connections on the device without the graphite and mercury electrodes in place – and they hadn't yet arrived. But he did fire up all four diesel electric generators, connecting them to a dummy circuit for testing. The circuit wires led up the hill behind the barn to two metal poles, held off the ground by old truck tires.

When he closed the circuit, the crack of sustained lightning echoed from the direction of the testing poles. He checked the power output gauge. It read .8 megawatts. Perfect. Resistance created by the lightning jumping the air space between the two poles accounted for the deficiency from the 1.1 megawatt expected maximum. There was plenty of electrical power available to energize the electro-magnet. The electrical system appeared to be operating correctly.

He hadn't been able to test everything, but this would have to suffice for today. He would ask John for the more powerful cooling system this afternoon. John also needed to get him those special electrodes and the argon gas. In the meantime, Farris would hide out in the lab. Maybe he would take the opportunity to supplement his prayer ritual. It had been interrupted by the demands of the potassium processing.

The Umbers, breathing heavily, continued shoveling and hauling the waste pile from Point A to Point B – occasionally stopping to smoke a cigarette. Every hour or so, Urland would grab two Old Style beers out of the large styrofoam cooler he had filled specifically for this job, and husband and wife would sit together on the concrete slab of the lean-to, and take a break.

CHAPTER 28

Wednesday, June 24th, in rural Ottawa County.

In Minnesota, if you are in the rock and gravel business, you can probably get a permit to store your explosives in a semi-trailer. You have to lock it, of course. You have to keep an inventory of your dynamite, blasting caps and so forth – although, you can pretty much make that up as you go. No one actually counts your explosives, or audits your inventory levels. Oh yeah, you can't leave your dynamite trailer parked in a residential neighborhood. But otherwise, pretty much anything goes.

John had been monitoring a limestone quarrying operation near the small community of Vasa, in Ottawa County, for almost a year now. He knew what time of day the explosives shipments arrived. He just didn't know on which days they would come. He couldn't think of a more sophisticated way to get this information than simply watching. So like a Vegas tourist at a quarter machine, he kept playing until he hit the jackpot.

It had been more than a month since he'd last seen the unmarked dynamite tractor-trailer arrive at the quarry. And there had been a lot of blasting, grinding and hauling of lime going on. Road construction season was in full swing. Another dynamite shipment should be due soon.

Today was his lucky day. In the predicted time slot, he saw the black Volvo truck-tractor and silvery metal trailer arrive at the quarry. It looked like many other semi-trailer combinations you might see on the interstate. But it didn't resemble anything else that traveled the rustic gravel road back into the quarry.

Having seen what he was waiting for, John slowly pulled the Chevy out from its hiding place behind an abandoned barn across the valley, and headed for the farm. When he arrived there, he knew he would have to share at least a few more details of the overall plan. Billy Bob and Lulu were getting restless.

It was about a thirty minute drive to the farm. As John was about to enter the driveway, he saw the sign he had asked Urland to make and display. It was four feet wide and three feet high, hand-painted on a piece of plywood, and planted in the ground with a single metal fence post. The post was apparently screwed onto the back of the sign, because there were some spots where the screws poked through.

The sign read, 'BEWAR OF DAWG.'

The letters were painted with a two-inch-wide brush in an unpracticed hand. Below the main message was an extra line that Urland and Brenda must have made up. Block lettered in the same style, but with a smaller stroke, were the words, 'Really Mean Basterd.' As he got closer, John could see a magazine picture of a drooling Rottweiler glued to the sign's bottom right corner.

He had to chuckle. At least making the sign had given them something to do. Nothing like a bit of arts and crafts to occupy the kids.

Half-way up the drive there was another wooden sign, this time nailed to a large tree. 'DANGER! WARNING! DON'T GO NO FURTHER! REALLY MEAN!'

John laughed again. The Umbers had certainly gotten into this project!

As he pulled into the turn-around, he saw Brenda and Urland sitting by the front door in plastic-webbed folding lawn chairs, cigarettes blazing, a cooler between them. He wondered if they missed the front porch of their ancestral home, back along the Oklahoma interstate . . . or wherever it was. He didn't see Farris; but he would almost certainly be sequestered in the lab.

John stopped to visit with the Umbers for a few minutes. Had they completed the waste pile moving assignment?

"Actually," Urland said, "we needed to call it a day. We'll hit 'er again tomorrow."

Since there was no firm deadline for this project, John nodded his approval.

Heading for the lab, John suppressed the ever-present ache that bored through his stomach and into his back. Damn cancer! He fumbled for a medicine bottle in his pocket and downed three small pills. Gotta keep this project on schedule – especially with someone 'watching his ass.'

Thus far, Farris had proven to be as capable a chemist as *Al Qaeda* had promised, albeit a pompous little shit. John knocked on the metal lab door.

"One moment," came Farris's voice from the lab. Presently, he opened the door a crack, saw who it was, then opened it the rest of the way.

"Just checking in to see how you're doing," John said.

"Since you finally got me the argon and the special electrical elements I was missing, I have been making good headway. Care to see?"

Farris couldn't resist the urge to show off to someone. And John was the only intelligent life form within earshot of the farm.

He waved John through the door ahead of him. The lab smelled like a swimming pool. Farris explained that chlorine gas was a byproduct of the chemical reaction. Though he had done a decent job of rigging a chimney and blower to vent the gas to the outside, there was still the piercing stench of it. John made a mental note to install a more effective chlorine venting system.

"I know it smells bad," said Farris, "but the chlorine levels in here are not toxic."

That was good to know.

On the lab table, a fire burned furiously beneath the potassium device. Even with the big new A/C unit on full blast, the radiant heat was fierce.

In a glass enclosure attached to and integrated with the cooking device, John could see what he assumed to be the molten potassium metal condensing on a white cooling plate. When the droplets got large enough, they would drip down the plate and into a ceramic tray. He remembered buying these trays for Farris long ago. John had had no vision at the time of their intended use.

Once in the tray, the molten metal cooled to a dull silvery-white as it solidified into ingots of pure potassium. The ingots were small. Maybe one inch wide, two inches long and a half inch thick.

Farris explained that the glass chamber – in fact, the entire apparatus – needed to be filled with argon gas at all times to avoid explosion. He indicated the blue rubber hoses attached to stainless steel argon injection nozzles on both the heating and cooling chambers.

Farris had devised a method of removing the ingots from the argon atmosphere, and bringing them out into the lab, without exposing the volatile metal to the air. He explained that the metal had to be quite cool before he could do this.

First he indicated to John a small spray nozzle at the top of the glass chamber. It wasn't connected to anything outside the device at present.

"Here is where I inject mineral spirits to coat the potassium before removal," Farris said.

Then he pointed at the lower edge of the glass chamber. John hadn't noticed before, but this edge was not made of glass. Farris explained that it was made of a custom polymer that could withstand both heat and substantial caustic chemical contact, while still remaining pliable. It looked sort of like a wide, clear windshield wiper blade.

It was time to switch the ingot trays and Farris wanted to demonstrate. John was a bit apprehensive. But he allowed Farris to proceed.

To remove the tray of potassium ingots from the apparatus, Farris first increased the argon flow to establish positive interior pressure. This assured that, if any gas leaked, it would be argon leaking out, rather than air leaking in.

From the corner of the lab, Farris retrieved a red, two-gallon weed sprayer. He pumped the handle to pressurize the sprayer, then connected its hose to the fitting on the top of the device. When Farris squeezed the sprayer trigger, a fine mist issued from a spray nozzle above the ingot tray. An oily sheen gradually began to appear on the otherwise dull ingots. He continued spraying until the oil began to pool on the tray. Then he released the trigger and disconnected the sprayer from the device.

The oil spray was necessary, Farris explained, to coat the potassium before it left argon isolation. Otherwise, the potassium would contact the water vapor in the air and the whole lab would go 'Boom!' He said it as though he needed to over-simplify for the infidel.

John ignored the insult. He had come to terms with the situation. He knew he had made his bed. Now he would lie in it – regardless of irritations.

To transfer the ingot tray out of the enclosed space, Farris used a flat metal handle, shaped like a football goal post. Holding it by the bottom of the 'post,' he inserted the handle through the windshield wiper slot and attached it to the ingot tray.

John held his breath as Farris slid the entire tray out of the glass enclosure.

Once the potassium was in open air, Farris moved quickly to a row of five-gallon, stainless steel chemical containers. Presumably, several of the containers in the row already held other finished potassium metal, submerged in large amounts of mineral spirits. Rotating a hinge on the handle ninety degrees, Farris lowered the entire ingot tray into the container and beneath the surface of the mineral oil. He then released the hinge, removed the handle from the container and looked at John with pride.

The kid's pretty impressed with himself, John thought. But as long as the process works, who cares what the little shit thinks.

"How much of this stuff are we going to end up with?" John asked.

"Best guess? That twenty-ton load of potash will yield about fifteen of those five gallon buckets."

"How much do the buckets weigh?"

"Potassium is one of the lightest metals. Its atomic number is 19 and its atomic weight is just over 39 – nearly as light as aluminum. The contents of the containers will weigh about the same as water. The buckets probably won't be completely full. So I would say they will weigh maybe twenty kilos each."

John did the math in his head. Twenty kilos would be just over forty pounds. Great! That was a lot lighter than John had feared. He had thought potassium might end up being as heavy as lead or something. Having these steel buckets weigh under fifty pounds made part of the job a lot easier.

"Farris. May Allah bless your service," John said, trying to keep their tenuous relationship intact.

Farris took offense at this non-Muslim's invocation of a blessing from Allah. But he let it go. Just another culturally ignorant American.

"I need to have a meeting with Urland and Brenda about some things. Is there anything else I can get you?" John offered.

"Iced tea, no sugar. Maybe a jug of it. With lots of ice."

It sounded as though he was ordering from the menu and John was his servant. Again, John tolerated Farris's arrogance.

"I'll get it up here as soon as we're done with the meeting."

John closed the metal lab door behind him and walked to the house. Urland and Brenda were waiting at the kitchen table, a beer in front of each of them.

"How 'bout a cold one?" Urland asked cheerfully. "Got plenty of Old Style."

"I know. I've been buying it," John said, with no small amount of sarcasm. "Thanks anyway, but I'll pass on the beer right now."

"Sure. No problem."

"Okay," John began. "Let's cut to the chase. I need you guys to be in top physical condition for your next big role in this operation."

Urland made a muscle with his right bicep, looking at it proudly. Brenda looked depressed.

"I need each of you to be able to lift and carry a five- gallon bucket of water at least a hundred yards without stopping to rest."

They looked at each other.

John continued. "There are some plastic buckets in the granary. Fill two of them with water. Then each of you can practice carrying one pail half-way down the driveway. You can stop at the 'Mean Dog' sign. Rest no more than one minute. Then carry them back up the driveway. When you can do this ten times in succession, resting no more than a minute at each end, you will be ready."

"Aren't we getting enough exercise moving the sand pile?" Brenda asked hopefully.

"Sorry. Different muscles," John said.

"Okay. Got it, Chief. Carry lots of water," reported Urland. Brenda still looked depressed.

"Oh yeah . . . please take a large insulated jug of iced tea up to the lab. Kid is dying in the heat up there. No sugar. Extra ice." John needed to keep Farris happy and hydrated for a while longer.

"Yeah. Sure." It was Brenda.

CHAPTER 29

Thursday, June 25th, on the Mississippi River near Red Wing.

United States Army Corp of Engineers Lock and Dam Number 3 is located less than a quarter mile down the Mississippi from the Prairie River Nuclear facility. Most of the dam projects on the river were built during the Roosevelt era as part of the CCC work program. Lock and Dam No. 3 was one of those projects and had been completed in 1938.

According to a recent official government report:

Lock and Dam 3 is connected to high ground on the Wisconsin side primarily by low-lying ground consisting of natural river levee banks, a series of sheet pile and rock overflow weirs called spot dikes and sections of constructed embankments that overtop during higher levels of river discharge. The constructed parts of the embankment system were not built to modern standards of engineering design, and have been deteriorating since the dam was completed despite a series of repairs.

The Wisconsin embankment conditions have reached an unacceptable level of instability and the system is subject to imminent failure.

Repairs to the dam were slated to begin next year. Now was the perfect time for someone to raise serious hell with the dam, if someone were so inclined.

And John was so inclined.

It was after midnight when John motored upstream from the Red Wing public landing in his sixteen-foot Sylvan aluminum fishing boat. It would be about a twenty minute ride up to Marsh Lake, adjacent to Lock and Dam Number 3. He had been there often, fishing for bullheads, catfish, carp and other bottom-feeding species. They loved the quiet, muddy water of the river shallows.

So far, the Sigler family's avenging angel was having a good day. The quarry company used much nicer explosives than he had dreamed possible. After cutting the padlock off the storage trailer, he could immediately see the stacks of wooden dynamite boxes – more than ample for his needs.

But the really sophisticated components were the detonation systems. Radio-controlled blasting caps, complete with paired transmitter/receiver packets. The dynamite could be detonated from a much greater distance than he had initially thought. This fact alone significantly decreased the chances of detection before detonation could be accomplished.

John had loaded his pickup with three boxes of thirteen-inch dynamite sticks and twenty blasting-cap/remote-control kits, then closed the door to the trailer to avoid any unnecessarily obvious signs of his visit.

In the morning, the owner would find the explosives missing. But he probably wouldn't report the theft. The surest way to lose your explosives license is to have some really good explosives disappear. The owner would adjust his blasting and inventory records as necessary – much easier than dealing with Alcohol Tobacco and Firearms concerning unaccounted-for dynamite.

As John's small boat approached the area near the dam, it left the main river channel to wend its way through the various sloughs, marshes and mud lakes that filled most of the three-mile-wide valley between the river bluffs. The main channel by the dam was only about 150 feet wide. There was also a significant side channel, which added another 350 feet to the total width spanned by the concrete Lock and Dam structure.

But John was not headed to the main dam. His targets were the earthen embankments and rock pile dikes that prevented the river water from circumventing the dam and surging through Marsh Lake.

The moon was nearly full and visibility was good. John wore denim shorts with a wet-suit top. He had a scuba mask, regulator and tank on board. Approaching the first earthen dam, he dropped anchor. With the boat floating lazily in the still water, he began his preparations.

He unpacked and organized everything for easy access. Dynamite, blasting caps and seven, one-foot lengths of straightened wire clothes hangers.

He knew from the boat's transponder reading that the water here was only about four feet deep. Nevertheless, he would be working underwater, so he strapped on the rest of the scuba gear and jumped in, feet first. Even though he could feel his feet sink into the muddy river bed about six inches, he nearly doubled over with pain when he hit the bottom.

After a moment to recover, he found that with a flutter kick he could raise himself high enough to access the contents of the boat, even though it hurt like hell. Reaching into a small canvas bag, he retrieved three white tablets, which he popped into his mouth and swallowed.

Using dynamite was not rocket science. Any kid who had played with cherry bombs had the general idea. The first order of business was drilling some holes in the dam. If an explosive blast isn't contained or directed, it tends to dissipate quickly, leaving little damage. The blast would be contained inside the holes, resulting in much greater devastation to the dam. John had a long, metal hand-drill in the boat for drilling.

He was about to grab the drill and begin placing the explosives when John heard the sound of an outboard boat motor on the main channel. He froze where he was, clinging motionless to the side of the boat.

Presently, the rev of the engine slowed and finally came to an idle. He could hear the boat's wake rippling onto the shore. They were close to his side of the channel. Then to John's horror, a searchlight aboard the unknown craft began sweeping the valley.

Shit! Probably the damn Sheriff's Water Patrol. He hadn't done anything to warrant their attention. Why would they be looking for him now? They *couldn't* find him now!

He thought the beam of light had come to rest on his boat for a few seconds. His heart sank. He remained still. What else could he do? Then the beam moved on, slicing across the mud flats and into the trees. After a short time, the light went out, the boat engine revved up, and the craft turned, heading back down-river – the direction from which it had come.

Still clinging to the boat's side, John breathed a sigh of relief. That had been too close. Now he needed to get back to work before there could be further interruptions.

Suspended in the water alongside his Sylvan, he first grabbed a few of the hanger wires and snapped them into a clip on his left calf. Then grasping the drill at its balance point, he lifted it over the side of the boat, letting himself sink into Marsh Lake.

The waters here were so silted and murky that, when submerged, he couldn't even see his hands. So everything he did underwater, he did by feel.

In a prone position, legs floating just above the river bed, John drilled the first hole in the dam. About two feet up from the bottom should be right. The drilling was easy in the fine soil. He bored six holes in this section of dam, each about four feet into the compacted earth. Next to every hole, he inserted a wire in the mud to mark his place. The holes were five feet apart, spaced evenly across the entire width of the small dam.

He returned to the boat, placed the drill back on board, and selected six sticks of dynamite and one blasting cap. He re-submerged. After some fumbling, he found the first wire. The dynamite fit nicely into the holes he had drilled. One stick first. Then push the first stick farther into the hole with the second. Same with the third. Then he prodded the third stick into the hole as far as possible using the wire. He moved on to the next hole – much easier to find since he had already established an underwater point of reference.

He repeated this procedure for the remaining five holes, returning to the boat for more dynamite. He also attached a blasting cap to the dynamite in the center hole.

John went through the same routine at a total of twelve separate earthen dam sections. Some of the larger dams required attachment of blasting caps in two locations.

In the rock pile dikes, instead of drilling, he wedged the dynamite between rocks by hand, placing them as deeply into the piles as he could. He spaced the sticks two feet apart and placed only one in each hole.

By the time he had finished, John had compromised a total of sixteen dams and dikes across Marsh Lake. When those structures failed, the entire river would surge through the openings. Very soon the new main channel of the Mississippi would flow through Marsh Lake, bypassing the nuclear plant – and its cooling water intakes – entirely.

John took great satisfaction in what he had accomplished today. His dead mother and father would be proud of their dear son.

CHAPTER 30

Friday, June 26th, at Red Wing.

Seated at the front porch table on Jefferson Avenue, Beth and I had just finished enjoying our evening meal of grilled walleye pike, new potatoes and sweet peas. We were in the process of finishing off a bottle of Kendall Jackson Chardonnay. Its fruity body and light oak were perfect with the walleye.

"I think I know how they're going to do it," I said.

"Who and what are we talking about right now?" Beth asked, very logically. Up until that point, our conversation had been about the daily news, our upcoming vacation plans and whether we should get a dog.

"Sorry. I've just let this nuke thing consume me. What I meant to say is, I know how the terrorists are going to attack the nuclear plant . . . sort of."

"What does 'sort of' mean?"

"It means I'm pretty sure of the method, but not the exact instrument."

"Well, now that we've cleared that up . . . ?"

"The terrorists plan to fly a plane into the spent fuel storage building," I continued. "The plane will contain a large amount of pure potassium metal, submerged in containers of mineral oil, or possibly diesel fuel. They intend to penetrate the building roof with the plane, thereby inserting the potassium into the pool."

"And what would that do?" Beth asked.

"The potassium will react violently with the water in the pool and result in a tremendous explosion and fire – essentially using the pool water as fuel. The explosion may also crack the sides of the pool and/or damage the fuel racks, though I'm doubtful. There is too much opportunity for the explosive force to go up, rather than down or out, when the potassium hits the water."

"Go on. This sounds creative." Beth was not patronizing me. She was sincere.

"In any case, the pool water will be gone and the stored fuel will immediately begin to heat up. The burning hydrogen released by the potassium/water reaction should accelerate the heating process, as would any burning fuel from the aircraft. And if the pool racks are damaged, the assemblies might tip into each other. That would also heat the fuel rods faster.

"The extreme heat creates an intense fire – a meltdown – releasing a steamy plume of radioactive and poisonous chemicals. It would be the equivalent of a nuclear attack on the sprawling residential neighborhoods of the Twin Cities metro area. Thousands, or possibly tens of thousands, would die within days. And the toxic effects on communities farther east, while less dramatic, could collectively result in even greater human casualties over time."

The idea was sobering.

"If the pool itself isn't cracked, doesn't the utility have a backup source of water to fill the pool and cool the fuel?" Beth was helping me think this through.

"I am told that they do. But I'm not convinced that the backup system would be effective with the pool emptying so suddenly and the heat developing so quickly. I suspect new water would just boil off. I don't know for sure. But this theory explains the missing lab equipment, the hijacked potash truck – since potash contains a lot of potassium – the involvement of a chemist, the international cell phone call, and possibly the motive for the professor's murder."

Beth leaned back from the table, wine glass held in both hands at breast level. "Where does the plane come from?" She was still trying to help me work out the kinks in my theory.

"Well, that's where the 'sort of' part comes in. It would almost certainly be possible for a small plane pilot to take off from the Red Wing Airport and hit the spent fuel building roof. I'm just not sure if a light plane like that would penetrate. Or if it could carry enough potassium. I don't have enough information."

Beth smiled at me. I could feel the warmth radiate across the table. "Babe, I think you have enough to take your theory to the authorities. Maybe they can fill in the blanks."

"I'll bring it to Gunner tomorrow. And if he won't listen, I'll find someone who will."

CHAPTER 31

Saturday, June 27ᵗʰ, at Red Wing.

It was 7:00 the next morning. I had already been sitting in one of the lobby's plastic 'torture chairs' for half an hour when Gunner came through the front door to the Law Enforcement Center.

Yes, he works on Saturdays.

I jumped up. "Gunner. I need to see you. In private." My expression and lack of donuts conveyed urgency.

Gunner looked like he had been bushwhacked, which he had. Without protest he directed me to the conference room just off the lobby and followed me in. "Now what's got your feathers in a bunch," Gunner said, mixing metaphors while sipping his convenience store coffee.

We sat.

"First, I need to know. Is there anything new on the murder case?"

"Not that it's really any of your business . . ." He paused for effect. "But we haven't been able to find the lab assistant or his car. His credit cards, telephone and bank accounts remain untouched since the night of the murder. His apartment has been re-rented to a new tenant. We got everything we could from there, which was essentially nothing, and then had to give the apartment back to the landlord. He was raising holy hell with the County Commissioners and at City Hall."

Gunner looked directly at me now. "Why? Have you got something useful to tell me?"

"Well. I'm afraid I don't know the location of your murder suspect," I confessed.

Gunner frowned.

"But I'm pretty sure there is going to be a terrorist attack on the nuke plant. And I think I know how they're going to do it."

Now Gunner really frowned.

I relayed to Gunner my theory and how it meshed perfectly with the professor's death, the potash hijacking, the cell call and the missing lab equipment – not to mention that the prime murder suspect was Arabic.

After he finished listening, Gunner took another sip of coffee from his paper cup. Leaning back in his metal conference chair, he looked straight at me and said, "You've got squat! Where you see terrorists, I see fertilizer. Other than racial profiling of our suspect, why do you think the nuclear plant is involved?"

I sat for a moment. "My gut?"

"Your gut."

"That, and the only worthwhile target within miles of here is Prairie River Nuke. Plus, I can show you and everybody at the nuke exactly how it could be done."

Gunner remained unconvinced.

"Okay. Let's look at it this way," I said. "Just suppose you possess the information I have just given you, and you keep it to yourself. Next week the Prairie River Plant gets dive-bombed by an airplane. All hell breaks loose. Worst nuclear event in history. Assuming you are lucky enough to survive, how are you going to feel?"

Gunner is a good guy and a good cop. He just doesn't like to play the fool in front of his law enforcement comrades. Sometimes a little fear can help a person do the right thing.

Gunner took a deep breath. I could feel the weather changing.

"We happen to have a Joint Enforcement Committee meeting Monday afternoon out at Prairie River. The FBI, the BCA, the NRC and a whole lot of other TLA's will be there. Why don't you come to the meeting and explain it to everybody?"

"Sure," I said. "What's a TLA?"

Gunner smiled. "A three letter acronym."

CHAPTER 32

Winter, spring and early summer, central Africa.

Al Qaeda had no intention of trusting execution of the Prairie River nuclear assault plan solely to three Americans and a young boy. While John Sigler, no doubt, considered attack logistics to be under his control, the council had taken its own measures to assure operational success.

For the past many months, three elite *Al Qaeda* guerrillas had been conducting specific training exercises at a base in central Africa. Their purpose was to bring strategic technology and military fire-power in support of the primary attack team at Prairie River.

The training base was arranged to simulate a small airport. Six months earlier, the runway proper had been overgrown with jungle foliage. Since then, local supporters had chopped, hacked, sawed and cut the tropical undergrowth until the runway emerged as a mile-long clearing of jungle grass. Workers had also erected beside the 'runway,' what amounted to a full-scale model of the buildings at the Red Wing Airport.

Rough-hewn, empty shacks, fashioned from indigenous tree trunks and branches, simulated the main terminal, the hangars and all of the airport out-buildings. Cleared dirt or grassy alleys were the taxiways. There was even an elevated, cruciform structure on the main taxi-way, intended to represent a large airplane.

To be sure, it would not have been prudent to land a plane here. But the replica was effective for its purposes.

Day after day, for months in the jungle heat, the three tactical operatives faced one simulated challenge after another. Their goal – protect the plane at all costs.

CHAPTER 33

Monday, June 29th, at the Prairie River Nuclear Generating Station.

On Monday afternoon, I pulled into the parking area at the Prairie River Personnel Training Center. There were already about a dozen cars parked in the lot. The Training Center is outside the 'critical zone,' so I could just drive up to the front door. No security at all.

I looked past the parking lot pavement at the chain-link fences with coiled razor wire on top, and at the nuclear generating station beyond. Even the look of the place close-up was awe-inspiring.

As the result of a security-related traffic snafu on the only road into the plant, and despite my usual preparedness in allowing extra travel time, I arrived a couple minutes late for the meeting. So when I entered the Training Center and knocked on the open conference room door, everybody stopped talking and looked at me.

"Hey, Gunner! Going to introduce me to your friends?" I asked. It was lame, but the best I could come up with at the time.

I had seen some of the faces at the table before. There was a City of Red Wing cop, a private security guy from the generating plant, the NRC onsite inspector, the Plant Manager, and an officer from the Prairie River Tribal Police. (The Rez is right next door to the plant.) Gunner was there from the Sheriff's Office. The other two guys had to be BCA and FBI special agents. I couldn't tell which was which.

Gunderson stood.

"Gentlemen, this is James Becker. He is a local attorney who expressed a concern to me this past weekend. I thought it prudent that you all hear for yourselves what Mr. Becker has to say."

He sat down.

Thanks a bunch for the rousing intro, Gunner!

The Red Wing cop was at the head of the table. Of course. The plant was within the city limits. The city would have primary jurisdiction. Cops are big on protecting their turf. The cop didn't invite me to sit . . . not that there was an empty chair anyway.

Red Wing Cop: "Okay, Mr. Becker. What is it that you'd like us to hear?"

Once again, I told my story.

When I was done, there were several comments.

Plant Security: "It's ridiculous to think that any private aircraft could successfully attack our facility. We have laser-guided guns and a rotating cannon that is capable of projecting more than 4500 rounds per minute of 20 mm lead. Not to mention numerous, more classified defensive counter-measures. Any small craft would be ripped to shreds before it even got near our fence."

"There was the case of that one guy who landed his plane on the White House lawn," I offered. "Sometimes it's hard to make that decision to pull the trigger. And as I have said, it may be only three seconds from legal flight to impact."

Plant Manager: "Even if a small plane managed to penetrate air defenses and crash into the spent fuel building, the roof and sides of that structure are plenty tough to repel a light craft. We reinforced them after 9/11. It's just not a realistic threat."

FBI: "And there's no way anybody's gettin' close to the plant with a commercial plane. Any commercial aircraft that far out of its airspace would set off buzzers and bells all over the place. Hell, we could probably get military defenses down here pronto. After 9/11, the National Guard is ready to do whatever it takes."

I doubted his statement about timing, but agreed it couldn't be a commercial plane for other reasons, so I didn't argue.

Prairie River Tribal Cop: "What about this potassium stuff? If someone gets that in the pool, are we in trouble?"

A concern from the man who lived next door to the plant. Good.

Plant Manager: "Of course not. No need to worry at all. We have multiple backup systems, redundancies, manual overrides. You know I can't discuss details without compromising security. But rest assured, potassium in that pool would not be a problem."

He was talking through his hat. He had never thought of potassium getting into the spent fuel pool.

I knew a little about the Plant Manager's history. A number of years ago he had been 'promoted' from plant maintenance to management. In the power generation industry, it is a well-known axiom that if you damage enough expensive equipment working your maintenance job, rather than fire you and risk a union challenge, the company will give you a spot behind a desk – just so you can't wreck stuff.

It had been a freakish mangling of bureaucracy when company ownership changed hands and the erstwhile maintenance man ended up as Assistant Plant Manager. After the former Plant Manager retired last year, the company just moved the Assistant on up into the vacant spot. It was my opinion that this particular gentleman had passed his Peter Principle Point several promotions ago. Nevertheless, he controlled operations at the plant and I would have to put up with him.

"Some folks are concerned about a zirconium fire in the pool and a massive release of poisonous iodine – not to mention a radioactive plume of cesium 137," I pointed out.

Plant Manager: "Who the hell made you the nuclear expert? I am not aware of any such concerns. And you have no idea what you're talking about."

"I could give you websites that explain it to you if you wish?" I couldn't tell for sure if his density was intentional, or innate.

Plant Manager: "I don't need any fuckin' websites from any fuckin' asshole know-it-all to tell me my own business. I know damn well this plant is safe!"

He was clearly getting worked up. When you know very little, you have to yell it really loud. I held my tongue.

NRC Guy: "I assure you, Mr. Becker, we take your concerns very seriously and will make certain that the scenario you have laid out is absolutely impossible."

The nuclear watch-dog for the public at work. He undoubtedly knew that the spent fuel pool was a weak link. But plant design was not under his control. And he had to trust the security team regarding possible attacks. He would probably do what he could. But I doubted it would matter.

The BCA guy wasn't going to have to deal with any of this business unless someone pointed him at a location he could swim to with a SWAT team. He just watched the proceedings with interest.

Deputy Chief Gunderson was notably silent.

Red Wing City Cop: "So if you have nothing further, we'll just thank you for bringing us your concerns and you may be on your way."

That was all I had to say. But it clearly had not been enough.

"Please review your security plans with my scenario in mind. Please." I was actually begging. Sometimes that works with bureaucrats.

Red Wing City Cop: "Thank you again for your input. We will certainly take matters under advisement."

I'd tried the polite approach. I now spoke calmly, but with deadly conviction.

"Gentlemen. You sit here in this room, insulated from reality, comfortable in your delusions that you are safe from international terrorism. In your imaginary world, your families are safe. Your neighbors are safe. We are all totally safe.

"Your delusions have led you to the conclusion that the nuclear catastrophe waiting to happen inside that fence across the parking lot is a fiction. Of course, you all know how extreme the consequences of a successful terrorist attack on the nuclear plant would be. But because of your fantasies, you discount the dangers – not only to yourselves and your loved ones, but to everyone in the eastern half of the United States, and possibly beyond.

But what if the worst possible scenario proves not to be a fantasy at all, but a deadly fact?

I'm telling you all right now that we are *not* safe! You no longer have the luxury of remaining comfortable in your delusions.

"Gentlemen," I said, eyeing each committee member in turn, "the wolf is at your door. It's time for you to step into the real world. Millions of Americans are depending on you for protection from a nuclear nightmare.

"Wake up and do your jobs!"

I turned and left.

When I got outside, I had to control my frustration. The Committee entrusted with nuclear security at Prairie River consisted of a bunch of over-confident, myopic bureaucrats, bent on avoiding occupational discomfort. Most of them couldn't recognize a terrorist if one stuck a pipe bomb up his ass.

I had expected better of Gunner.

Security had certainly gotten lax at Prairie River. It made me nervous. Even if my plane attack scenario proved folly, what other terrorist approaches were they leaving undefended?

I sat in my car with the windows open, stewing, until Gunner came out of the building. He saw me and kept walking, head down, toward his car.

"Hey, Gunderson," I yelled through my window. "Come here! I need a word."

Reluctantly, he came over to my car and got in the passenger seat. He faced straight forward and remained silent.

"Way to hang me out to dry in there, Gunner!"

I was pissed.

"Damn it! I told you that your story was lame. Don't blame me because everyone else thought so, too."

"What's your usual order of business in there? Trying to figure out how to divide six bananas between seven people? I think my IQ dropped ten points just by osmosis. And damn it, Gunner, you know in your gut that there is a risk here. And you know the consequences."

There was a long pause. I stared at Gunner – he, at the windshield. Finally, he spoke.

"Okay. You're right . . . Shithead!"

I choked down a laugh.

"I didn't like the answers I was hearing in there any better than you did. A lot of huffing and puffing and just plain bull. I'll do what I can . . . unofficially. How can I help?"

"I don't know right now. But I'll think of something. Thank you."

"Yeah. Yeah. Yeah."

CHAPTER 34

Thursday, July 1st, near Red Wing.

It was 6:30 in the morning when the phone on John Sigler's bed stand rang. He was disoriented at first – partly from fitful sleep, and partly because of the heavy dose of Oxycontin he had taken to make any sleep at all a possibility.

He reached for the handset, but the stab in his gut laid him flat on his back.

The phone kept ringing.

John slid sideways to the edge of the bed and gradually rolled off it and onto his knees. From this position, he was able to answer the call.

"Yeah?"

"Sigler?"

It was the man with the Midwestern accent. His overseer.

"Yeah. Whatta ya want? It's pretty damn early to be calling."

"The bosses want you to do something. That damn lawyer's been sniffin' all over town with talk of a potassium bomb and an attack on the nuke plant."

Still on the floor, John rolled onto his back, the phone at his ear. "Well shit! Ain't that just peachy! I thought you guys were gonna take care of him."

"You just do what I tell you and everything's gonna be fine."

"Yeah . . . just peachy!"

"He's looking for a potassium bomb, but can't tie it to the nuke. So we need to give him a potassium explosion. You understand?"

"You want me to waste some of that high-powered stuff we've been cooking for months to set up some kind of diversion? You're shittin' me."

"Listen up," the man said. "Here's what you're gonna do."

*   *   *

John didn't like the plan. But he feared that if he disobeyed orders, the whole shootin' match might go south. Where would he be then? No bomb. No retribution. Nothing to show for his patience and labors.

He would go along with the plan.

CHAPTER 35

Saturday, July 4ᵗʰ, at Red Wing.

Every summer, Beth and I enjoyed sitting on our front porch while we watched Red Wing's Independence Day fireworks display. The firework shells were launched from an island on the far side of the main channel and detonated above the Mississippi itself. We lived close enough on Jefferson Avenue to appreciate the entire experience. We could even hear the "ooos" and "ahhhs" of spectators from Baypoint Park – the official viewing location – and the appreciative horn-tooting from pleasure boats as their passengers watched at anchor in the river.

The generosity of a local pyrotechnic engineer significantly enhanced Red Wing's annual display. He was a nationally-recognized importer and wholesaler of firework shells – some, up to 18 inches in diameter – which he regularly donated to benefit Red Wing's celebration. As a result, it was always a great show. Being able to enjoy it from our mosquito-free porch was a bonus.

Shortly after the fireworks started, an earth-shaking vibration rolled through our neighborhood. At first I thought it was a new type of pyrotechnic. I was impressed by the sub-sonic rumble I felt coming up through my feet, and the dramatic rattling of our windows. But when the fireworks display suddenly came to a halt, and the sound of police sirens echoed from downtown, I knew in my gut that what I had heard was not part of the show.

Something else had happened.

*   *   *

With a significant portion of the Red Wing police force on vacation for the holiday, and most who remained on duty working traffic control at the fireworks display, local law enforcement was caught short-handed and unprepared when the explosion rocked City Hall. By the time police arrived at the scene, there was little for them to do but cordon off the area in an effort to protect bystanders from injury.

As crowds gathered at the police lines, they marveled at a watery inferno emanating from a huge hole in the street just outside City Hall's main doors. Shooting nearly fifty feet into the air, the eery juxtaposition of multi-colored flame mixed with spraying water held the gawkers transfixed.

Some viewers maintained that the explosion had resulted from a large firework shell gone astray. Others even said they had seen a shell hit the street. Still others claimed to have seen firework-like sparks jetting from the turbulent crater after the initial detonation.

As imaginations ran rampant, rumors of an errant cruise missile began to circulate.

The fire department scrambled its men and equipment, fogging the fire from all sides to contain the heat from the flames. The local utility raced to cut off the source of natural gas feeding the inferno. And Red Wing Public Works located the appropriate water valve to seal off the ruptured main.

In less than twenty minutes, the water and gas were turned off and the show was over. The Mayor had arrived. Holding a bull horn, he announced that the explosion was most likely caused by a gas leak under the street. In any case, he said, everything was now under control. No one had been injured. Everyone should disperse and go home.

* * *

Technicians worked through the night to re-route water, sewer and gas lines, restoring utility services to surrounding homes and businesses. Most were re-connected and operating by sunrise.

The crisis appeared to have passed . . . for now. But exactly what had happened was far from clear.

* * *

At 8:00 a.m. Sunday morning, Gunner and I accompanied a group of forensic specialists, all of whom were closely examining the scene of last night's explosion. The hole had been pumped nearly dry – its contents collected in a tanker truck for later analysis. Rubber-booted BCA crime scene investigators worked down in the crater, sampling water, mud, piping and every tiny bit of material that might not belong there. Since Gunner and I were not officially part of the investigation, we could only observe the goings-on from street-level with interest . . . and concern.

The BCA had brought its Portable Crime Lab down from St. Paul to aid with preliminary findings. It was parked crossways in the street, just down the block from the twenty-foot-wide, ten-foot-deep crater.

I stepped as close to the edge of the hole as I dared, hoping to overhear snippets of conversation between the investigators.

"This is really strange," one technician was saying to another. "I expected to find a place where the gas line exploded outward. But it looks like the blast force came from the sewer line and then bent the gas line here." He pointed with his foot.

"So the sewer line ruptured first? And then the gas and water lines later?" his co-worker was saying.

"I can't think of any other explanation."

"That's one helluva fire cracker down the toilet!"

"Take plenty of pictures. Swab the lines for chemical residue and let's get this stuff to the lab."

"Roger that."

CHAPTER 36

Monday, July 6th, at Red Wing.

I was at Becker Law Office when I received Gunner's call.

"So, have you learned more about the City Hall explosion," I asked.

"Yeah . . . as a matter of fact. And I think it helps solve your mystery of the missing potassium machine."

"Stop right there. I'll be at your office in five minutes. I want to hear this in person."

After asking Debbie to direct my calls to Karen, I hopped in the Pilot, arriving on the L.E.C. doorstep three minutes later. Gunner was waiting in the entryway as I pushed through the doors.

"C'mon in," he said, waving me into the inner corridor.

When we got to Gunner's office, he had to sit in his chair before speaking. I remained standing. I was too anxious to sit.

"So you said this solves the potassium puzzle. Give me the scoop."

"The initial reports are back from the BCA lab. As you overheard yesterday, the explosion originated in the sanitary sewer line."

"Okay," I said. "I already knew that."

"But what you don't know is that the bomb inside the sewer line was no ordinary bomb."

Gunner paused.

Sometimes I could just throttle him and his dramatic pauses.

"So what was unusual about it?" I managed, without jumping across Gunner's desk.

"The bomb was made from potassium!"

I sat down.

"I'll be damned. Tell me more."

"Somebody apparently wrapped a few ounces or so of pure potassium in some kind of pouch, then stuffed it into the sanitary sewer system. It was only a matter of time before the sewer water dissolved the pouch and the potassium and water would explode.

"So that solves the mystery of the potassium. It was used to make this bomb."

"So the pouch was made of some kind of water-soluble material," I continued. "Do we know what that material was?"

"The report I got doesn't say. Why does it matter? Your potassium was in a pouch and it blew up."

"The makeup of the pouch might say something about the sophistication of the bomber," I responded. My mind was still processing this new information. "Do they know where the pouch entered the sewer line?"

"No." Gunner looked irritated that I hadn't immediately embraced his resolution of the missing lab device mystery. "And they will probably never know. The stuff could have been flushed down any toilet, or jammed into any floor drain, then floated downhill to City Hall. There's no way to estimate how far the damn thing may have traveled before exploding."

I stared at the ceiling. Gunner fidgeted in his chair.

"I don't think I'm buying this scenario," I said after a moment.

"What! There was definitely potassium residue . . . and shreds of the dissolvable pouch. And it exploded right in front of City Hall. What's not to buy?"

Gunner was more frustrated than angry.

"Gunner, listen. Think about it. If you wanted to make a big hole in front of City Hall, how many ways could you do it?"

Gunner thought for a moment. "I s'pose a half-dozen or more."

"Any of them involve potassium?"

"'Course not. I'd probably use dynamite, gun powder or homemade plastique. And I'd either shove it down the storm drain out front, or climb down a manhole and put it right where I wanted. Remote detonator or a long fuse would work."

"What's your point?"

"So there are lots of other ways to blow up a street . . . right?"

"Okay. So what? He decided to use potassium because he's a chem geek."

"Gunner, no 'chem geek' is going to risk his life manufacturing elemental potassium when a jug of nitro would work just grand. No way."

"So what's *your* theory as to why there was potassium in that hole?" Gunner crossed his arms over his chest.

I paused a moment in thought.

"Here's what I think," I replied. "The bad guys know we're looking for a potassium bomb. I don't know how they know – but they do. So they give us one."

"So you're saying this explosion was a diversion? And their real target is somewhere else."

"That's the only logical explanation for finding potassium in that hole."

Gunner still didn't look convinced.

"Gunner. Try this one on for size. S'pose our bomber . . . for some inexplicable reason . . . had a thing about using a potassium bomb. Why not cause more damage? Why not put the pouch in a rail car of ammonia? Or the storm drain of a gas station? Or a lavatory at a government building?

"Why just a harmless hole in the street? It'll be fixed up good as new by next week."

Gunner considered my arguments.

"Okay. It doesn't sound likely that someone would kill a man, steal his potassium machine, and then just use it to blow up a street.

"But maybe the location was a mistake. Maybe he intended to bring down City Hall. That might be worth the extra effort to some radical."

"But Gunner . . . we're still down to the same thing. Why potassium? Gasoline in a stairwell, a stick of dynamite in the basement, a fertilizer bomb parked out front, a Molotov Cocktail on the tarred roof – all of them would do a better, and a more certain, job of destroying City Hall. If our bomber is smart enough to make pure potassium, he's too smart to miss his target.

"No way this was the real attack. I'm more convinced than ever that the nuke is the goal. And we now know that Ahmed's been able to make at least *some* pure potassium for the attack."

"Wait a minute. How are we sure it's Ahmed?"

"He's the chemist. He's the guy who is capable of distilling the pure potassium, using a *unique* machine that only he could have taken from the University Lab. Farris Ahmed is definitely connected with this bombing. Unless you know of other manufacturers of elemental potassium?"

Gunner eyeballed me with irritation.

"Beck. I should be getting used to losing these arguments with you. But I gotta admit you make sense . . . dammit!"

I laughed.

Gunner smiled.

"Glad to hear you're still onboard. Because even though this explosion doesn't solve our potassium riddle, it does raise a question that needs investigating."

"Which is?"

"Farris Ahmed, or his conspirators, must know that we suspect a potassium bomb. Hence, the diversion. How did they find out?

"The only people I've talked with about potassium are you, Beth, Bull, Dr. Downing and the nitwits at the nuke security council. Somebody leaked something to somebody. Maybe you could track down the leak? That might get us closer to Ahmed."

"Sounds like traditional police work, thank god. I'll see what I can find out."

"¡Muchas gracias!"

"Yeah. Yeah. Yeah."

CHAPTER 37

Wednesday, August 5th, at the Ottawa County farm.

Nearly two months had passed since Farris started processing the potassium chloride. It was now early August. John was back at the farm again today. Urland and Brenda had supposedly been working on their water bucket conditioning for weeks. It didn't show. It probably wouldn't matter. At least it had kept them busy and tired them out.

On the other hand, Farris had just about completed his work on the potassium. The pile of chloride outside was almost gone. And the lab now held eighteen steel buckets filled with pure potassium ingots submerged in mineral oil.

"When do you think we can wrap this up, Farris?" John asked.

"I can finish the rest of it tonight or tomorrow," he said, sounding tired.

"How much more product do you expect to yield?"

Farris, looked at the apparatus and went outside to check the chloride pile. When he returned, he said, "Maybe one more container . . . maybe."

"Okay. I'd like you to finish up the pile; but we need to be ready to move this stuff by the weekend."

"I will complete it."

CHAPTER 38

Friday, August 7ᵗʰ, in Red Wing.

It had been three months since the professor's death. It was a Friday afternoon in early August. Sunny. Eighty degrees Fahrenheit. I had been at the office since noon. I needed a break. I thought everyone else could use a break, too. So I closed the office and sent everyone home at 1:00. An extra half-day of vacation. What a guy!

As I shut off the lights and closed the door, I heard Frank come out of his office into the darkened interior space.

"Karen? Karen?"

Time for an afternoon off, Frank. Life is short. Enjoy the day.

Before Frank could catch me leaving, I was in the Pilot and out of the parking lot. I dialed Beth on her cell.

"My boss gave me the afternoon off sweetums. Care to sip mint juleps on the patio with your best guy?"

"Sounds heavenly. I'll be home in about an hour. I just need to check out some new jewelry designs at the Art Center."

I wasn't sure an hour would do it. So when I arrived home, I immediately changed into shorts and T-shirt, grabbed a tall aluminum bottle of Budweiser, and moved to one of the green lounge chairs on the back patio. The icy beer slid smoothly down my throat, quenching more than just thirst. The bottle emptied quickly.

Gunner hadn't yet been able to identify the information leak in our inner circle. That wasn't surprising. It was likely that every cop in Red Wing knew about my hair-brained concerns. They had told their spouses about the nut attorney. They, in turn, had told their friends.

Gossip moves quickly around a small town. Both the nuke, and potassium, had probably been widely discussed – mostly in a casual, and likely humorous, context. I was sure Gunner was doing his best. I wouldn't bug him for a progress report.

I reclined in the chair.

Taking a deep breath, I let my body sink into the lounge – muscles relaxed, jaw loose. I closed my eyes against the near-midday sun, consciously enjoying its warmth on my face.

The next thing I heard was Beth's voice.

"You're getting a bit fried, Babe."

I felt my forehead. Yup. Toasty.

Leaning my head forward, I squinted at her as she walked past me toward the house. "Gotta change. Be out in a minute."

"Doll, would you mind bringing the sunscreen and an aluminum Bud for me when you come out."

"No problem," I heard faintly from inside the house.

As I sat in the afternoon sun, awaiting my cabana service, I heard an airplane approaching. It sounded quite low. Leaning forward on the lounge chair, I searched the sky in the direction of the sound. A single-engine Cessna barely cleared the hill behind our house, roared over my head and continued on into the valley.

Most planes don't fly so low over our neighborhood. Jefferson Avenue is several miles from the airport, in a direction perpendicular to its runway(s). But once in a while some punk has to show off by buzzing the bluffs. It's illegal, but hard to prove.

Beth joined me on the patio. A quick kiss, plus delivery of my sun screen and a second ice-cold Bud. Life could not be better! Beth oriented her matching lounge chair for maximum sun, and lay back. She hadn't fried herself earlier.

I applied the sun screen liberally, even though it was probably too late to do much good, and resumed my lounging position.

"Any good bargains today?" I enquired, my eyes closed once again.

"Didn't buy anything. Saw some interesting designs at the Art Center though. There are some very inventive artists who live around here and sell their creations at the Center."

Another plane flew over. This one sounded different than the planes we usually hear in Red Wing. Again, I sat forward and searched the sky.

I could hear the plane clearly, but couldn't seem to pick it out. Finally I spotted it. I had been looking much too low in the sky. It was a large, twin-propeller plane, at least ten thousand feet up.

I lay back into the lounge.

"Beth? Is there something going on around here with the planes? That's a strange looking bird. And before you came out, some yahoo in a Cessna barely cleared the bluff."

"That air show is this weekend, Babe."

I sat bolt upright.

"What air show?"

"Wings of Thunder or something like that. There have been posters in all the store windows for months." Beth looked at me over the magazine she had been reading. "You don't get out much, do you?"

"Not in the right places, apparently. Wasn't it advertised in the paper?"

"Sure. They had a whole special section in last weekend's edition."

I usually ignored the 'special sections' in the local paper. They ordinarily dealt with gardening, crafting, baking, or youth sports, none of which interested me. I wished I had seen this one though.

"Listen Doll. I've gotta make a call."

I went into the house and dialed the number for the Law Enforcement Center. "Chief Deputy Gunderson please. Tell him it's Becker. And please tell him it's important."

A moment later, he answered.

"Gunderson."

"Gunner, I think I need your help now."

"What can I do?"

CHAPTER 39

Friday, August 7th, from Thunder Bay, Canada to Red Wing.

Among the aircraft that had flown to Red Wing for the show was a four-seater Cessna, fitted with pontoons instead of wheels. The aircraft had departed Thunder Bay, Ontario, Canada Friday morning with a flight plan filed for a fishing trip to Lake Saskatoon. But its passengers weren't fishermen. They were three of *Al Qaeda's* most deadly operatives – members of the elite Special Forces of the *Jihad*.

The plane disappeared from Canadian radar just as it arrived over the lake. Since Lake Saskatoon was in a remote, heavily forested area, Canadian air control assumed the plane had made the planned water landing. It had no further interest in the craft.

Instead of landing on the lake, however, the Cessna had dropped very low over the trees and turned southeast, toward the American border. Skimming the tree-tops and hugging the rugged contours of southern Ontario, the plane soon crossed over the Rainy River and into the State of Minnesota, U.S.A.

When the Cessna carrying the Arab terrorists returned to radar height about 100 miles after entering the U.S. from Canadian airspace, there was no requirement of a flight plan or identification, so long as the plane stayed below 3,000 feet.

American laws did not even require it to have a radio on board. Canadian/American air security was practically non-existent – at least concerning small planes.

Only four-and-a-half hours after taking off from Thunder Bay, the small plane cleared the wooded bluffs of the Mississippi river valley, about ten miles southeast of Red Wing. Dropping below the bluff tops, the plane changed course, swinging to the northwest, following the river's course upstream.

Less than ten minutes later, at about 1:30 Friday afternoon, the Canadian pontoon plane made a water landing on a back channel of the river. It didn't take long to find an inaccessible and inconspicuous mooring spot on the edge of a mud lake about two miles downstream from Red Wing.

The three passengers exited the plane, sinking into the muddy lake bottom. There was some gear to unload and an exact route to be found. But they had plenty of time to make their way upstream to the Red Wing Airport in time for this weekend's action.

CHAPTER 40

Friday, August 7th, in and around Red Wing.

The air show was Saturday and Sunday at the Red Wing Airport. I had told Gunner my concerns. He'd agreed to do all he could to step up security at and around the airport. He was going out on a limb for me. And I appreciated it.

The show was a flying museum of World War II era Air Force planes. Actually taking off and landing from the Red Wing airfield there would be: a P51 Mustang fighter, a P40 Warhawk fighter, a four-engine B17 Flying Fortress heavy bomber, a twin-engine B25 Miss Mitchell medium bomber, a four-engine B24 Liberator (affectionately known as the 'flying boxcar' because of its large, flat, ugly sides) and a number of other, less famous, vintage warplanes.

Additional appearances would be made by the Blue Angels precision flying team and other jet aircraft. The fly-by appearances were generally made by planes that could not safely takeoff or land at Red Wing due to the length of the runway.

Airplane enthusiasts would descend on the Red Wing Airport for the weekend. Some would fly their own planes into neighboring airports today. But most would drive. In any case, the skies over Red Wing and the rest of the Mississippi valley promised to be alive with air traffic for the next two days.

I would have enjoyed the show myself, if I didn't have other things on my mind.

CHAPTER 41

Friday, August 7th, at the Ottawa County farm.

Friday evening out on the farm, John, Urland, Farris and even Brenda were loading the steel containers of potassium into the back of a black Ford pickup. The pickup had a white hard-shell topper, so it would be difficult for anyone to see its unusual cargo. Everyone was being extra careful.

All nineteen containers fit fine. John found some boards and a few blankets and arranged the containers tightly together on the pickup bed. He didn't want any shifting or tipping during transport.

When the potassium had all been loaded, John carefully placed several large, military-green satchels in the very back of the truck box, segregated from the potassium cans by the wood and soft materials.

Everyone promised not to touch anything on the truck bed without John's approval. No one wanted the product of all their work to climax prematurely. And most of them didn't want to die, at least not yet.

They left Farris's car hidden at the farm. Urland drove his Buick. Farris drove John's Chevy. John drove the pickup with its precious cargo. They were headed to what John called the 'staging area.' Urland would follow John. Farris would follow Urland. Everyone would take great care to obey all traffic laws en route.

They started their respective vehicles and rolled slowly down the dirt driveway. A minute later, the small convoy turned left onto the gravel public road and headed toward Red Wing.

Half-a-mile up the road, in the dusky light of sunset, a neighboring farmer observed the passing of the unusual parade from his front porch. Turning his head to one side, he spat brown juice into a coffee can.

CHAPTER 42

Saturday, August 8th, on Jefferson Avenue.

I woke up early Saturday morning. The sun was barely lightening the starry eastern sky outside our bedroom window. I was lying on my left side, watching Beth sleep. She was on her right side, facing me. Her fine, straight, sandy-blonde hair draped seductively across her left cheek.

I appreciated the curve of her neck, the soft tan skin on her bare shoulder, the little pout her lips made as she slept.

Her eyes popped open, as if she had sensed me watching her.

"It's early," she said sleepily, rolling onto her back.

She stretched both arms, arching her back and shrugging the sheet off her trim torso, exposing the pink cotton tank top, pulled taut over her athletic body. As she stretched, the top slipped up, showing off an inch or so of silky skin above her pajama bottoms. I fully appreciated the view, as I always do.

"Beth?"

"Um hmm?"

"Something very bad may well happen this weekend at the nuclear plant. Everyone is going to do their best to stop it. But there are enough unknowns that there is no guarantee it can be stopped.

"If something bad does happen, I don't want you to be in Red Wing. I want you to drive somewhere to the west. Hang out with friends in Mankato. Or check into a hotel for the next few days and explore some new stores.

"The girls are all right at their west-coast internships. But it's not safe for you to stay here in town."

Beth had been listening while lying on her back, eyes closed. Now she rolled to face me, her head resting blissfully on her pillow, eyes open and calm.

"Babe. I'm not running away from Red Wing. I'm staying here with you."

"That's part of why you might as well leave," I argued. "You're not going to see much of me this weekend, even if you stay. Bull and I are helping with security at the air show."

Beth smiled. "Does Gunner know that?"

"He will . . . sooner or later. I'm sure he just forgot to invite us to the party."

She laughed, rolling over on top of me and forcing me onto my back. She was now on her knees, one leg on each side of my pelvis, her upper body braced on straight arms. She gazed deeply into my eyes – or maybe it was the other way around.

"I'm not running from terrorists, Babe." She leaned down and kissed me, a long wonderful kiss. I ran my hands up her strong back, pulling the tank top with them. She shook her hair in my face playfully.

Somehow our pajamas wound up on the floor. And we appreciated one another even more.

CHAPTER 43

Still Saturday, August 8ᵗʰ, in and around Red Wing.

The air show was slated to officially commence at 9:00 a.m., but I could hear planes humming over Jefferson Avenue beginning at 7:00. It was now 7:30. I had showered and dressed. Beth had showered, but she was draped in her pink satin robe. We were still in our bedroom.

Beth and I faced each other, my hands resting lightly on her hips, hers on my back.

"If I don't leave right now, you're going to drag me back into bed, aren't you?" I said.

"I don't recall having to drag you anywhere just a while ago."

"Okay," I said, pulling away from her gently, but with purpose. "A good part of me would absolutely like to stay here, if I could."

"I bet I know which part."

"Okay. Okay. I gotta go." I kissed her briefly on the lips. "Don't know when I'll be home. And I might need to have my cell off sometimes. So don't worry."

She held my face in both hands. "Be safe," she said, looking back and forth between my eyes for assurance that I would do so.

"You know me, Doll. I never take unnecessary risks."

"I know," Beth said. "It's the necessary ones I'm worried about."

"I'll be safe," I said.

With that, I forced myself to leave.

As I drove my Pilot the approximately five miles to the airport, I tried to focus myself for the day. I hadn't brought my gun. Security probably wouldn't let me on the airport premises if I were armed. Or some FBI goon might see my gun and overreact by shooting me.

I wasn't really sure how I was going to help without a gun. But there was no real choice today. I told myself that sometimes eyes and ears are more important than weaponry anyway. My role this day would have to be that of an informed observer. Someone to blow the whistle if something suspicious arose.

I would have preferred the gun.

Unarmed, I was probably going to be worthless. Still, I had to do what I could.

As I neared the airport, I could see the mass of automobiles collecting in a field several hundred yards from the entrance. I guessed there were already more than a hundred cars here, though some probably belonged to pilots and crew members. Apparently, no unauthorized persons would be allowed to enter the airport by car.

That was good.

I was unauthorized. I parked the Pilot in a location outside the airport where I thought I would be able to make a hasty exit if necessary.

As I traversed the grassy field toward the airport entrance, I noticed that a makeshift barrier of wooden snow fencing had been staked the entire length of the airport access area. The fence wasn't going to stop a determined invader. But it was better than nothing. I saw at least one Red Wing city cop walking the fence line. That was also good.

I presented myself at the show admission booth. Tickets to the event were twenty dollars a day. I peeled two bills off my money clip and handed them to the ticket woman. She stamped my hand for today and gave me a ticket for access to the grounds tomorrow. I slipped the ticket in my back pocket and went straight to the main terminal.

The place was packed with pilots and crews. Most of the building was reserved for their use only. Civilians like me were only allowed access to the rest rooms in the terminal entryway. I walked into the entry alcove and scanned through the interior window for Gunner. After a moment, I spotted him talking with the airport employee. I moved to the glass door to enter the terminal interior.

A uniformed rent-a-cop security kid stopped me at the open doorway. He didn't have a gun, just a night stick and a tin badge.

"Sorry. No admittance without a security clearance badge," he said.

I looked past the fake cop, yelled at Gunner and waved. Even at this distance I could see him roll his eyes. He came over to where the security guard and I were standing.

"He's with me. Give him a badge."

"Yessir!"

I thought the kid was going to salute.

I stepped through the doorway and pinned the plastic badge on my chest as I walked. 'Security. All Access.'

"I was hoping to not have the pleasure of your company today," Gunner said, looking straight ahead as we made our way through the terminal crowd. "Didn't really expect it though."

"Always nice to be welcome," I said.

*   *   *

The conspirators had arrived at the staging area Friday night at 9:30. The staging area turned out to be John's home. It was a small brown house, situated at the end of a long dirt road, and atop one of the many Mississippi river bluffs near Red Wing. The truck, with its precious cargo, was secreted in the garage. The other vehicles were parked on weedy areas to the side of the road.

This morning, the terrorists needed to go over the final attack details.

Brenda and Urland were responsible for disabling any guards at the airport. Deadly force was acceptable. But rifle shots were not permitted. Shooting would draw too much attention. After the guards had been dispatched, John would bring the truck alongside the plane and the three of them would load the containers. John was fairly confident in Urland's ability to deal with the guards. He was stupid, but brutal.

For now, Farris was to assure that the chemicals remained stable and functional in their garage storage. If the heat in the garage became a problem, the truck would need to be moved, or the containers taken to a cooler location.

Farris and John would also do a dry-run to the mud lake later today. The Umbers would stay at the homestead and guard the truck while the other two were gone.

John had been growing increasingly fatigued lately. And the stabbing pain in his abdomen was approaching unbearable. Even the Oxycontin and Oxycodone the doctor had prescribed no longer seemed to dull the pain. He wouldn't let it show to the others. And he was damn well going to see this thing through. But the narcotics, and the symptoms they masked, did not make it easy.

*   *   *

Gunner ushered me into the conference room. It was otherwise unoccupied. "What can I do for you Beck?"

"How about a sit rep?"

Gunner looked at me sideways.

"You know damn well what I mean," I said.

Gunner outlined the security arrangements for the air show. The FAA had cleared the pilots and crew members in advance. They all had official photo IDs. Besides the photo ident, each pilot and crew member had already appeared in at least a dozen previous air shows in the past year.

"The FAA feels pretty comfortable with the credentials and trustworthiness of that group. And I feel pretty good about them, too.

"On the ground," Gunner continued, "an FAA guy checks everybody's ID before they can get on board a plane. Same FAA security man that has been working these shows for several years. He knows the faces of all crew members and won't be fooled by a fake access badge.

"The FAA has also established, and is broadcasting on the appropriate frequencies, a 'no-fly' zone within a two mile radius of the nuke plant below 15,000 feet altitude."

"Two miles isn't very far," I noted.

"The whole damn airport is only six miles from the nuke. They have to be able to take off and land."

"I suppose," I conceded.

"May I continue?" Gunner could be a wise guy sometimes. But I let it slide. I was, after all, on his territory.

"Please do."

Gunner turned to the large airport map on the conference room wall. "The City has got three guys patrolling the fence 24/7 on rotating shifts." He indicated the fence location on the map. "They are required to check in with each other every fifteen minutes via radio.

"I have two deputies on site. One is in cargo shorts and a tan safari shirt, circulating among the fans outside. The other is dressed like a crew member and spends his time in 'crew only' areas, mostly looking and listening."

Gunner wasn't done yet.

"The Prairie River Plant Security Team is over-staffed and on elevated security status. We'll hope they don't get trigger-happy and shoot down some stupid tourist trying for a photo-op over the plant. They wouldn't tell me their rules of engagement.

"The FBI has someone on site here at the airport, too. They won't tell me who. It would be nice if some of these other guys would share info with us mere mortals. I hope we don't end up shooting him if he flashes his gun."

"Or her," I added.

"Or her."

"The FBI has arranged for a National Guard F-14 to be available on emergency standby at the St. Paul Airport. Don't think the fighter would get here in time to engage if anything went down. But fighter availability looks good to the public in case we screw up."

"Politics."

"Makes the world go 'round. Anyway. Where was I? Oh yeah. The BCA has an observation team set up on one of the bluffs around here somewhere. They'll be in place day and night until the show is over. Exact location is – surprise, surprise – 'need to know.'

"We tried to get permission to set up a metal detector at the entrance and deploy explosive-sniffing dogs on site. But the mayor vetoed it. He wants the 'appearance of normalcy.'"

"Hasn't the guy ever seen *Jaws*?" I remarked.

"More politics. Fact of life.

"Other than me, that's about it. At least that's all I know about. It would sure be easier if agencies would share more information. But everybody has their own turf to defend."

"Doesn't Wisconsin want in on the action?" I asked.

I can offer no explanation for the fact that the Red Wing, Minnesota airport is located on the Wisconsin side of the river. But it is.

"Hell no! They just want somebody to blame if the shit hits the fan. Lewiston County will send in the posse if a firefight breaks out. That's all they would commit to. They think the whole 'terrorists attacking the nuke' thing is funny, by the way."

"Tell 'em to get in line," I said.

"I gotta admit that, at times, I'm feeling pretty stupid myself," Gunner said. "I mean, setting up all these resources to defend against a damn improbable event. But don't worry. I'm here. So I'll do my part. Just feeling a little dumb, that's all."

"I understand completely. And I've gotta thank you again for all your help."

"Yeah. Yeah. Yeah.

" So what are you gonna do?"

"I plan to just hang out around here. Mingle. I'm unarmed. If I see anything unusual, I'll let you know. Should I call on your cell or what?" I asked, feeling useless.

"Cell will be fine. My ass would be grass if anybody heard you on our radio frequency."

"Okay then," I said.

"And Beck."

I had started to leave, but turned around to face Gunner.

"Don't screw anything up."

"Have I ever let you down before?"

Another eye roll from the Chief Deputy.

CHAPTER 44

By nine o'clock the area around the outside of the terminal was filled with eager spectators. They were lined up along another snow fence segregating the runway from the throng. Several of the classic warbirds were parked at various locations on the taxiways between hangars.

A popular activity was having your picture taken beside the P51. You could also buy separate admission for $10.00 and get an inside tour of the mammoth B17 bomber. The entire time, awe-inspiring WWII war planes were taking turns roaring down the runway on takeoff, doing high speed fly-bys, and performing daring aerial acrobatics, before touching down to the cheers and applause of the crowd.

For obvious reasons, the Red Wing Airport was closed to all civilian air traffic during the show. The FAA had also cleared airspace inside a five mile radius for air show use only. Any gawkers hoping to get a bird's eye view from their private planes were going to be disappointed.

The five-mile airport radius and the two-mile Prairie River no-fly zone overlapped to form a sort of Venn Diagram, the overlap zone being space within which even the air show planes were not permitted. All pilots in the show had both zone demarcations graphically displayed on add-on cockpit GPS units.

It didn't pay to sacrifice safety to preserve technological authenticity. Using this bit of 21st century technology, the show planes had no problems staying inside the airport clear area and outside the nuclear plant no-fly zone.

The show was truly spectacular. So much so, that I occasionally found my eyes straying to the aerial display in progress, instead of paying attention to the folks on the ground. I had to remind myself that the most distracting moments in the air would also provide the best opportunities for foul play below. I needed to improve my concentration.

Although I hadn't been able to spot him, I knew that Bull was here somewhere, also observing the crowds and crews. But I still needed to do my job. Too many operations fail because each person assumes his backup has the situation under control, while the backup assumes the same of his principal.

Images of the Chernobyl aftermath flashed in my head.

Focus.

I walked the length of the spectator area observing faces, postures, behavior. I was looking for indications of tension, frayed nerves. Or for a person who seemed disinterested, not paying attention to the show for no apparent reason. Or for a facial expression of determination, agitation, maybe even unnatural calm.

I saw the plain clothes deputy. He was doing pretty much the same thing as I was. I hadn't made the Fibbie yet.

The day marched on.

Lunchtime had come and gone two hours ago. I allowed myself a hot dog and Diet Mountain Dew from an on-site purveyor.

During a short break in the action, fans stormed the concession stands and portable biffies. I remained on station, working through the crowd. Real men don't pee when duty calls. Well . . . some do, depending on the duty. I had once been deployed under circumstances where I had to remain perfectly still for entire days, under a pile of hay. In that situation, peeing on station is part of the assignment.

But I digress.

The B17 was due to take off next. You could feel the subsonic rumble of its four engines as it taxied to takeoff position. When it was at the absolute end of the runway, the bomber made a 180 degree turn to make its run into the wind. The B17 was a lot of propeller plane to lift off and clear fifty feet of altitude before passing the end of the runway.

The Flying Fortress was ready. All eyes were locked on the plane except for mine and the deputy's. I heard the engines rev up. The pilot would hold the brakes until the engines were up to speed, then let her go.

As the B17 thundered toward the terminal, the tarmac trembling, the engine noise was impressive. The roar did a red shift as the plane passed the terminal with its landing gear barely ten feet in the air. I sneaked a quick peek as the historic bomber climbed upwind and upstream, toward the nuclear plant.

If that pilot were willing to die crashing into the Prairie River Nuke Plant, there was no way anyone was going to stop him. Fortunately, this particular pilot was more interested in making a safe landing back at the airport . . . but not before climbing to about a thousand feet above surface and making three memorable passes almost directly above the runway.

On final approach, the plane appeared to slow nearly to a stall. In reality, it was still traveling about a hundred knots when the wheels hit the runway. It just seemed incredibly slow to anyone who had seen a commercial jet land.

CHAPTER 45

Still Saturday, August 9th, in the Mississippi river flats, upstream from Red Wing.

John and Farris took the fishing boat down to the river late Saturday afternoon. Trailering the boat behind an old Ford pickup, the two had driven to a remote public launch on the Wisconsin side of the Mississippi. The launch was rustic. No concrete or asphalt. Just two dirt tracks through the grass leading to the water's edge. This launch location was also seldom-used – its most attractive characteristic.

Back at the house, John had explained to Farris everything he needed to know about the boat. Now John wanted to confirm that Farris could execute the plan.

With John watching from beside the truck, Farris slowly backed the trailer into the water until the boat floated. He got out of the truck and tied a good length of bow rope from the boat to the trailer hitch. The last thing he wanted was for the boat to float away in front of the infidel. Now he could safely release the trailer crank, loosen the cable and unhook the boat.

When the Sylvan floated freely in the water, he let it drift out past the end of the trailer, paying out bow line as it went. Then he towed the boat back to shore, heaving it far enough up onto the grass to keep it in place for the time being. Finally,

Farris drove the truck and trailer up the ramp and out of the water, parking them in the weeds to one side of the launch.

Returning to the boat, he pushed it back out into the water, jumping into the bow when it floated freely again. John climbed in, too.

Farris lowered the outboard motor into the water. With the gear-shift in neutral, and the manual throttle advanced just slightly, he grasped the starter rope by its black rubber handle and pulled hard. The motor revved to life – pouring oily blue smoke into the air. Farris released the starter rope and throttled the Evinrude back to an idle.

Ready to go. So far, so good.

John had mounted a GPS display on the starboard side of the boat, near the stern. Farris could easily face this direction as he maneuvered the tiller with his right hand. The GPS unit displayed a detailed course through the shallows. Farris eased the gear shift into forward. Watching both the water ahead and the GPS, Farris tried to keep the boat on the displayed course.

"Don't look ahead, Farris. It will be almost completely dark when you do this for real. Navigate using only the GPS."

Farris focused on the display. This was actually easier, more like a video game. He had played plenty of those during his indoctrination to western culture.

John had charted this course several days ago. It should be perfect. But things change on a river, sometimes unexpectedly. Best to be sure.

Farris continued following the green line on the display. Turning to port here, to starboard there. Always moving at a bare idle. After about thirty minutes, Farris reached a point on the display where the green line ended and a red 'X' appeared. Here he shut off the motor and dropped the anchor, securing the anchor line to a cleat on the top of the bow.

When Farris finally looked up, he saw that he was in the middle of the river valley, almost equi-distant from the bluffs on the Minnesota and Wisconsin sides. There was no river current here, at least none that Farris could detect. The boat seemed to swing with the light breeze. He was in the middle of one of the mud lakes that filled the river basin. More importantly, he was within radio transmission range of the dynamite-rigged dams.

On the way back to the landing, Farris followed the same GPS line in reverse. All went well.

Praise Allah! This was easier than he had feared.

He did it! Thank God! The know-it-all can follow directions.

They secured the boat back onto the trailer and returned to the staging area.

Mission accomplished for today.

CHAPTER 46

Back at the Red Wing Airport.

Saturday's air show continued with more of the same. Nothing remarkable. There were plenty of strange people, to be sure. But no obvious security risks. Until . . . just after the B25 Miss Mitchell bomber made the last scheduled landing of the day, a man suddenly broke from the end of the throng of spectators and trotted parallel with the runway, away from the terminal and toward a patch of woods. I was maybe 150 feet behind as I started to jog after him.

He was wearing a khaki-green T-shirt, green camouflage baggy shorts and black athletic shoes. As he neared the woods, I caught a glimpse of Bull running through the trees just inside the edge of the foliage. He was on an intercept course with the runner. I began to walk. If the man saw me running after him, he might panic and do something stupid.

As he approached a particularly thick area of brush, the man slowed to a walk. Then he came to a complete stop, still partly in my view.

I stayed quiet and remained vigilant.

Oh shit! He was taking a leak.

Probably figured, no doubt correctly, that with the show ending, the lines for portable johnnies would be long. I stayed where I was and watched, just to be sure. I could no longer see Bull. After about a minute, the suspect zipped up his shorts, found his way out of the brush and started jogging back to the crowd.

Some security guard! Pee patrol. We go where others went. Or is it *vice versa*?

I turned and walked back toward the exiting herd. A plane tractor was pulling the now silent B25 to its parking space on a taxiway just south of the runway. All three bombers – B17, B24 and B25 – were positioned for maximum effect. 45 degrees toward the runway. Facing the spectator area. Ready to 'fly and defend,' or whatever their motto had been in the Big War.

I stayed at the airport until it was nearly dark. The crowd was gone. The air crews had left for their hotels, or beers, or whatever they did on Saturday night of a two-day show. The only people remaining at the airport that I could see were the three Red Wing cops (now stationed at various locations around the airfield), the airport employee inside the terminal behind the counter, Gunner and me. One of the city cops had a German Shepherd on a leash. The airport employee would be finishing up flight summaries for the day. Then he'd be gone, too.

I approached the Chief Deputy.

"Long day?" I asked.

"Another one tomorrow. But so far we've thwarted the evil terrorist cell plotting to destroy freedom and all that is right and good in this world."

The last was delivered with no small amount of sarcasm.

I couldn't really blame Gunner. If it weren't for me, he would be home with his wife playing cribbage or something.

"I'd call it a successful day. No incidents," I replied.

"What about the unauthorized urinator?"

Gunner did not miss a thing!

"You saw that, huh? I collected a sample. You can give it to the Feds to analyze. He seemed pretty suspicious to me."

Gunner smiled a tired smile.

"We've already had one shift change on the patrols. Another one comes on at midnight. Go home. Get some sleep."

"Thanks, Doug. You, too."

* * *

Across the river, near Red Wing, one of the strangest terror cells in recent history waited for its chance.

CHAPTER 47

Sunday, August 10th, in and around Red Wing.

Sunday morning I slept in until 6:30. Saturday had been a long, slow day. Today promised more of the same.

I showered, put on some khaki shorts, a white pique golf shirt and my Adidas running shoes. Before leaving, I leaned over the bed and kissed Beth on the cheek. "I love you."

"You, too, Babe. Be safe."

When I arrived at the Red Wing Airport, it was 7:45. Things were noticeably less busy than the day before. Fewer cars in the lot. Fewer spectators milling around. I showed my admission ticket at the 'gate.' No hand stamp today. I guess the 'All Access' badge would have gotten me in free. Too bad I didn't know that yesterday.

I displayed my badge toward the rent-a-cop in the terminal. He examined it and allowed me inside. Gunner was behind the counter talking with a uniformed City cop. I waited for the conversation to end. The cop passed me on the way out of the terminal. Gunner was examining an air show flyer as I approached him.

He looked up.

"Just refreshing my memory on today's schedule. A little different than yesterday's," he said.

"Yeah. No fly-bys from remote airports. But there are plane rides this afternoon," I noted. "Any special security before those passengers get aboard?"

"The passengers must check-in for their flights at least one hour ahead of time," Gunner recited. "A city cop will be there to check IDs. She'll run every name through the BCA and FBI databases to make sure we don't have felons. She'll also check the FAA 'no fly' list. Any red flags and they'll have to take a ride another day.

"Right before boarding, one of my deputies will check hand-bags and such. And everybody will need to pass a hand-held metal detector scan."

Gunner looked at me for a response. "Does that work for you?"

"I assume all the law enforcement folks have seen pictures of the missing lab assistant?"

Gunner gave me annoyed.

"All right. Sorry. Just trying to be thorough."

"Beck. If someone plans to fly a plane into the nuke plant, they're not going to be able to do it from this airport – at least not today."

"Okay. I trust your judgment."

"I can't tell you how relieved I am," said Gunner, dramatically wiping his brow. Whew!

"I'll stay out of the way. As a special favor, I'll also make sure no one tries to pee on your unmarked car. I have recent on-the-job training in urinator apprehension."

Gunner allowed a small chuckle. "On that, I will depend."

*   *   *

The *Al Qaeda* tactical support team had worked its way slowly and cautiously up the river valley during Friday and Saturday nights, mostly slogging through sloughs and shallow mud lakes, avoiding the main channel with its boat traffic. They had slept during the day on Saturday, hidden by the dense river growth of late summer, totally invisible in the back waters – even from the river itself.

Now on Sunday morning, they were hunkered down a mere 500 meters from the Red Wing Airport. They wore their grass and weed camo suits – making them look like moving weed piles. The swamp grasses, scrub ash and even the muddy water made for perfect cover.

They had no direct view of the airport from here. But the activities there were clearly audible.

Air traffic was constant as planes passed above them, one after the other. Never knowing. Never seeing.

The team would try to rest here for as much of the day as possible. Very soon though, they would need to approach the airfield proper. So much depended on them. Perhaps every-thing depended on them.

*   *   *

A few of the show planes were warming up their engines by about 8:30 Sunday morning. Their takeoffs, aerial maneuvers and landings began promptly at 9:00. The morning schedule was pretty much the same as Saturday's. I did my usual strolling and scoping-out of the crowd for evil-doers.

As I walked, I began to doubt myself. Maybe I was wrong about this terrorist thing. No one here looked like a threat to civilization. But I was doing a job. There was a small chance it might be extremely important. Regardless of how boring, I would keep my focus.

I kept scanning for anomalies. Probably a man over thirty without a beer-gut would qualify as anomalous in this crowd. I walked for hours. Ever-vigilant.

I did notice one difference in the show this morning. After concluding their routines, a number of the planes did not land. Instead, they buzzed the runway, wagging their wings goodbye, and roared off down the river valley. I began to wonder when the last of the show planes would be gone.

It was about 12:15 in the afternoon. Seeing no immediate threats in the overweight audience, I decided to grab a hot dog and chance a visit to the flight center. I got the dog and chowed it in two bites, followed by a plastic bottle of Diet Dew.

The rent-a-cop didn't try to stop me this time. As I walked inside the terminal, the airport employee was standing behind the counter chatting admiringly with some of the show pilots.

I stood at the end of the counter with my finger in the air.

"Excuse me."

He hadn't heard me.

"Excuse me. Sir!" Much louder.

The airport guy reluctantly left his war buddies and came my way. "What d'ya need?" he asked, not really sounding as if he cared.

"Will all the show planes file flight plans before leaving here?"

"Sure. They're already in the computer – have been since we booked this show last summer."

"May I see them please?" I glanced down at my official 'All Access' badge. His eyes followed mine.

"Okay. I'll set you up in the flight center." He waved at me to follow him.

We walked about three steps down the hall into the 'Pilots Only' area. He stepped through the doorway on the right and beckoned me inside. I walked past him into the flight center.

"You can use the computer terminal over there." He gestured generally toward the only computer in the room.

"Thanks," I said. But he had already left.

After I figured out how to access the flight records on the computer, it was pretty easy to locate the show plane departure times. The small planes would all be gone soon. Just the three bombers would remain to give thirty-minute rides to anyone willing to pony up $500.

The B17 was scheduled to depart Red Wing at 8:00 p.m. The B25 at 8:15. The B24, however, was going to spend the night. It would be leaving at 7:00 tomorrow morning.

That seemed odd to me. I went back to the terminal counter to bother the civil servant some more.

"Hey!" I called.

He reluctantly came my direction.

"I've got a question," I said.

"Yeah?"

"How come the B24 is spending the night? Everybody else is gone today."

The airport employee looked irritated at my question.

"The Liberator is scheduled to visit the Duluth Air Force Base tomorrow morning as a surprise for the airmen there. It was part of the original plan. The B24 crew made hotel arrangements in Red Wing. We've got security scheduled to babysit the plane while it waits here overnight."

"Thanks," I said.

"You're welcome."

He said it in such a way that I knew I wasn't.

I stepped outside the brick terminal building and looked around for Gunner. I didn't see him, so I called him on his cell.

"This better be good, Beck. I'm working, you know."

"Need to see you," I said. "It's important."

"Let's meet at your car in fifteen. Maybe you'll get in it and leave."

"Gunner," I said, "it's a truck – but you may be right about me leaving."

"I'll look forward to it."

I don't know what I do to deserve this sort of treatment; but it happens to me all the time.

It was about 1:00 p.m. when Gunner approached the Pilot. I was waiting, leaning against the front fender like a gunslinger staying loose.

"What's up?" Gunner asked.

"The rest of the afternoon is all plane rides, right?"

"Yes."

"And all the planes will be heading out of Dodge before 8:30, except the B24?"

"Apparently you already know that to be the case. We're leaving a deputy to guard the plane. Is that what this is about?"

"Not really. I can't expect you to leave a whole squad here all night for one plane. But I have a favor to ask."

Gunner's eyes rolled. He was getting good at that. "I can't wait to hear this!" he said, as if he could.

*   *   *

Beth was surprised to see me jogging up our front walk on Jefferson Avenue at 1:30 Sunday afternoon.

"Home early today?" she asked, from her seat on the front porch settee.

"Sorry. Just a short stop for supplies."

I hastened inside and began collecting things. Beth followed me into the house.

"Any signs of trouble?" Beth asked, wearing a bit of a worried expression on her face.

I stopped what I was doing and walked to where Beth stood, trying to project calmness and confidence. I put my arms around her waist and gave her a gentle kiss on the lips.

"Everything is going fine. Gunner has done a great job. But you know me. I prepare for every contingency. And I'm feeling lucky. You know I'm a big believer in luck. And the more I prepare, the more luck I seem to have."

I knew I had stolen and bastardized that quote. But it fit my approach to life.

"I think I just heard Thomas Jefferson roll over in his grave," Beth said.

At least I had loosened her up a bit.

"There is going to be one plane left at the airport overnight. I'm going to help with additional security until they leave in the morning. I should be home no later than 10:00 tomorrow."

"I'll miss you," she said.

"Me, too. But right now, I need to focus – focus and prepare."

She understood and left me to my work.

I changed clothes into camo shorts and a black T-shirt. Then I resumed collecting gear, stuffing all of it into a medium-sized, khaki-green duffle. I thought I had everything I needed. I sure hoped so.

Best to leave on a light note.

"June Dear, I'm off to the office," I called, as I stood in the open front doorway."

"Ward. Don't forget to pick up the Beaver," Beth replied from the kitchen.

At least someone got my jokes. I hoped Beth and I would be able to share jokes for many years to come. But all that depended on what might happen later today.

Back in the Pilot and on the road again, my mind was processing logistics. I had a pretty good idea of what I wanted to do. But I hadn't studied WWII bombers as part of my Agency training. There were some variables to be dealt with.

At the airport, the crowd had thinned considerably. The show was over except for the bomber rides. There were a surprising number of people willing to pay $500 for a rough ride in a piece of outdated technology. But I suppose the nostalgia is a strong draw.

I grabbed my duffle bag from the passenger seat and strode through the entrance, which was no longer being monitored for interlopers. The show was over, after all.

I hunted down Gunner. His security people were still on station, though some had been re-purposed to metal detection and checking IDs. He was leaning against the brick wall of the terminal building, observing the joy-riding assemblage.

He saw me approaching.

"All quiet on the western front," he remarked.

"Glad to hear it."

"All passengers have checked in for the B24 flights. They only take eight sightseers up at a time. Unless we get some late-comers, which I doubt, the last flight should be about 6:30. I've saved you a seat."

"Thanks, Gunner. By the way, I need to bring this bag on board with me." I lifted the duffle in his direction. "And it won't make it through a metal detector."

I gave him apologetic.

"Great! Can't you ever do things the easy way? What's in there . . . never mind. I don't even want to know."

"Can you get me in? Bag and all?"

"I'll arrange it somehow. Now if you don't mind, I'll continue my work."

"Thanks a million, Gunner!"

It was only 3:00. I had some time. I'd better eat and drink now. I wasn't going to get a chance later.

The hot dogs were passable. The Diet Dew quenched my thirst. I also ate a soft, salty pretzel with cheese to fill in all the gastro-intestinal cracks. After eating, I bought two more 24-

ounce bottles of Dew and put one in each of my large front pockets.

Then I was off to the terminal to do some computer research on the B24. I wanted to see pictures, diagrams, operating specifications, whatever I could find.

Preparedness, you know. Godliness, you know.

To my disappointment, there were multiple configurations of the B24 interior. I couldn't find a schematic for the exact plane sitting on the runway. By 5:00, I had learned all I was going to get from the computer. I went outside.

As I'd expected, the line for the B24 ride was still twelve or fifteen people long. The B17 had concluded its tourist duties, as had the B25. Both planes were maneuvering for a spot at the gas pump – 100 Octane, low lead. The crews would fill up the tanks and secure the planes before grabbing dinner. They'd no doubt depart the airport at 8:00 and 8:15, as per their flight plans.

I moved outside for some fresh air. A bench was available on the runway side of the terminal. I sat there, duffle in my lap, and watched the B24 load, taxi, takeoff, land and unload. Twice.

There were still six people left for the last ride of the day. Some of them must not have been in line when I counted. On the previous two flights, I had made note of the boarding procedures. Passengers were ushered into the large plane by climbing up a set of portable stairs and ducking through the rear hatchway.

Gunner came over and sat on the bench beside me.

"Okay. It's all set. I've talked with the ride security folks and the crew. While the other passengers are being metal-detected, you and I and one of my deputies will walk to the back of the plane, and you'll just hike right up the stairs like you've got a job to do. Then stuff the duffle somewhere so none of the passengers will get nosey. Got it?"

"Where do I go again?"

"Oh, shut up!"

*   *   *

The *Al Qaeda* tactical team had arrived at their final destination near the airport by 2:00 Sunday afternoon.

First, they laid out some traps, alerts and counter-measures, just in case someone should approach their position. It was unlikely that anyone could sneak up on them, especially with a guard posted. But this team was professional. They were prepared.

Next, they set up various electronics. Radar equipment. Sound gear. Several video vantage points – both optical and infrared. Two of the guerillas crawled even closer to the runway. Preferred shooting lanes were established. The airport layout was just like their African model. *Al Qaeda* intelligence had been flawless.

They had already changed out of their weedy camo suits and into more functional, operational attire. They placed weeds or leafy branches as needed to provide superior camouflage. Then two returned to the willowy grasses lining the main channel adjacent to the airport, leaving the third on watch. They re-checked their weapons and ammunition. Finally, they tested electronic communications. Everything worked as per its design.

Let the infidels try to stop them. They were ready. They were skilled. And they were lethal. But for now, they would wait and watch.

CHAPTER 48

When the B24 landed and discharged its eight passengers through the rear hatchway and down the portable stairs, the three of us headed for the back of the plane like we were supposed to be there. While Gunner and the other deputy appeared to check the hatch and adjust the steps, I trotted up and into the plane.

I found a stowage box and opened it. Empty. I placed my duffle carefully into the box and closed the lid. Perfect fit.

A crewman appeared at the top of the stairs. "All set?" he asked, tossing me a noise-reduction headset. I gave him a thumbs up and stood as much out of the way as I could, given the confines of the plane.

As the other passengers filed aboard, the crewman handed out headsets to each of them and showed them their seating options – floor or bench, at various locations throughout the plane. Only the nimble chose to scramble through the crawl-way, located between the bomb bays, to the front part of the fuselage. The rest of us sat in the back.

We each had an original-equipment, khaki-tan seatbelt for our laps. I found both ends of mine, latched them, and pulled the belt tight. The crewman helped others secure their belts.

Presently, the crewman gave us the same speech he had delivered to every group this afternoon. The history of the aircraft. Its significance to the Allied effort in winning WWII. He ended with some rules to be observed during the flight.

"You will remain seated during takeoff. When it is safe to move around, you will hear a horn. At that time, you may release your safety belts and move about the plane.

"You will note that there are openings in the sides of the plane where the machine guns stick out. There is also a gun turret in the rear, which you may enter. You may attempt to shoot the machine guns if you wish. They have been disabled.

"This craft has a top speed of nearly 300 knots. So please, do not stick your head, hands, feet or any body part you hold dear, outside of the airplane.

"When we are ready to descend for landing, you will hear another horn. At this time you must promptly retake your seats, fasten your safety belts and prepare for a crash landing. The landing gear haven't been very reliable today, and if we need to ditch, we don't want y'all to get injured."

He looked at me and winked. The rest of the passengers turned a little green.

"Okay. Please put on your headgear and we'll be on our way."

That concluded the presentation.

Even through the headset, I could hear the B24's engines rev higher. Gradually, we started to move.

The plane rumbled and bumped like a lumber wagon all the way down the taxi-way. At takeoff, we could hear the engines wind up to full throttle. Despite the sound protection, the engine noise was even more impressive from inside the plane than it had been alongside the terminal.

The runway proved as bumpy as the taxi-way. But then we lifted off, and the whole plane felt different. The ride was still bumpy and incredibly noisy. But you no longer felt kidney-punched every two seconds.

We climbed slowly, periodically banking slightly to the left, presumably to remain in the airport's vicinity. A couple minutes into the flight we had leveled off. The horn sounded.

The passengers hastily unstrapped and began moving around. Most wanted to see out the open, side windows, or sit in a gunner's seat. Some chose to venture through the crawl-way to the front of the plane. Some of those in the front came to the back.

I wasn't there for the ride . . . though it was an interesting experience. I preferred Bull's Diamond DA40. But this ride was smoother, actually, than I had expected.

After about twenty minutes, the horn sounded again. Everyone scrambled to return to their seats as if their lives depended upon it. I knew the pilot would allow plenty of time for everyone to sit and buckle up before final landing approach.

I re-took my original seat and fastened my belt. After everyone was strapped in, the crewman poked his head through the crawl-way to make sure that was the case. He gave us a thumbs-up or thumbs-down motion. We all responded with a thumbs-up.

Soon I could feel the plane turn right and begin to descend. The descent continued. A left turn this time. Further descent, then another left turn. I could feel the landing gear drop down. We should be headed for the runway at this point. There were some thumps and a shudder as the huge plane touched down. We were safely on the ground. No need to ditch today. Whew!

After we had taxied to a stop near the terminal, the crewman reappeared and opened the plane's rear hatchway, pulling the door up and in. Stairs with a railing appeared outside the opening. The crewman collected headgear and thanked each passenger as he or she filed out. They all seemed pleased to have survived. And they had a tale to tell. The day they flew in a B24.

After the last of the other passengers had left, the crewman turned to me.

"We're going to gas 'er up so she's ready for takeoff in the morning. We've also got some post-flight inspecting to do. So plan on hearing some bangin' around for a while. If you need to get out, this rear hatch is the easiest way. We'll leave the stairs for you if you like."

"Thanks. But I'd rather you didn't. I do have one favor to ask, though?" Seemed like I'd been saying that a lot lately.

"What's that?"

"I know you and everybody else probably think I'm crazy. But I have reason to believe someone will try to steal your plane tonight."

"I understand that's why you're here. And what is your favor?" He was trying to be accommodating.

"I would appreciate it very much if you could somehow disable this plane so, in the unlikely event that some unauthorized person should get inside, it would not be possible to take off."

The crewman thought for a moment.

"Okay. I don't expect any attempted theft. But it's easy enough to make 'er unflyable. I'll see to it before we leave."

"Thank you so much." I was relieved that he had acceded to my request.

"No problem. Enjoy your night."

With that, the crewman closed the rear hatch, and disappeared through the crawl-way to the front of the plane.

I had might as well get comfortable. I couldn't really set up until everyone was off the plane. I did retrieve my bag from stowage and checked to make sure the contents had survived the flight. They looked okay. I would check more thoroughly later.

*   *   *

I stayed where I was while the crew jockeyed the plane to the fueling station and gassed up. Not until they had parked the bomber for the day did I begin my preparations for the night's possible activities. As the crewman had indicated, I continued to hear crew voices and various thumps, clangs and rattles as they went through their post-flight routine. But so long as the plane wasn't moving, I could work.

I had to assume this plane would be crashing into the Prairie River Plant tonight. Any other assumption made my presence here useless. I also had to assume it would be carrying quite a bit of potassium, for the same reason.

The first order of business was to determine where the potassium would be placed.

If I were the terrorists, I would want it near the front of the plane, so it could easily spill out into the spent fuel pool. I worked my way forward through the crawl-way, bent over, but still barely able to walk in the confined tunnel.

At the front end of the crawl-way I could see the cockpit ahead. The cockpit entrance was at the same level as the platform on which I was now kneeling. Between me and the cockpit, on a lower level, were the navigation station to the right, and a set of stowage cabinets to the left.

I climbed down the ladder into the small space between the station and the cabinets. Slightly forward of my position was a second steel ladder leading to the main access hatch on the top of the plane – ahead of that, a third ladder leading up to the cockpit.

Although I didn't know what sort of container or containers the potassium would be in, I suspected there would be quite a lot of it. The space where I was standing was not only too small, but there was also a rigid bulkhead between me and the front of the plane. This bulkhead would block the release of potassium from this area during a nose-down crash. It would not be a good spot for the cargo.

The cockpit was too small.

As I surveyed the remaining options, I decided that the crawl-way itself was the perfect location. It was at the same height as the glass cockpit. There was nothing between the crawl-way and the cockpit entrance that would hinder the potassium flying or spilling into the cockpit and beyond. And the crawl-way was easily accessible for loading, both from front and rear.

Having learned what I could in the front section of the fuselage, I worked my way back through the crawl-way tunnel to the aft section and down the stairs. There was plenty of room for the potassium back here. But both bomb bays, right and left, would impede movement of the chemical to forward areas when the plane crashed. This would not be a good location. But one never knew how smart one's adversaries would be. I had to be prepared for the potassium to be located here in the rear as well.

Where to hide? I needed a location to await the terrorists, elude detection during loading, and still be able to emerge when necessary. I looked around.

The bomb bays on the B24 were unique for their time. The interior hatchways opened like a roll-top desk, with the door rolling up into the top of the bomb bay itself. I decided to try the port door. I rotated the latch a quarter turn and lifted. By god, it opened!

It was pretty dark inside. I went to my bag, took out a small LED flashlight and shined it into the darkness of the bomb bay. No bombs. That was no surprise. There was, however, a conveniently smooth section of lower bomb bay door where I could set up shop. The spot was perfect – unless the bad guys decided to open the bay doors during flight, in which case I would be exiting the aircraft rather abruptly.

I grabbed my duffle and rummaged inside for a coil of electrical wire. Then I opened the rolling door as far as necessary for me to reach the interior latch. I wrapped that latch securely with the wire. I needed to be able to close the hatch door once I got inside the bomb bay. If the door rolled too far up and open, I wouldn't be able to reach the latch without the wire.

I tossed the rest of the coiled wire into the bay. Then I opened the rolling hatch door far enough to allow me to enter the bomb bay comfortably. Backing in, feet first and on my stomach, I slid down the lower bay door, pulling my duffle behind and above me.

I turned on the flashlight again, this time setting it on the floor – which was actually a bomb bay door – to provide general illumination. Pulling gently on the electrical wire, I was pleased to find that the hatchway door rolled easily down to the bottom latching position. There was the same quarter-turn locking mechanism on this side of the hatch.

After closing the latch, I wound the lever repeatedly with the wire so there was no way anyone might be able to enter the hatch from inside the plane – at least not without a can-opener. With that accomplished, I settled my *derriere* on the aft slope of a lower bay door, put the duffle on my lap, and dug into my survival kit.

CHAPTER 49

One of the *Al Qaeda* military operatives kept constant watch on the airfield. Now that all the plane noise had ceased, using binoculars and a parabolic microphone, he could both see and hear everything happening outside the airport.

It was odd, he thought, that a crewman from the bomber was removing a piece of gear from the cockpit. He looked more closely. It was actually several pieces. The crewman handed each piece to a fellow crew-member on the ground.

He turned up the gain on his microphone to hear better.

"Put these in the terminal basement under a bunk bed," one man said.

"What are we doing this for?"

"Never mind. It's no big deal. Just put them where I asked. I'll re-attach them first thing in the morning."

"Okay."

The operative knew that this conversation, and the missing equipment, would be important. He crawled back to report to his team.

*   *   *

Besides the wire, the flashlight and the cell phone in my shirt pocket, I had brought in my duffle the following:

- a 16-ounce bottle of water – it might get hot in here for a while
- a roll of duct tape
- a wearable LED head lamp
- a small AM/FM radio with a single ear bud
- a cigarette lighter
- extra batteries for everything (even though I had tested the current batteries before leaving the house)
- three, standard, eight-inch road flares
- a medium-sized multi-tool
- my .40 caliber short barrel Beretta, in its holster
- four extra .40 caliber ammo clips, fully loaded
- a hi-tech parachute I had picked up a couple years ago at an extreme sports shop. It was a much smaller package than a typical chute. This type of parachute was supposed to be good for base jumping – from bridges and the like – but I hoped it would work for my current situation as well.
- several protein bars (just in case I needed nourishment)

I laid all of the above out before me. To this assortment, I added the two plastic bottles of Diet Dew from my pockets. I would almost certainly need them later, if trouble should arise – and again, that was the premise under which I was operating.

I strapped my head lamp on and lit it up. Now I could turn off the other flashlight and save it, just in case. The beam of the head lamp was not particularly bright. But my eyes adjusted quickly and soon I could see rather well in the dim light.

I unpacked and laid out the parachute. I wished I had had the chance to test the chute before now, but it had been an impulse purchase two years ago. I hadn't actually ever used it. After reading the rather worthless instructions, I re-folded the chute, slipped it over my shoulders and adjusted it to fit.

I made sure I knew exactly where all the straps, latches, adjustments, and most importantly, the rip cord were located. I needed to be able to work the chute in complete darkness, if necessary. And I always assumed all contingencies were necessary.

I examined the road torches to confirm the correct ignition procedure. My gun I placed in an easily accessible position on the floor, making sure to chamber a round. The extra ammo went into my pockets, along with the flares. I tested the cigarette lighter. It worked fine. That went into another pocket. I clipped the multi-tool to my belt.

I probably wouldn't need all of this stuff. But I couldn't say which items I might not need. So I had brought them all.

Next to godliness, you know.

I checked my watch: 9:00 p.m. The noises of the crew outside had ceased. I knew there was a deputy out there guarding the plane. I hoped he or she was good at his or her job. Maybe my services wouldn't be needed.

A worthless assumption. I discarded it.

I called Bull's cell. He answered on the first ring.

"Yeah."

"Good evening to you as well."

Silence.

"Do you still expect to observe developments from a reasonable proximity, enjoying the peaceful night sky while I sit here in this sweaty sardine can?"

"That's my plan."

"Will you be available if I should need assistance?"

"Do my best."

"And I will do my best to not require your assistance. Good luck!"

Click. Not a single word wasted.

I settled back against the curvature of the bomb bay door and tried to stay alert for whatever might come.

CHAPTER 50

Very early Monday, between the airport and the Prairie River Plant.

At 2:30 Monday morning, Farris was on station – kneeling on the aluminum bottom of the small boat, in the darkness, in the middle of the mud lake. The shift change was just occurring at the Prairie River Nuclear Generating Station.

It was about to begin. The plan was swinging into action. Farris prayed to Allah that the Great Satan would suffer at last.

Farris had already organized the transmitters on the wooden boat seat in front of him. John had numbered them in the sequence in which they were to be activated. That was their precise order here, from right to left.

Farris picked up the first transmitter. He checked his watch. 2:30 exactly. He slid the actuator to the 'On' position. A red light blinked. He depressed the round 'Detonate' button with both thumbs.

At first he heard nothing and thought the dynamite hadn't worked. But then, in the moonlight, he saw a fountain of water erupt from the mud lake between himself and the ever-glowing lights of the Plant. A second later, the water around him rippled and he heard a muffled thud.

Yes!

He moved on to transmitter number two, slid the actuator, pushed the button. Again the splash was first, followed by the ripples and the thud. Now he moved through the twenty transmitters as rapidly as he was able, no longer waiting to see or hear the explosions.

After the last detonation, he could hear the sound of alarm bells ringing at the Power Plant. Something good had happened, he knew.

His heart pumped in his throat and his mouth went dry. Praise Allah! It is working. It is working.

*　　*　　*

Just as the 2:30 shift change was taking place at the Prairie River Nuclear Generating Station, a control room alarm went off. The Operator saw the blinking red light and checked the monitor below it. Tiny green ripples traced a jagged line across the screen.

The alarm had been triggered by a seismic event. In other words, sensitive electronic monitors had felt the earth shake, and they were alerting the humans to the anomaly. It was a small blip. Nothing to be concerned about. It happened every once in a while.

The Operator reset the alarm and it was silent. Moments later, the alarm went off again. More ripples on the monitor.

What the hell?

The Operator tried to reset the alarm again, but the ringing wouldn't stop. He stared at the monitor. A nearly solid line of ripples wriggled its way across the screen. He had never seen anything like this before.

Protocol called for him to trigger a plant-wide alert. Reluctantly, he went to the wall panel, opened the metal door and pulled the 'Seismic Alert' lever down.

Now bells were ringing all over. Everyone seemed to stop where they were. Loud speakers announced, "Seismic Anomaly. Seismic Anomaly." The verbal warning was computer-generated and repeated every thirty seconds.

Every employee had a station to monitor in the event of this type of alert. Employees moved quickly to their stations. Most stations ended up being manned by two people. Because of the pending shift change, neither was sure which of them was in charge.

After about a minute of sustained 'seismic anomaly,' the ripples on the Operator's monitor stopped, and a flat, steady line reappeared. The Operator tried resetting the alarm again. The bells and announcements ceased.

The Operator's voice boomed over the loud speakers, "Inspect stations. Report to supervisors."

No one knew what had just happened. The Operator was pretty sure everything at the plant was working okay, though. There were no other alarms or red lights on his panels.

When after five minutes, all supervisors had checked in, reporting no problems, it appeared that no damage had been done. Nevertheless, an incident like this one required immediate reporting to the Plant Manager and the NRC. In fact, the Operator in the control room knew the automated system had made those calls already.

CHAPTER 51

I had decided to turn off my headlamp while I sat in the darkness of the bomb bay. I might need to be able to see in the dark. I should let my eyes adjust as much as possible. This had already been a long night. And it would only get longer.

As I shifted position, trying to keep my muscles from tightening up, I thought I heard a muffled sound, like thunder in the distance. I held myself motionless, listening. A few seconds later, there it was again. I was sure the acoustics of the cylindrical metal bay distorted the sound. I kept listening, not moving, muscles tensed, adrenaline pumping.

There it was again.

It seemed to be echoing down the river valley from upstream. Like sustained thunder. Or a series of depth charges. That is actually what it sounded most like – the sound of depth charges heard from inside a submarine. I knew that sound intimately. I did not associate it with pleasant memories.

As I tried to interpret the meaning of the low echoes, I heard a thud and a grunt from outside the plane. Then loud voices.

Man: "Got him right on the nut with the old Reggie Jackson commemorative, Brenda. Stee - rike three! You're outta there!"

Brenda: "Should I take his gun, Urland? What if he wakes up?"

Urland: "I'll make sure he's out first . . . . Okay. Go ahead and get his gun."

Brenda: "I got it Urland."

Urland: "All right. I'll tie him up and haul him outta sight somewhere before somebody sees him. You call John."

While I continued to listen, I sent a text message to Bull. "*sos @ rgk need u asap.*" RGK was the official designation for the Red Wing Airport.

As I tapped on my cell, I could hear what I presumed to be the deputy, my first line of defense, being dragged away from the plane.

Brenda: "Hello? John? It's all clear. Come on in."

A few moments later, I heard the man and woman talking to each other. They were some distance from the plane now. They sounded excited and were speaking quite loudly. A few seconds later, I heard the sound of a vehicle approaching the plane. It pulled up along the left side of the fuselage, adjacent to the forward roof entry hatch.

Urland: "We got 'im, John."

John: "Shhh!" He spoke in a loud whisper. "We don't need to let all the neighbors know we're here. There are houses just past the runway."

There were some metallic clanking noises, then the sound of a ladder being leaned against the fuselage near the plane's nose.

Urland: "You know, I'm not one to complain. But do we have to haul this stuff up that ladder? Wouldn't it work better to put those steps over there up to the back. It's a lot lower."

John: "We need this stuff up front. So that's where it's going. Why do you think I had you hauling all those buckets around to get in shape? "

Urland: Loud whisper. "Sorry, John. What do you want us to do?"

John: "Brenda, get up in the pickup and hand the buckets to Urland. Urland you get on the ladder, so you can reach the buckets from Brenda. I'm going inside the plane. You need to lower the buckets down to me one at a time. Real careful. Got it! So don't screw this up!

"Let's get started."

I heard someone climb the ladder and open the forward hatch. More sounds of climbing inside the plane. Then there was a lot of grunting and whining from outside. The bucket brigade was struggling to get the buckets up the ladder.

When I heard grunting from inside the plane, I assumed that a bucket had been delivered. There were footsteps and movement on the crawl-way, nearly to the back of the bomb bay. Then a metallic thunk.

A metal bucket finding a home onboard?

I thought about trying to stop the enemy now. But without knowing exactly how many there were, how they had been trained, or what weapons they possessed, trying to take them all out from my starting point in the bomb bay didn't seem like a good bet. Besides, if the crewman had effectively disabled the plane, there was no real danger to the plant. Now was not the time to intervene.

There was more movement toward the front of the plane. More grunting and whining, mostly from the woman. Another bucket stowed near the rear of the crawl-way. At least the stuff seemed to be in containers of manageable size. I had predicted the location correctly. And no one was trying to get into the bomb bay.

Everything was as I had anticipated. The real bitch was that, if this plane got off the ground, it was headed for a really rough landing.

CHAPTER 52

It was just after 3:00 a.m. and both the Plant Manager and NRC inspector were in the plant control room.

Plant Manager: "I know what I heard on the phone, but give it to us both one more time."

Operator: "Okay. First there was a seismic alarm. I checked the monitor and it seemed isolated. So I reset the alarm.

"Just as I was going back to my desk, the damn thing went off again. This time, when I tried to shut it off, it just kept ringing, and the monitor showed nearly constant, low-level, seismic activity. So I triggered the general alarm, just like the book says."

He looked at the NRC guy. "Everybody got to stations right away. And a minute or so later, it was all over. Nobody reported any systems compromised and all my controls and monitors read normal.

"Damned if I know what it was."

Plant Manager: "Well, whatever it was seems to be over."

But before he'd finished his sentence, another alarm bell went off. The Operator scanned his panels and moved to the red light.

Operator: "The water level in the river is down two feet from what it was an hour ago. The cooling system computers monitor any significant change in river water level. That's what triggered the alarm."

Plant Manager: "What in the name of . . . what's going on here?" The Plant Manager scratched his head, then pounded his fist down on the Operator's table. "Damn it! Get me the Army Corp emergency line. It's their damn river!"

The Operator picked up a line to the switchboard. They would have the emergency number and connect him.

NRC: "With an unexplained drop in river level, and primary cooling of the reactors dependent on river water, I am officially notifying you to shut down the reactors immediately."

He said it directly to the Plant Manager. And it wasn't a request.

Plant Manager: "Damn it. That'll cost the rate-payers millions. Can't we hold off for a while, just until the Army Corp weighs in."

NRC: "I cannot do that, sir. Shut down both reactors . . . now!"

The Plant Manager looked like a defendant who had just been read his death sentence. An unscheduled shutdown would, indeed, cost the company millions, and maybe him, his job.

He turned to the Operator. "Initiate controlled shutdown – Reactors 1 and 2."

CHAPTER 53

Back at the Red Wing Airport.

It was taking the bad guys quite a while to load the plane. I had counted nineteen buckets in the crawl-way. Maybe Bull would get here soon.

I heard John's voice from above the forward entrance. "Okay. That's it. Pull the wheel chocks out. Then get that ladder and truck outta here. I gotta get this plane off the ground."

The forward hatch slammed shut.

*   *   *

The first thing John noticed when re-entering the enclosed plane was the strong smell of the mineral oil. He had unlocked the container covers so the contents could more easily spill out on impact.

Although it smelled bad, he knew the mineral oil fumes were not likely to catch fire. He had confirmed that with Farris. Their flash point was simply too high. The smell he could live with – at least as long as he needed to.

He had never flown a B24. His experience was with small aircraft. But he was certain that, if he could get this plane off the ground, he could hit the spent fuel building. When it came to flying, landing safely was the only really hard part. And he didn't need to be concerned with that.

He could fly this mother.

He stood at the base of the ladder leading up to the cockpit, gripping the railings purposefully. It was against his nature to be a *kamikaze*. He was a fighter, not one to give up.

But this wasn't giving up. Not at all. The cancer would take him soon anyway, and then how could he avenge his family's suffering? This was definitely *not* giving up. This was achieving his life's goal. Fulfilling his purpose. Finally the government and the nuclear establishment would pay for what they had done to the Siglers, and many others, at TMI.

He mustered his resolve and set to the business of getting the plane on its way toward his destiny.

Lowering himself painfully into the pilot's seat, he immediately saw something was wrong. The rudder pedals were both missing. He checked the co-pilot's station. Gone from there, too.

Shit! They took off the fucking pedals. Now what? He couldn't fly the plane without the damn pedals. He didn't know what to do. Shit!

As he was trying to decide, he heard the butt of a rifle banging on the side of the plane.

"You in there. Show yourself."

A man's voice he didn't recognize. A foreign accent of some kind.

This couldn't be true. How could the police have found out so quickly?

"We are friends," the man called. "We have the parts you _ need."

A trick? Or a miracle? He might as well find out. He wasn't going anywhere the way things were right now.

He climbed out of the pilot's seat and crawled agonizingly up the ladder to the top hatch. He took a deep breath of the oily air and opened the exit.

Outside, he could make out a man dressed from head to toe in black – his face also blackened with military grease. His uniform was muddy and soaking wet. In one hand, he held a black automatic rifle – in the other, two missing rudder pedals.

"Here are the parts you need. Do you require assistance attaching them?"

John did not understand what was happening. But he knew he wanted the pedals.

"No. I can do it. Can you throw them up, one at a time?"

The soldier put down the rifle and tossed John the pedals.

"Now put them on and get moving. We cannot wait for more infidels to arrive."

John glanced left and right, seeing two more of the black-faced soldiers.

"Thank you," John managed.

He disappeared back into the plane and closed the hatch. Once he was back in the cockpit, attaching the pedals was easy – just four, keyed pins. Praise God! He was back in business.

CHAPTER 54

When I heard the cursing coming from the cockpit I had to chuckle to myself. As serious as this drama was, one had to appreciate when a good idea worked out. They'd captured the plane, but now they couldn't even fly it.

Then I heard a banging on the left side of the fuselage. Who was this? Bull? Gunner?

Then I heard the really bad news. Someone else was outside the plane. A man with a thick Arabic accent – and they had found the missing parts. Who were they? And why hadn't the crew taken the parts to Red Wing?

Damn!

Maybe this would still slow them up enough for Bull and the cavalry to get here. I sure hoped so. It looked like my Plan B had been thwarted.

*　　*　　*

John had found an abbreviated starting checklist for the B24 on the internet, and had memorized it. He had also memorized the cockpit layout. He ran through the starting procedures in his head as he executed them in the real B24 cockpit.

--   Turn fuel supply to 'ALL.' *Check.*

-- Turn on Master Trim Panel switch. *Check.*

-- Set cowl flaps to the 'FULL OPEN' position for Engine 3. *Check.*

-- Turn Master Ignition Switch to 'ON' position. *Check.*

-- Set magnetos for Engine 3 to 'BOTH.' *Check.*

-- Turn on the boost pump for Engine 3. *Check.*

-- Set the mixture for Engine 3 to 'FULL RICH.' *Check.*

-- Make sure fuel pressure is 15 psi. *Check.*

-- Open the throttle slightly. *He shoved the throttle slide for engine three ahead a bit. Check.*

-- Press and hold the engine 'START' switch until the engine starts. *He pushed the button and held his breath. The propeller on engine 3 began to turn over. Soon engine 3 burst to life. He waited a moment to be sure it was running smoothly, then throttled it back to idle speed.*

-- Turn on the 'GENERATOR' switch for Engine 3. *Check.*

All he needed to do was repeat this procedure for engines 4, 1 and 2, in that order. This was easier than he had feared.

Soon he had all four engines running smoothly.

He took a deep breath and released the brakes. The plane began to roll slowly forward. To turn he would adjust the engine speed on whichever side he needed to move faster – left turn, more speed to engine 4; right turn, more speed to engine 1. Rotating the yoke in the cockpit would also encourage the turns.

Steering in this manner, he worked his way toward the end of Runway Number 9. Tonight he would be taking off headed down-river. He would have preferred to go west, up the river and directly to the nuke. But the wind was from the southeast and he needed to take off into the wind. It was unavoidable. And it would only add a couple minutes to the flight.

As he approached the end of Runway 9, he swung the big bird wide, turning 180 degrees. He was now pointed down the runway and into the wind. He held the brakes.

Takeoff Procedure:

-- Cowl Flaps: 1/3 Open. *Check.*

-- Flaps: 10 degrees down. *Check.*

-- Fuel Mixture: Set to 'FULL RICH.' *Check.*

-- Elevator trim: 2 degrees nose-up. *Check.*

-- Rudder trim: 3 degrees right. *Check.*

-- Aileron trim: Neutral. *Check.*

-- Power: 49" Hg/2700 rpm. *Check.*

At this point, something shattered the port cockpit window. He looked outside. What he saw resembled a scene from the Gaza Strip. The three muddy men in black were dodging around the terminal building and hangars, shooting rifle bursts around corners.

Damn it! The cops must be here.

Illumination flares lit up the sky over the runway.

With the port window gone, he could hear automatic rifle fire on the tarmac, pitched above the low engine sounds. Explosions from the area of the hangar village echoed inside the open cockpit.

Why had he stopped to look . . . even for a moment? He needed to ignore the firefight and get the damn plane in the air.

-- Liftoff speed: 120-130 mph. *Check.*

-- Apply power smoothly and gradually. *He pushed the four throttles forward about one quarter. Then he released the brakes.*

Here we go . . . .

CHAPTER 55

Gunner had been sleeping hard when he received Bull's call. But the message had him wide awake in seconds. Help was needed at the Red Wing Airport. Someone was trying to steal the B24.

He first contacted his own office and mobilized as many Ottawa County Deputies as he could. Then he scrambled the BCA SWAT team, using the emergency communication link established specifically for that purpose.

With everyone else already headed toward the airport, Gunner quickly pulled on his own uniform, clipped his sidearm onto his belt and raced for the squad car parked in the driveway.

It was a tense four-minute drive for Deputy Chief Gunderson. He was hearing things on his police radio that he didn't want to hear. But even considering the radio transmissions, nothing could have prepared him for what he found when he arrived at the Red Wing Airport.

His deputies and the SWAT team had beaten him to the airport. And it looked like they had attempted to establish a perimeter around the hangar village. That was standard procedure. SWAT would surround the opposition and then use its superior weaponry and tactical training to quickly overwhelm its adversaries.

But the tactics clearly hadn't worked here. The perimeter was in disarray. Tan-uniformed county deputies and black flak-jacketed BCA SWAT members alike were scrambling madly for cover.

What the hell was happening?

Gunner's car screeched to a halt in the asphalt parking lot. He grabbed his shotgun and raced toward the action. The air hung thick with blue smoke. And the unmistakable smell of freshly-fired gunpowder was everywhere.

Now that he was outside his car, Gunner could hear automatic weapon fire coming from the vicinity of the brick terminal building. It must be the fierceness of the criminals, he thought, and their strategic location behind the only defensible structure at the airport, that had scattered the law enforcement personnel.

As he ducked behind one of the hangars in the darkness, Gunner found the SWAT commander. He was cool-headed, but clearly concerned.

"What the hell's goin' on out there?" Gunner whispered.

"You tell me. You invited me to this party. Those assholes have got Kalashnikovs, hand grenades, RPGs, and god knows what else. We're totally defensive here."

Then the realization hit Gunner. These weren't the kind of criminals he was used to dealing with. They were terrorists! Actual goddamn terrorists!

"*Al Qaeda*," Gunner said solemnly. "It's fucking *Al Qaeda*."

The two officers looked at each other for a moment. Neither could seem to get his head around the thought that *Al Qaeda* was really here . . . in Red Wing . . . or that the men they were fighting were highly-lethal, brutally efficient, soldiers.

SWAT possessed tactics, coordination and firepower that was more than ample to overwhelm typical Midwestern thugs. The commander now realized that this was a military situation – not a routine drug bust. Attempting to surround the terrorists had been the exact wrong decision. The maneuver had allowed the terrorists to assess the numbers and weaknesses of their targets.

He should have used his superior man-power to establish positions to the enemy's flank and rear before attempting an assault. A few well-placed sniper bullets from behind the adversaries might have made short work of this situation. As things stood, those options were no longer available. Any police moves to circumvent enemy defenses were met with a hail of fire.

"They're going to fly that plane into the nuke," Gunner said, referring to the B24 that had already begun taxiing toward the runway. "We've got to stop it from taking off."

The SWAT commander immediately directed his troops to concentrate as much of their fire as possible on the plane.

"Aim for the engines and the fat part of the wings. That'd be where the fuel tanks are," he ordered. "Don't waste your shots on the tires. There are too many and they're too tough."

The commander was right about the tires. But it was unfortunate that he did not know that the B24 had an extremely unusual fuel tank location – between the wings and above the fuselage. So although the SWAT members and deputies did their level best to halt the bomber by aiming at the engines and wings, their bullets had no effect on the rolling behemoth. They couldn't even slow it down.

As the officers tried to maintain a steady stream of fire at the bomber, the terrorists continually hampered their efforts. One by one, fire from the Kalashnikovs chewed up the corrugated steel and wood hangars behind which the officers had been forced to take cover. And RPGs flattened any parts of a hangar that survived the rifle fire. The police had to keep falling back to new defensive positions, just to avoid being slaughtered.

Eventually, the plane had taxied beyond reasonable shooting distance. And law enforcement focused their efforts exclusively on self-preservation.

By this time, an additional posse of deputies from Lewiston County, Wisconsin had arrived at the airport – raising everyone's hopes that the increased manpower would make a decisive difference in the battle.

The SWAT commander tried to advise Lewiston of the tactical situation. But like the Minnesotans, the Lewiston Deputy couldn't conceive of a true military action happening in his county.

After an initial headlong rush into the fray, it hadn't taken long for the Lewiston force to come to grips with the situation. They soon sought cover alongside their Minnesota counterparts. Ultimately, the additional forces could do little more than add their Hail Mary shots to those of the other officers.

Hopes for law enforcement survival were fading fast. But as best they could, the officers bravely continued the fight.

The SWAT team had devised some alternate tactics to expose the enemy. Illumination flares now filled the air over the terminal – above the area from which the Kalashnikovs seemed to be firing. The added light allowed the officers an occasional glimpse of the black-clothed guerillas as they darted in and out of positions inside and around the brick terminal building.

The terrorists quickly countered the flares with smoke grenades, once again occluding all view of their movements.

As the fighting raged amid the blue chemical smoke, Gunner could hear the B24 roaring down the runway and into the air. They had failed to stop the plane. Would they even be able to stop the enemy?

Once the plane was safely away, it was obvious that the terrorists were on the advance. Their previous priority had been protecting the plane. Now they were attacking the law officers in earnest.

Having been driven backward from tin hangar to tin hangar, the police officers had all eventually ended up in about the same place – ducked behind the final row of hangars at the edge of the airport, shooting blindly around corners at their seldom-seen opposition. This is where they would have to make their stand.

Portable mortar fire began to rain down around the police force. Thank god the enemy had made a small miscalculation, and the initial shells were landing twenty meters behind the law enforcement positions. It was only a matter of time before they realized the error, and the mortar rounds would begin decimating the troops.

The SWAT commander and Gunner had stayed close to each other during the fight. Now the commander turned to Gunner.

"Any idea how we get out of here with our skins?"

"Can we get some people behind them . . . along the runway?"

"I've already tried sending some men to do just that. But the taxi-ways have trip wires that set off grenades. And as soon as anyone clears the buildings and heads toward the runway, they're sitting ducks for the Kalashnikovs. It would take too long to send personnel all the way around the runway outside enemy firing range. I'm afraid that's just not an option."

Gunner was silent, trying to envision a path to salvation.

CHAPTER 56

As soon as I heard the first engine start, I knew I could move around without fear of being heard. If I could act quickly enough, maybe I could get to the pilot before takeoff and still avoid the risk to the plant. The noise in here was deafening, but I didn't dare wear sound-protection for fear of missing something crucial.

Moving off my backside and onto my knees, I hooked the Beretta on my belt. Next I reached for, and found, the tangle of wire I had placed around the interior latch as a lock. The wire unwound smoothly. I rotated the latch counter-clockwise a quarter turn. With the hatch barely open, I scanned for enemies in the aft cabin. It was very dark, but I saw no one.

Suddenly the air seemed drenched in chemicals. I had been spared the odor while isolated in the bay. The fluid in which the potassium had been submerged was definitely mineral oil. I knew the smell. Unclarified mineral oil smells like burning lubricant – the same sort of smell you get if you drip motor oil on a hot engine. The odor was overpowering.

Ignoring the stench, I rolled the hatchway door the rest of the way open, and slowly pulled myself up from the darkness of the bomb bay, into the darkness of the aft cabin. From there, I carefully made my way up the ladder to the central crawl-way and peeked over its edge. I would have to climb higher to see the pilot over the containers. I worked my way farther up until the cockpit was barely visible.

From this vantage point, I could occasionally see a silhouette of the pilot's right arm as it moved to push buttons or flip switches – part of the start-up procedure. The rest of the pilot's body was obscured by the thick metal portside bulkhead. The bulkhead was too thick for my Beretta to penetrate. The only way I could possibly get a shot at the pilot was to climb over all the containers, which completely clogged the crawl-way.

There wasn't enough space for me to go over the containers. I didn't have time to move them, one at a time, as I worked my way forward. And if the pilot happened to look back while I was in the middle of the pack of containers, I would be stuck, unable to move in any direction – a sitting duck.

As much as I would have liked to end this whole operation quickly, an attempt right now would have been foolhardy, rather than brave. Again, I would have to wait.

I thought I heard sounds outside. But the reverberations of the engines in the empty plane kept me from telling what they were. I hoped the posse had arrived. If so, I should stay low and try not to get shot.

I climbed back down the ladder and flattened myself on the floor of the aft compartment. Whether help had come or not, this was where I needed to be right now.

CHAPTER 57

At the Prairie River Plant.

The Plant Manager had just gotten off the phone with the Army Corp of Engineers.

The Ottawa County Sheriff's Department and the Red Wing Police had been receiving calls from residents of low-lying properties along the Mississippi. Citizens were reporting flood waters in their basements. Local law enforcement had done their job and forwarded the issue along to the Army Corp.

The only conclusion the Corp could come to was that there had been a catastrophic failure at Lock and Dam Number 3. The Corp was sending out a helicopter in an attempt to better assess the situation.

The Plant Manager relayed the news to the NRC inspector.

NRC: "What's the river level now?"

Operator: "Down six feet and still dropping."

Plant Manager: "Bring the backup cooling system online." He was talking to the Operator. "Just to be safe," he said to NRC.

The Operator approached a panel containing a circuit breaker labeled: 'Backup Cooling Water Pump.' He pulled the breaker into the 'On' position. A green light illuminated. The backup pump had started.

Plant Manager: "Even if the river keeps dropping, we get our backup cooling water from an artesian well. Five hundred feet deep," he said, to no one in particular. Everyone in the room already knew that. The Manager was starting to come unglued.

An alarm bell sounded in the control room.

"Now what?" The Manager was getting hysterical.

Operator: "I've got a red light on the backup pump temperature. It's overheating."

Plant Manager: "Check the damn water flow rate!"

Operator: "Sir. The flow rate shows zero at the well head. Sir, we need to shut down the pump before it burns out. "

Plant Manager: No response.

NRC: "Shut it down."

The Operator flipped the breaker to the 'Off' position. The red light went out.

The Operator called the maintenance supervisor on his walkie.

Operator: "We've got a main pump overheat on the backup cooling water system. And the flow meter shows zero. Fix it . . . now!"

The maintenance department head sent two men immediately to the pump house. As soon as they got there, they could see the problem.

Maintenance: "The main water valve is closed. Do we have permission to open it?"

Operator: "Are you sure? My board shows that valve as 'Open.'"

Maintenance: "Sir, I'm standing right next to the valve. It is closed."

Operator: "Yes. You have my permission. Open it immediately."

Maintenance: "Yessir!"

As soon as the two maintenance men grasped the wheel to open the valve, they discovered another problem.

Maintenance: "Sir?"

Operator: "Now what?"

Maintenance: "Sir, someone has cut the valve stem inside the bonnet. We tried to turn the valve open and the whole wheel and stem came out in our hands."

The Plant Manager had heard everything. This can't be possible, he thought. Both cooling systems can't fail at the same time.

Plant Manager: "What the hell is going on?"

NRC: "Isn't it obvious? Your plant is under attack! I will notify the FBI immediately. If we have a spent fuel pool incident right now, we are in serious trouble. Change your security alert status to 'Red.' Send out security personnel to clear a larger perimeter around the plant. And tell air defense to shoot down any aircraft within a one-mile radius."

NRC picked up his cell and speed-dialed the FBI liaison. He explained the situation and requested that the FBI deploy the fighter jet from St. Paul.

FBI: "We can't do that, I'm afraid. We sent it back to Duluth Air Base at 21:00 hours. We were told the air show was over."

NRC: "Well, get whoever and whatever you can down here right now. WE ARE UNDER ATTACK!" NRC ended the call.

NRC: "I hope to hell that paranoid lawyer from Red Wing wasn't right." It was said to no one in particular. "'Cause if he was . . . we're all seriously screwed!"

Just then, the Plant Manager's radio went on.

Air Control: "Sir. Air Control. We've just picked up an aircraft departing Red Wing Airport."

Plant Manager: "If it comes anywhere near this plant, shoot it down! Damn it! Find a way to shoot it down!" The Manager's voice was cracking as much as his sanity.

CHAPTER 58

Onboard the B24.

Other than keeping his head down, John tried to ignore the firefight outside. Some of the explosions made it difficult. But he needed to keep going. Everything depended on it.

He slid the throttles forward in unison. The engines revved higher. He struggled a bit to keep them in sync, avoiding unnecessary vibration and uneven thrust. Whenever he failed, a throb of harmonics emanated from one side of the plane or the other, and he would make minute adjustments to the throttle levers.

The plane was on track, rolling faster and faster down the middle of the runway. Finally the throttle slides were at full open. John glanced back and forth between the runway and the land speed indicator dial. 80 mph. 90 . . . 100 . . . 110 . . . . The plane was pulling to port now, as the operating manual had predicted. He turned the yoke a bit to starboard to compensate. 115 . . . 120 . . . 125.

He pulled back slightly on the yoke, still turning right just a little. He could feel the front of the plane becoming lighter, the front wheel barely on the concrete. He pulled back harder on the yoke. The front wheel lifted from the runaway. More pull on the yoke. The back wheels left the ground and the vibrations changed instantly from the wheel clatter on the runway to the creaking and popping of the metal plane as it strained against the increasingly strong airflow.

*   *   *

So much for the rescue. We were racing down the runway on takeoff. The best laid schemes . . . .

I was down to my final option. For now, I just needed to be sure I wasn't seen until after we were airborne. Then it wouldn't matter.

I crouched inside the dark, rumbling, metal hollow of the 'flying boxcar' and waited for my chance.

I steadied my breathing. In and out.

Relaxed my muscles.

Now, focus on what you need to do.

For some reason, as I opened my mind, relaxed my muscles and controlled my breathing, a song seeped into my head: "This train is bound for glory, this train."

I couldn't remember when I had last heard that song. Why now? There didn't seem to be any glory in this flying boxcar's future. And at least one of the people on board was bound for Hell.

Maybe two.

CHAPTER 59

At the Red Wing Airport.

As he strove to come up with a miracle plan, Gunner thought he heard engine sounds coming from the direction of the river. He lay down flat on the concrete behind the hangar. Crawling on his elbows, shotgun in hand, he slithered to an edge of the tin building. Peering around the corner, he could see nothing at first. But the engine sounds were getting louder.

Then he saw them.

What the hell?

Barely distinguishable through the dissipating smoke, and dimly illuminated by the dwindling flares, two silhouettes seemed to rise from the waters of the river itself. Whatever they were, they were large, they were black, and they were headed this way.

As the spectral images approached, Gunner could hear the increasing growl of powerful engines, the whine of high-velocity turbines, and the rhythmic thumping of helicopter rotors. Finally, he could make them out.

They were Apache Attack Helicopters. Their distinctive shape and signature nose-down attitude were unmistakable. But Gunner saw no markings to indicate whether they were friend or foe – only their menacing blackness.

Turning his head over his shoulder, Gunner called to the commander.

"Have you got choppers coming?"

The commander was seated on the concrete, with his back straight against the metal hangar. He was staring out into the darkness.

"No such luck," the commander managed.

"Well . . . somebody does. And if it's the bad guys, we're gonna be dead sooner than we thought."

Trapped behind the last row of hangars, dozens of police officers waited in silence as the Apaches closed in on their position. There was nothing to do but wait. Their fates were now in the hands of others.

By this time, all gunfire had ceased. A deadly calm had fallen over the airport grounds. It seemed as though all combatants knew that the resolution to this battle would come from the air – and probably swiftly.

Moving at a steady clip, the Apache gunships roared past, sweeping directly over the place where the officers were hunkered down. Airborne sand and pebbles stung the faces of deputies and BCA alike as they crouched behind waste barrels and hangar supports. The Apaches couldn't have been more than a hundred feet up.

After flying over the nearly defenseless police force, the pilots deftly maneuvered the gunships, first directly behind, and then flanking, the law enforcement positions. They were hovering now, gun turrets twitching robotically beneath their cockpits.

Questions raced through Gunner's mind. Where had the helicopters come from? Whose side were they on? And how had he ended up in the middle of this smoldering slice of Hell?

The Apaches began to nose forward – first toward, and then past, the hangars where law enforcement had made their last stand. The entire corp of police officers, Gunner included, breathed a collective sigh of relief as the aircraft passed them by.

The gunships continued their advance, moving slowly toward the terrorists, held aloft it seemed, by sheer force of will.

It was then that the beleaguered police force first heard the thunder of the Apache's 30 mm chain guns – a sound that dwarfed the comparatively feeble twitter of the terrorists' weapons as they returned fire. Enemy bullets sparked off the Apache's heavy armor plate, ricocheting in all directions.

But these were true war machines – built specifically to repel the kind of attack the terrorists had mounted at the airport.

The gunships remained in formation, continuing inexorably forward, their chin-mounted chain-guns ripping through metal, wood and brick. For a while, return fire from the Kalashnikovs was intense. But the Apaches remained undamaged.

Since the helicopters were drawing all enemy fire. This would have been a perfect time for the police to beat a hasty retreat. But no one could move. They were frozen by the chilling presence of the deadly war machines, and the other-worldly scene unfolding before them.

In a matter of minutes, it was over. All ground fire had ceased.

And the Apaches' weapons, too, fell silent.

The awestruck police officers continued to watch the hovering gunships – unable to speak, or even to comprehend the spectacle they had just witnessed.

One by one, the officers stood.

At first, there was silence in the group. Then someone started to applaud. Others joined in. Soon hats were flying in the air, while cheers and whistles erupted from the former dead men.

Although the shooting was over. The gunships continued circling the airport for several minutes more, using their onboard technology to confirm complete destruction of the enemy.

"Chief Deputy Gunderson," Gunner's radio crackled. "This is Blackdog One. Do you read me? Over."

Gunner was still in shock. The entire scenario at the airport had been surreal. With some fumbling, he managed to unclip the radio from his belt.

"You got Gunderson," he replied, trying to sound composed. "Over."

"Chief Deputy, we confirm three hostiles down, but are unsure if any might still be hiding in the buildings. We show nothing obvious on infrared. But you're going to need to send your team in to flush out any stragglers. Over."

"That would be our pleasure, sir. But may I ask to whom I am speaking? Over."

"Captain Michael Turner, U.S. Army Special Forces. Please proceed with cleanup, sir, while we fly cover. Over and out."

The SWAT commander insisted that his team was best trained and armed to clear the buildings. Gunner had to agree.

So the commander gave the necessary orders and the cleanup of Red Wing Airport got underway.

CHAPTER 60

Onboard the B24.

The plane was climbing nicely. But there was more shudder and more drag than there should be – even in an old plane like this one.

Landing gear! He needed to raise them.

John knew where the levers were. He lifted all the gear at once with his left hand on both levers. His right arm still fought the plane's desire to turn to port. In all the noise, he couldn't hear the front landing gear retract into the nose of the plane. But he felt a thud under his feet. And when the rear gear folded out and into their specially-designed spaces in the wings, the plane immediately felt different. Better. Smoother. Like grease had just been applied up and down the outside of the craft and it was slipping through the air on the new lubrication.

He continued straight forward on a heading of 270 degrees. He wanted to reach at least 1400 feet on the altimeter before he tried to turn. He knew the land was 900 feet above sea level at the Red Wing Airport. He might need all of the additional 500 feet to turn this beast without dropping out of the sky.

At 1400 feet his airspeed indicated 165 knots – sufficient to attempt a slow turn. He held the yoke with both hands and applied equal pressure to the rudder pedals. It took more strength than he had anticipated just to keep the plane headed straight. He didn't know what to expect in a turn.

Despite the muscle strain, he knew any movements of the yoke and pedals needed to be subtle. He allowed the yoke to rotate a bit counter-clockwise, while shifting slight foot pressure to the left pedal. The plane rolled to port, more than he wanted. Again using both yoke and rudders, he turned back a bit to starboard.

He glanced at the altimeter. He was losing altitude. Of course. He knew better than this. He needed to increase elevation during a turn. He pulled back on the yoke to raise the nose and compensate for the reduced lift of the angled wing surfaces.

Slowly but surely, the plane returned to 1400 feet and gently rolled around a sweeping left hand turn. John glanced up from the instrument console.

Shit! He could see lights straight ahead of him through the canopy. At 1400 feet?

Damn it! The bluffs.

He pulled back on the yoke as hard as he could. It would not yield easily. But the nose did pull up. He couldn't have cleared the bluff top by more than a couple hundred feet.

Perspiring profusely, he kept the plane climbing to 2500 feet, then reduced the throttle until he was cruising at 210 knots.

The plane still felt nose-up, even in level flight. The flaps!

He reached across with his right hand and returned the flaps to their neutral position. The nose went down and the plane felt more level. He could finally see a decent horizon over the console against the night stars.

*   *   *

I wasn't able to stand during takeoff. So I lay on the floor of the aft compartment, holding onto a safety belt strap until we were in the air. I was lucky that he had needed to takeoff to the east. That gave me an extra few minutes. That extra time might be all I would need.

As we were climbing, the airplane wobbled, rolling left and right unpredictably. An inexperienced pilot. But it made my job harder. I had to keep my balance.

I would have preferred to put my parachute on. But there wasn't enough room in the crawl-way for me to work with the extra bulk around my torso. Reluctantly, I left the parachute secured to a safety strap on the wall. Then I worked my way to the front of the aft compartment and climbed the ladder to the crawl-way.

On hands and knees, I maneuvered toward the forward area and what I hoped was the potassium. There just wasn't room for me to stand and move safely with his erratic flying.

I didn't care if he saw me now. What was he going to do? Let the plane fly itself? And even if he had a gun, he wouldn't risk detonating his cargo – at least I hoped not. And if he did shoot at me, I could hide behind the containers. And if that didn't work . . . I would have to hope he was a poor shot.

Unfortunately, I was in a similar predicament. I couldn't get close enough to shoot the pilot and still expect to make a safe exit from the diving plane.

Slowly, I worked my way forward on the crawl-way. Just ahead in the near total darkness, I could see the first canister. Stainless steel. I hoped the canisters weren't locked somehow. I didn't know if my multi-tool would get me into a locked steel container.

But locking the containers wouldn't make sense. They needed to spill their contents on impact. Still, you never know.

After being thrown side to side a few times, I reached the first canister. I grabbed its lid on both sides and lifted gently. Even in the noisy aircraft I thought I heard a sucking sound, as if a seal had been released. I lifted the lid and set it aside.

Just as I did so, the plane banked sharply to port. Mineral oil slopped from the open canister – through the cat walk, onto the other canisters and onto the legs of my camo cargo shorts.

With my pants soaked in slippery oil, I braced my back against the metal grid on the starboard side of the crawl-way until the left turn ended and we leveled off. I looked into the open container. All I could see was more mineral oil, its surface maybe six inches down from the top.

Steadying myself on one knee and one foot, I lifted the lid off a second canister. Again, all I could see was the dark reflection of the mineral oil. But the potassium had to be in there.

Suddenly the plane jerked upward into a steep climb. I was nearly thrown off the crawl-way, but managed to catch a grip before falling. Both of the open canisters spilled backward, emptying their entire contents of mineral oil. Remaining inside were dozens of silvery-white ingots of potassium!

I had to move fast now. The potassium was still coated in oil. But the oil would evaporate. I didn't know how fast.

*　　*　　*

John knew he had strayed farther into Wisconsin than planned. But no harm done. He would have a longer, straighter approach in which to make sure he hit the final target. He was beginning to get the feel of this bird. Even so, the yoke still fought him, trying to turn the plane to port.

It was time for another turn. He allowed the yoke to move just a bit counter-clockwise again, making corresponding adjustments to the rudder. This time he pulled back on the yoke at the same time and maintained his altitude during the ninety degree turn to the east.

Now he could see the lights of the nuclear plant glowing on the horizon outside his missing port window. If he flew a bit farther east, he could swing north and descend straight onto the plant.

As he continued on his course, John noticed a small reflection of light on the glass canopy. Where was that coming from? It quickly grew brighter. Soon he could also see light shining into the cockpit from aft.

What the hell?

He allowed himself a quick look over his right shoulder toward the rear of the plane.

"Jesus Christ!"

CHAPTER 61

At the Prairie River Nuclear Plant.

The nuclear plant was a combination of chaos and sepulchre. Security forces scrambled around outside the fences. Men dressed all in black. Black flak jackets. Black helmets. Black Colt AR-15 assault rifles. Other employees milled about solemnly – nothing for them to do with the reactors shut down.

To aid with night vision, each security guard had an infrared viewer on one eye. Computer-controlled pole cameras also sought temperature changes in the brush. Guards visually scanned for any signs of warm bodies creeping through the sumac, or lying in the swampy hollows. Dogs hunted the woods ahead of them. The security circle slowly expanded until it reached a quarter mile from the fence.

Security: "Sir, we are secure to 400 meters beyond critical perimeter."

The Plant Manager was starting to get a grip.

Plant Manager: "Good. . . . Good Chief. Ah . . . maintain that perimeter and do whatever you need to keep intruders out."

Security: "Yessir!"

Plant Manager: "And Chief. . ."

Security: "Yessir."

Plant Manager: "Patch the air control officer's audio into our com link up here in the control room. And for God's sake, keep your eye on that damn plane."

He looked warily at NRC. The Manager knew he sounded more, ah . . . collected than he had moments ago. Could he hold it together through this thing?

Then he spoke to NRC.

Plant Manager: "Don't worry. We've got everything covered."

NRC looked at the Plant Manager with a mixture of pity and contempt.

NRC: "Covered? You've got shit covered!"

The Plant Manager staggered in shock.

NRC: "Your primary cooling water supply from the river is in serious jeopardy. Your backup system is non-functioning and we don't yet know how long it will take to get it fixed. Security patrols are creeping all over the grounds ready to shoot anything that moves. Your fuel pool will overheat and melt down if the river level drops further. And a goddamn unknown aircraft is in the air within a few miles of where we are sitting – its intentions unknown, but assumed to be bad!

"Exactly what have you got covered?"

The Plant Manager's head sank until his flabby chin rested on his chest.

Air Control: "This is air control. The unknown aircraft is at an altitude of 1400 feet, bearing one-seven-eight degrees. Heading toward Wisconsin. At this height, he might not clear the bluffs."

FBI was on the phone.

NRC: "Patch him into the com link with all of us, security, operations, air control . . . everybody that matters. We don't need anyone dropping the ball because of a communications failure."

FBI: "What the hell's going on down there? The Corps says the dam at Lock Number 3 is probably out and they expect River Pool 3 to drop to near zero – even in the barge channel. Have you got the plant safely secured?"

NRC: "Not by a damn shot." He repeated the situation to FBI.

Air Control: "The unknown aircraft has cleared the Wisconsin bluffs and is now on heading zero-niner-zero degrees at an altitude of 2900 feet. Approximate airspeed is 220 knots."

FBI: "Have we been trying to identify this craft or raise it on the radio?"

Air Control: "Yessir. Continuous automated requests for communication and warnings to stay more than two miles from the plant. The aircraft transponder is inactive."

FBI: "Does that mean that this aircraft, whose identity and intentions are totally unknown to us, is headed along the Wisconsin border, roughly parallel with the river, at a ground speed of over 200 miles per hour, and is closing on the plant?"

Air Patrol: "Yessir, it does."

FBI: "What is the distance from the aircraft to the plant?"

Air Control: "Most direct vector . . . approximately six miles, sir."

FBI: "Security. Make damn sure your air gunners are ready! I think you're gonna need 'em."

Security: "Yessir!"

NRC and the Plant Manager stood and looked at one another in disbelief. This wasn't happening. It couldn't be happening.

Air Control: "The unknown aircraft has altered course. Its heading is now zero-two-zero degrees at an altitude of 2700 feet and descending. Approximate airspeed is 230 knots. It's headed right toward the plant. Current distance . . . five miles. At present speed, aircraft will be on site in approximately 50 seconds."

NRC and FBI together: "Shit!"

CHAPTER 62

Back inside the B24.

The plane had leveled off. But just as I was regaining my footing, we again banked into a left hand turn. Once more, I was flattened against the right, cage-like side of the crawl-way. I guessed we were now heading upstream along the Wisconsin border, somewhere above the bluffs.

I had to work fast.

The B24 leveled again. I forced myself back into the one knee, one foot position, and with some effort, stood the two spilled containers upright.

Reaching one hand into each pocket, I produced the 24-ounce bottles of Diet Dew. After the burning mineral spirits had dehydrated the air, I needed to make sure there would still be water available to ignite the potassium. Diet Mountain Dew wasn't water. But it would work fine.

I laid one bottle of Dew on its side in each open steel can, directly on top of the oily potassium ingots.

Now, for the moment of truth.

With my left hand, I pulled the two road torches from my pocket. I was pretty sure the mineral oil fumes wouldn't explode. And I knew the flames wouldn't spread nearly as quickly as they would with gasoline. But there was a lot of spilled oil between me and my exit strategy – the rear hatchway. And my parachute might also be soaked with oil. These torches burned really hot – around 1400 degrees Celsius. So I hoped this would work, and that I would still escape, quite literally, with my skin.

Whether I would survive or not, at this point I was committed. I had no other options. Countless lives depended on me bringing this bomber down before it could reach the nuclear plant.

I removed the safety caps from both flares, exposing their ignitors. I struck the first flare on the rough base of the second. It sparked to life, sputtering and spewing drops of burning-hot phosphorus all over the place. I didn't have time to check the status of the fire that I knew was growing around me.

Acting as quickly as I could, I lit the second road flare from the flame of the first. Then I dropped one flare into each open canister and dove out the rear of the crawl-way. There were streams and puddles of burning oil all around me. My left shorts' leg had caught fire. But it hadn't yet had the chance to spread. I snuffed the pant fire with my hands.

I searched for my parachute in the now well-lit cabin. As luck would have it, one of the plane's lurches had flopped the parachute off the wall and onto a bench seat. As far as I could see, the chute remained oil-free.

The fire was spreading everywhere.

Just as I tried to slip my arms into the parachute, the plane banked left once more. The turn launched me into the starboard wall – but I stayed on my feet, and was able to keep the parachute dry.

We must be close to the plant by now. Probably near or over the river valley.

The plane leveled again briefly, then nosed gently downward. We were starting to descend. The pilot must have seen the fire by now. But he had no real options either. He would try to complete his mission before the plane blew up.

I stumbled to the rear hatch and found the release. Rotating the handle counterclockwise, I swung the hatch up and into the plane. At least with the plane in a descent, the burning oil tended to run toward the front of the fuselage, instead of toward my exit.

Knowing that the Diet Dew bombs could detonate at any moment, I put one hand on each side of the hatch and flung myself out of the plane, head-first into the blackness.

*   *   *

When John saw the flames, he knew he had a serious problem. He just couldn't figure out what had happened, or anything to do about it.

Had the mixture become unstable and spontaneously combusted? Had someone sabotaged the plane? Had a bullet hit the potassium? It didn't matter. His only option was to strike the plant before the plane exploded.

He executed his final turn and made a beeline for the plant. If it was God's will, he would make it there before the plane blew up. What else could he do? He concentrated on the job at hand.

Bring this present home to Nuclear America, Johnny Boy!

*   *   *

FBI: "How soon can your air defenses engage?"

Security: "We have no realistic chance until the aircraft is less than a mile-and-a-half out."

FBI: "Jesus Christ! How long will it take him to cover that last mile-and-a-half?"

Air Control: "At his current ground speed of 310 miles per hour, about twelve seconds, sir."

FBI: "Twelve fucking seconds? Even if you hit him you might still end up with hunks of airplane in your yard, just from the momentum! Twelve seconds! Jesus!"

Security: "Air control, give me a countdown to impact, starting at fifteen seconds."

Air control: "Yessir."

Security: "Gunners: Lock laser sights on target. All guns begin firing on my mark."

It was silent in the control room. The reactors and their related pumps, fans, turbines and generators had all been shut down. The power plant was feeling more and more like a tomb.

Air Control: "15 - 14 - 13."

Security: "Fire. Fire. Fire."

The sound of the plant anti-aircraft batteries rattled and thudded a steady staccato.

One second later:

Air Control: "Sir, the target is off the screen."

Security: "What? Keep firing. We can't have hit it yet."

Firing control: "We cannot locate the target, it has disappeared."

Security: "Keep firing. Best guess. Tower, do you see anything?"

Tower: "Big ball of purple flames in the air. Looks like an explosion."

Security: "Cease fire. Tower, do you see anything else. Any aircraft?"

Tower: "Holy shit! Excuse me sir. There was just an even bigger explosion when the debris hit the water. Looks like fucking fireworks out there. Just spewing up out of the river. The whole valley is lit up."

Air control: "We still show no aircraft on the scope."

Everyone in the control room looked at one another. There was only static on the com link.

After nearly a full minute of tense silence:

Security: "Sit-rep. All units report to your supervisors. Stay alert. This could be a diversion. Air defense, hold fire. Remain at high alert, security level 'Red.'"

NRC: "I think we just dodged one big fucking bullet!"

FBI: "No shit!"

Operator: "Maintenance. What's your e-t-a on fixing that pump?"

Maintenance: "We need a part from Michigan. They'll fly it in to Minneapolis yet tonight. Should be fixed by about noon today."

Operator: "Screen house. What's the water level?"

Screen House: "Down eight feet and holding steady. We're starting to suck mud though. Don't know how long we can keep the screens clear."

FBI: "I'll call the Army Corp and see if we can get more water released from Pool 2. They can open the gates at least part way to give us a couple feet of water in the channel. Is there anything you can do on site to increase cooling water flow?"

Plant Manager: "I don't know. Can't think of anything. Let me think. I don't know. Huh?"

Operator: "We have enough fire hoses and portable pumps to draw water from the pond behind the plant. That will help some. We can also use the fire hydrants in the plant. And we can connect regular garden hoses to all the water faucets and add that in, too.

We should be okay until the pump is fixed, especially if the Corp can give us a little more water in the river. With the borinated cooling water in the fuel pool intact, we've theoretically got 26 hours before it boils off – even with no river water. If that pool water had emptied, though . . . ."

NRC: Shaking his head. "State of the art nuclear technology and we've got to hold it together with duct tape and baling wire."

NRC turned to the Plant Manager: "Sir, you have a new job starting right now. I don't know what it is. But you are no longer running this generating station, by order of the United States Government. Operator, you are in charge for the present."

Operator: "Yessir!"

CHAPTER 63

Back at the Red Wing Airport.

The BCA SWAT team maneuvered methodically through the airport hangars, gradually closing a ring around the terminal building. Soon the entire airport had been cleared. There were no further hostiles to be defeated.

Gunner radioed the Captain that the airport was secure and asked what had happened to the B24.

"We were too late to engage the B24, sir. Had it still been flying when we arrived in the area, shooting it down would have been our priority. As things stood, the best we could do was lend you a hand down there."

"Do you know what happened to the bomber?" Gunner asked.

"I am informed that it exploded in mid-flight and splashed down somewhere upstream."

"Any survivors?"

"Sorry, sir. That's all I know."

"Thanks for the intel, Captain."

Gunner didn't know if he should be relieved that the bomber hadn't impacted the nuclear plant, or sad because he might have lost a friend.

"Will you be landing here so we can thank you properly?" Gunner asked finally.

"Sorry, sir," the Captain replied. "Just doing a favor for our C.O. Gotta get back to base. We've all got our regular tours at daylight."

"Well, please pass along one helluva big 'Thank you' to your C.O. from all of us down here on the ground. You sure saved our bacon." Gunner knew he spoke for everyone concerned.

"Roger that. Our pleasure to be of service.

"Oh, and one more thing, sir. My C.O. said you should say 'Hi' to somebody named 'Beck' for him.

"You have a nice night, sir."

With that, the two lethal war birds lifted and banked northwesterly, vanishing into the night sky.

The SWAT commander asked Gunner, "What the hell does that mean: 'Say Hi to Beck?' Who's Beck?"

"Nobody you know," Gunner said, as he listened to the choppers echoing up the valley. "Good man, though."

CHAPTER 64

Monday morning, August 10th, in and around Red Wing.

I was covered in mineral spirits, mud and river water. I looked bad and smelled worse. But I had a pulse. Thankfully, the parachute had performed as designed and my landing in the muddy river bottoms hadn't been unduly abrupt.

Since the fireworks from the bomber's explosive entry into the river had lit up the valley, I could see that my splashdown site was much closer to the Wisconsin side of the river than to Minnesota.

Shedding the parachute and any other unnecessary weight, I had swum and slogged my way to the Wisconsin shore. From there, a bewildered resident had allowed me to use his cell phone to contact Gunner, who had sounded pleased to hear from me. He had even sent a squad to retrieve my reeking remains.

Right now, it was 5:00 a.m., and I was getting Gunner's vinyl side chair disgustingly dirty and smelly. Despite my condition, Gunner appeared uncharacteristically happy to see me in his office. Bull was there, too.

I thought Gunner might ask me some questions about my ordeal. But he was far too pumped-up about his own recent encounters to be thinking about mine.

"While you were busy joy riding in that plane," Gunner reported, "Bull and I captured two outlaws and defeated an army of very mean sons-of-bitches. Military types, with automatic weapons, grenades . . . the works. One helluva fight."

"I caught the crooks by myself," Bull said.

Gunner flashed him a dirty look, but continued with his story.

"Bull called me when he got your SOS," Gunner was saying. "We mobilized our forces and got our people over there *tout de suite.*

"Seems Bull arrived at the airport a bit before we did, though. On the way in, he found these two hicks" – Gunner showed me mug shots – "attempting to flee the scene in their pickup truck. He blocked their path with his Cherokee and convinced them to surrender."

"How'd he do that? Offer moonshine?" I still had a sense of humor.

"I believe he offered them the business end of his Browning 12-gauge over-under."

Gunner could tell a pretty good story.

"In lieu of that option, they could lie on the ground until the Sheriff's posse came to save the day."

"Everything goin' fine 'til cops show up," Bull said. "Nice and peaceful. Bad guys all trussed up. Cops get there and all hell breaks loose."

"Why?" I asked both of them. "What happened?"

Gunner spoke first. "Freakin' terrorist army, that's what. They were military-types . . . armed to the teeth and hell-bent on destruction. Swarming all over the place. We had my crew, BCA

SWAT and Lewiston County all there, and we still couldn't put a dent in 'em."

"Was just three guys," Bull said.

Gunner gave him the hairy eyeball.

"I didn't see you helping out," he said accusingly to Bull.

"Hell, I figured your goddamn brigade could maybe handle three hostiles on your own. I left my hostages tied to a tree and moved to take out the pilot. Got the cockpit window when he was at the end of the runway gettin' ready to roll. But never had a decent shot at the guy."

"Anyway," Gunner continued, wisely refusing to engage Bull further, "they were three of the meanest bastards you'd ever run into. Automatic weapons. RPGs. Probably some laser-guided shit, too."

He looked pointedly at Bull.

Bull looked at the ceiling.

"So how did you finally finish them off?"

"Actually," Gunner said, "I think you finished 'em off for us." He gave me a look I couldn't quite identify.

I leaned over Gunner's desk, picked up his coffee cup and gave it a sniff. "What the heck have you been sippin'? While you were at the airport, I was busy tryin' to save my own backside on that airplane."

"Maybe so," he went on. "But you got some buddy who's a Special Forces C.O. who decided to do you a favor by sending us a couple freakin' Apaches to squash the bad guys. They did a damn fine job of it, too."

"They did," Bull agreed. "Damn fine job."

"I guess if you don't ask, you don't get," I said cryptically.

Bull smiled.

Gunner looked at both of us. "Now what's that supposed to mean?"

Neither Bull nor I spoke.

"Aw c'mon," Gunner pleaded. "Gimme a break. Where'd those choppers come from?"

"After I texted Bull," I said, "I sent another SOS to a guy I used to work with. I guess he decided my heart was pure and my cause was just."

"All right. That'll do it." Gunner had had enough. "You military comrades can keep your secrets. I don't care. We got ourselves some big time criminals. And we're gonna go get us another one or two in just a bit."

"Honestly, Gunner," I complimented, "you did a great job!

"So is one of the hicks you caught the chemist who murdered the professor?"

"Ahem. Actually, no. But Urland and Brenda . . . don't ya love those names . . . Urland and Brenda Umber . . . are gonna lead us to the terrorist hideout right now. BCA SWAT is geared up and ready to pounce."

Gunner was hyped up for more action.

"Mind if I tag along?"

"Well. Since you were a bit of a help in misdirecting the airplane . . . and your Special Ops buddies did save our cans . . . and your goofy theory of this whole nuclear thing turned out to be more than horse-hockey after all, I suppose I've gotta let you come along. But try to stay out of the way.

"And Jesus, you stink!"

Gunner just had to have the last word.

*   *   *

Two deputies covered the back seat of Gunner's unmarked car with a canvas tarp and let me sit there. Gunner had all the windows wide open the whole way to the 'hideout.' No one else chose to ride with us.

While we were driving, I asked Gunner if he had had any luck with my hunch concerning the possible connection between the Ottawa County plot and the Mongolians' re-entry into my life.

"Actually, I did," he said, glancing in the rearview mirror. "And I'm afraid I owe you a big apology."

"An apology? How's that?"

"Turns out the guy that got your daughter in the soup – and the guy who leaked our info to the terrorists – was one of my own deputies. A new guy.

"When you told me your theory that an *Al Qaeda* informant had been at the Lab when you were there, I ran a thorough check on everyone who'd been on the grounds that day – including my own troops.

"Turns out that Deputy Watson had a connection to *Al Qaeda* from his army tour in Afghanistan and somehow slipped through our screening process. We brought him in this morning.

"Watson normally handles Water Patrol in the summer. But he was in the car at the Lab when you stopped by there. And he called in your visit to his superiors. They must've figured out the Mongolian connection to get you out of town, and maybe out of their lives permanently. I s'pose *Al Qaeda's* got connections all over the place."

Gunner checked the mirror again for my reaction.

"I'm really sorry."

His voice was definitely contrite.

"Huh," I said.

"What's that s'posed to mean: 'Huh'?"

"I'd've put my money on the groundskeeper – the guy with the Panama hat."

I knew Gunner's eyes were rolling somewhere in his head.

"Hey. Don't feel bad," I acknowledged. "There's no way you could have known your deputy was involved. Don't worry about it. One more terrorist off the streets and where he belongs."

I was just pleased to have the Mongolian saga, finally, behind me.

We were now approaching our destination.

Slowly, our parade of vehicles drove up the dirt drive to the old white farm house with the dark green trim.

Being the trained experts in this kind of thing, the SWAT team went in first, stopping their vans about a hundred feet short of the house. The vans' back doors swung open and the SWAT officers piled out, wearing their black SWAT gear that said 'SWAT' plainly across front and back.

They fanned out – weapons at the ready.

As they skulked closer to the house, I was sure they would see the huge, yellow semi-truck and trailer parked around the corner in the turn-around. And they'd probably be focused on the smallish Arab man standing on top of the semi tractor holding a burning Zippo lighter in his hand.

So as SWAT closed in on the semi-truck, I ducked into one of their vans, borrowing an appropriate weapon. Then I made my way quickly forward, jogging parallel to the driveway, through the yard and on a more direct route toward the truck than SWAT had taken.

"This truck is filled with nitrogen fertilizer," the Arab man was yelling at the SWAT officers. "I have soaked it in diesel fuel. I intend to blow myself and all of you infidels to pieces. Praise be to Allah! You will all rot in Hell. And I shall receive my reward in Paradise."

No one on the SWAT team seemed prepared to shoot, lest the lighter might fall into the open trailer of fertilizer, that did, in fact, smell like diesel fuel.

While SWAT had been holding its position, I kept advancing – maneuvering ever closer to the truck. I now stood within about thirty feet of the man ranting on its top.

Out of the corner of my eye I could see Gunner back on the driveway, waving his arms wildly, and mouthing the word, "No" in my direction.

Too late to change my mind now.

"Here's your reward!" I yelled, like some cowboy who'd had a few too many at the Long Branch Saloon. I brought up the weapon I had been hiding alongside my leg and let him have it – twice, in rapid succession.

Both shots hit him squarely in the chest. The young terrorist tumbled backward onto the hood of the semi-tractor, and then onto the ground. He was writhing in pain. But there was no blood. SWAT team members moved quickly to disarm him from his lighter, and then took him into custody.

Gunner came running up and scolded me.

"What the hell are you doing? You could've gotten us all blown up."

I ejected the spent cartridges from the bean-bag gun.

"Not with *that* truck," I said.

"And why the hell not?"

I calmly closed the weapon's breech and leaned it against a nearby tree.

"First of all, there's no way that guy got his hands on enough diesel fuel to make a proper bomb with *that much* fertilizer. And if he had, it would've been dripping out the bottom of the truck."

"And reason number two?" Gunner was still hot.

"Even if he *had* gotten enough diesel fuel to get the right explosive mixture, the bomb wasn't contained. I could see some of the nitrogen piled up over the top of the trailer. The best he could do with an uncontained mixture like that is make one helluva campfire."

Gunner shook his head at me.

"Beck," he said. "You are one lucky sonofabitch!"

"Thomas Jefferson," I said.

"Godliness," I said.

CHAPTER 65

Back in Red Wing.

Given my current state of attire, cleanliness and aroma, I elected to leave the Pilot parked at the airport for the day. A kind deputy agreed to give me a ride home – as long as I brought along my 'Haz-Mat' tarp. I was happy to oblige.

When I finally poured out of the back seat of the cruiser, together with the tarp ("No thanks. You can keep that." "Okay."), I looked and smelled like I had fallen into a chemical spill at a fish farm. Beth tried to come over to meet me, but I waved her off. Seeing I was okay despite my appearance, she agreed to let me clean up a bit.

I rinsed myself off in the back yard with our garden hose for fifteen minutes before I felt clean enough to enter the house. After a thorough going over in our real shower, several times, lather-rinse-repeat, I finally looked, and smelled, human again.

Beth handed a bath towel to me over the glass shower door so I could dry myself. When I exited the shower, she was waiting and jumped into my arms, wrapping her tanned legs around my waist. I didn't even have a chance to properly secure the towel.

*   *   *

Some brunch, a bottle of champagne and a couple hours later, Beth and I were lying close in bed. Each of us had small beads of perspiration on our foreheads. Neither of us cared.

She threw back the sheet and we lay there, side by side on our backs, waiting to cool down after our recent exertion.

After a bit, Beth said, "So are you going to tell me how you got to be in such a state of disrepair?"

"Disrepair? I'm hurt. I thought I did okay just now. Maybe not great . . ."

Still lying on her back, Beth slapped me in the stomach with the back of her right hand.

"Ouch!"

"You know what I'm talking about," she said. "Tell me about your night."

"You'll be able to read all about it in the newspapers tomorrow. Lock and Dam Number 3 gave out due to age and deterioration. The Prairie River Nuclear Plant was shut down as a precaution.

"In an unrelated incident, a former postal worker stole a B24 and crashed it into the Mississippi. No survivors.

"The Ottawa County Sheriff's Department and BCA SWAT team apprehended a suspect in the murder of Professor Donald G. Westerman, PhD. They never comment on an open investigation, but they're pretty sure they've got their man.

"Oh yeah . . . one more thing. Urland and Brenda Umber were booked into county jail for grand larceny and car-jacking relating to the disappearance of two semi-loads of fertilizer.

"I think that's about it."

"And where were you exactly when all of this happened?" Beth asked.

"Well, I took a plane ride, shot off some fireworks, did a bit of sky-diving and took some target practice with a bean bag gun."

"So how did you end up so dirty and stinky?"

She really knew how to hurt a guy.

"I spilled some of the fireworks stuff on my pants. And my parachute landing was a bit off course – hit the middle of a mud lake, actually."

"Was your muddy parachute adventure anywhere near the plane crash and/or the nuclear plant?"

She clearly had skills as an interrogator.

"Sort of both."

She rolled on top of me and tousled my hair. "Babe. You can't keep playing Rambo. I like our life here in Red Wing. And I'd really love for us to grow old together." Her voice was playful, but poignant at the same time. She worried for my safety – for our lives together.

"Doll," I said, looking up into her gorgeous green eyes. "I can't stop being who I am. And part of that will always involve taking calculated risks. Would I be the same husband if I spent my days cooped up in that law office, or my evenings in front of the television?"

She didn't answer. She understood, but still looked worried.

"Remember when the Agency told us we shouldn't have kids? That it was too dangerous?" I asked.

"Yes."

"But we knew we could have a family and keep us all safe, so we did it anyway. A calculated risk. What would our lives mean without our girls today? Seeing them mature into adults and go off to college, all grown-up and independent. What would our purpose have been – what would it be now – without them?"

Beth smiled down at me.

"You're right, I suppose. We can't stop living life, hiding in corners to avoid possible negatives. Risk is part of life, and for us, maybe more than most. Sometimes I just can't help worrying about you. That's all."

"Worrying is fine. And I love you for that. But you know we have to be who we are – both of us."

She nodded. I pulled her close. We lay like that for a bit, her body on top of mine. Silent.

Beth spoke first.

"So how are you going to compensate me for all the duress you have caused of late?"

"How 'bout I make us a gourmet dinner?"

Beth pushed herself to her knees, sitting on my hip bones and stomach.

"I've told you before. You don't know how to cook."

She playfully tousled my hair again and rolled off me, across the bed and onto her feet.

"Where are you going?" I asked.

Standing there naked in our bedroom, she looked at me and smiled. "To sign you up for a cooking class."

She turned and headed for the shower.